Pursuit

of

Power

LB Swanson

PURSUIT OF POWER Copyright © 2022 by LB Swanson
All rights reserved.

First Edition 2022

ISBN 9798987538302 (paperback)

Published by Romans 12:2
Dunlap Illinois

For Dusty, A, K,and M.

Thank you for believing in me and encouraging me to pursue my dreams. I love you all – you make my heart happy.

1
Magdalena

Tree branches tangle and tear at her short blonde hair and bloody her cheeks as she runs, barefoot, in the thick white snow that blankets the forest floor. The moon is high as it dances between the heavy clouds to cast shadows in the dark, shadows that look like the men chasing her. She wills her eyes to focus on the figure running ahead of her, guiding her. Her breath, coming in short, fast bursts, creates little puffs of water vapor visible in the full moonlight. Her white nightgown whips in the wind around her knees, making her appear ethereal in the winter moon.

She risks a glance and quickly looks behind her. The dense forest is all she sees, with its tangle of naked branches and sparse spots of green from their coniferous cousins. The shapes and the shadows and the now falling snow create monsters within her mind. She tries to blink them free but her imagination holds steady to its haunting fantasy. She sees the men in their fur skins and blackened teeth. She sees them coming after her, and she knows she isn't going to be able to outrun them. The men are wolves, and they can smell her for miles. *They are the men of the mountain. They have come for me.* She knows this must be true. All her life she has feared the day she might be discovered. For on that day, the evil would descend the mountains of Crask and come looking for her. It is too much, the fear and the running and the cold on her skin. She imagines them reaching out and grabbing at her nightgown, their hands like teeth ripping and pulling her back, dragging her through the night and up, up, up, deep into Crask mountain.

She can't breathe. She pulls air, willing her lungs to fill. Spots of light dance through her vision. She tries to blink them away, but more come with each bat of her eyelids. The dots in her vision and the noise in her head are disorienting. Through the whipping snow, she can no longer see the outline of who she is following. The high-pitched ring that vibrates between her ears muffles even her own cries for help as she trips over a fallen tree. Her body slams against one of its still standing brethren, and she weakly attempts to wrap her arms around its trunk to prevent sliding further into the snow. Resting her forehead on the rough bark, she cries. She is no longer able to run. Drops of blood mix with her tears and fall from her face, dotting the white snow below.

"No! Lady Magdalena. You have to move!" Liri screams at the crumpled form at the base of the tree. Magdalena looks up to meet Liri's green eyes, full of fright, and musters merely a shake of her head. She weakly tries to push Liri away, convince her to run, but Liri stands firm, her thin lips set in a tight line. The wind blows her long, almond-colored hair, into her face. She pulls her pale fingers through the unruly strands and lets out a disparaging sigh.

"We must keep moving, my lady. We are close to the house. We can make it. Please," Liri begs with the strangled tears heavy in her throat.

"Go without me, Liri. It is me they want anyway. Please, I can't breathe, let alone run any further."

"Get up now. We go together or we die together. Do you understand that?" Liri grabs and pulls hard on Magdalena's arm. Magdalena understands that Liri's dedication to her mistress will get her killed if she doesn't go willingly. She can't lead another friend to death's door. Magdalena dares one more look back as she wipes blood from her lips, the streak dark against the fair skin of her cheek.

Hand in hand, they begin to run once more, Liri dragging Magdalena on unsteady legs deeper into the forest. The snow begins falling harder now as the wind howls through the weighed-down limbs. Their pace is slow, but Liri is determined. She leads the way, and Magdalena doesn't know if it's by knowledge, instinct, or luck, but as dawn approaches, the two see the puffs of smoke rising in the distance signaling the cottage they have traveled all night to find.

The home belongs to the family of Astrid, the maid they left behind. The maid Magdalena left behind. The two come to a stop at the tree line. Hands on knees, they force air into their lungs in huge, expansive gasps. Magdalena's head vibrates with a throbbing ache as she looks down upon the small cottage. A short stone fence wraps its arms protectively around the tiny home of wood and stone. There is one barn behind the cottage whose thatch roof is sagging from the weight of all the snow. She can see dots of tiny hovels throughout the snow-covered field and can almost feel the breath of life snuggled within. Pigs or lambs, perhaps. She can spot shadows moving in and out of the firelight that flickers through the small windows that appear on either side of the worn wood door. *They are awake.* She tilts her head to the dawning sun and watches the smoke stretch lazily out of the stone chimney to melt into the early morning sky. A deep sigh escapes her parted lips.

Seeing the little cottage now doesn't bring hope. It doesn't bring a breath of relief. For Magdalena, this house only brings guilt, guilt that where there should be three, there are only two. She is frightened of the vision that surfaces from somewhere deep in her mind. It is one where she is caught, and dragged to the mountain, where she finally faces the fate that was always destined to be hers, rather than facing the people within the home below, admitting to them what she did, admitting she even exists at all.

"It is safe. Let's go," Liri instructs as she begins to descend the snow-covered hill. Magdalena stands still for a moment. She watches her maid slip and trip in the deep snow, body turned sideways to counteract the slope. She looks over her shoulder and into the forest. Her body twitches to turn and run, to take her chances out there.

***

Magdalena can see the glow of daylight through her closed eyelids. She reaches a hand to her eyes to rub the heaviness of sleep from them. The pain this causes is instant and sharp, and she is reminded of the welts that cover the skin of her face from the branches whipping as she ran. She eases one eye open and then the other. She scans the room, trying to recall a memory, an anchor from their early morning arrival. Her eyes travel across the worn floorboards and up the walls. The triangular shape of the room suggests she is in some sort of loft. There is the bed she is currently occupying and another across from her, blankets folded and tucked neatly. A wardrobe stands against one of the tallest walls, with two doors that open in the center and a single drawer below. There is a small table with a hairbrush and a basin for water. It is a drab room by anyone's standard, with one notable exception: the room contains hundreds of handfuls of dried herbs and plants that hang from the highest points of the wooden rafters. As she lies on her back and looks up, it is as if she is enveloped in a canopy of various shades, shapes, and textures of green leaves with bits of pale purple, pink, and white scattered throughout. She is unable to identify what the plants are, but she is amazed and strangely comforted by their presence.

She runs her hands over the brown blankets that cover her body. They are thick and warm, and the material lightly scratches her palms and the bare skin of her legs. The smells of honeyed oats and the murmurs of conversation waft up from a hole in the floorboards where the top of a ladder pokes through. Magdalena fixes her eyes on the herbs and tries to breathe fully into her lungs, hoping to inhale some of their magic. Expanding her chest, stretching the skin of her stomach, she holds the air inside her body, along with it the wave of nausea threatening to escape should she move or part her lips in the slightest. The expelling force within proves to be too much for her to contain, though, and she rolls to her side, letting gravity pull her body to the rough wood floor below, where it falls with a loud thud. She crawls on her hands and knees to the chamber pot in the corner and vomits into it.

Her head bowed over the bowl and her legs tucked underneath her, Magdalena gulps air between the spasms of her stomach. Without hearing her approach, she feels Liri's cautious hand rest gently on her heaving shoulder. Magdalena shakes her head from side to side in an attempt to discourage the comfort that is being offered. Liri, however, is not fazed and rubs slow circles in the middle of Magdalena's back.

At last, feeling that there is nothing left to expel, Magdalena crawls away from the chamber pot. Her body weak, her throat sore, and her face stained with tears, she doesn't even try to pull herself back into the cocoon-like warmth she just left, and instead, she sits on the floor, back resting against the side of the bed, legs stretched out in front of her. Liri moves in close to her, and Magdalena takes her hand. They sit for a while, not saying a word, just crying silent tears side by side, hand in hand.

"How did this happen, Liri? How did they find out about me?" Magdalena whispers into the space between them.

"I don't know, my lady. Maybe they don't know at all. Perhaps you are still safe. What if your father failed to deliver his offerings at the last full moon and that's why they've come?"

"For twenty years he has kept me a secret. He has hidden me against all laws of our lands. He has convinced everyone I am his oldest son and his heir. There is no way that after doing all he has to keep me alive, he would make such a silly error as forgetting the offerings." Magdalena's tone is sharper than she intended.

"I am sorry, my lady. Of course he didn't forget." Liri's voice catches in her throat.

"No, Liri, I am sorry for getting angry. Tell me, what is happening below?"

"I was sent up to get you by Sybbyl, Astrid's mother. She has prepared food. There are some clothes in the wardrobe for you. We are to eat and await the arrival of a man named Brom. After hearing what had happened, and, well, seeing you like this," Liri starts, motioning to Magdalena's body, which appears unbound for the first time since she began to show signs of womanhood, "Astrid's father, Hagen, rode fast to Kaelonoch. He thought for sure there would be an attack on the village. With the treaty now broken, he believed the men we saw at the castle would move throughout the countryside seeking their vengeance. Magdalena, there was nothing amiss. None of the men we saw at the castle had made their way to the largest village in Masunbria. Why is that? It doesn't make sense. If they came down from the mountains, it is war they want. Punishment. Hagen decided to wake a friend there, the tavern owner. Brom. Magdalena you should know, Hagen told him about you." An insecurity coats Liri's throat at this admission, and she chooses not to meet Magdalena's eyes.

Magdalena nods slowly as she silently adds the three new people to the very small list of those that know of her existence.

"Brom sent Hagen home to guard the house, and he himself took off at full light for the castle," Liri continues. "They say he

LB SWANSON

will return and tell us what he finds. Magdalena, Astrid never arrived here. She was supposed to meet us, but she hasn't come."

Liri doesn't say more as she erupts into tears once more. Magdalena knows though. She knows what Liri is too afraid to say. *Astrid has surely been taken because of you, Magdalena.*

"I can't face them, Liri."

"You don't have a choice, I am afraid. They are the only thing keeping you safe at the moment and the only way you will get news of your family. You need to find out where your parents are so you can get back to them. They are the only ones who can protect you. You know this."

Liri is right. Liri is always right. Magdalena nods in resignation. She pulls herself to her feet, dresses in the borrowed clothes that were once Astrid's, and lets Liri lead the way down the ladder and into the belly of the cottage.

"My lady." A small, gray-haired woman attempts a smile in greeting, but it never reaches her eyes which brim with pools of confusion, fear, and sadness. Pools that Magdalena herself is responsible for. "Please, will you sit?" She motions toward the wood table that occupies the center of the one large room that makes up the first floor of the cottage. Magdalena looks at the bench seat and down to her borrowed dress. The action seeming incomprehensible with the unaccustomed bulk of flowing fabric, she chooses the chair at the head of the table instead.

"Magdalena, please, call me Magdalena."

"What a beautiful name. You look just like your mother; I don't think I noticed that before. I am Sybbyl, and that there is Hagen." She motions with her wooden spoon to the man sitting in a worn chair near the hearth, eyes focused on the licking flames. She spoons a sticky mound of oats into the bowl before Magdalena, and the plop of the mixture hitting the wood surface sends her stomach in a lurch once more. Reaching into her apron pocket, she plucks out a handful of dried herbs and sprinkles them across the lumpy surface.

"They will help with the pain and the nausea," she offers with a small wink. Magdalena reaches for the spoon. She hesitates over the bowl, her stomach warning her that it will rebel if she dares. But her twenty years of manners and civility win, and she lowers the spoon into the lumpy mixture. She forces her mouth to chew and swallow as if she has never eaten a day before. She looks up to meet the gray eyes of an expectant Sybbyl. Magdalena can see in her face that this is all Sybbyl can offer right now. Feeding her husband and her guests. She is waiting for Magdalena to offer her the only thing she can in return. Gratitude. Smiling warmly, Magdalena thanks the woman and, for good measure, scoops another blob onto her spoon.

"I am grateful for the kindness you have shown Liri and me. Once we have eaten, however, we should begin to make our way back to the castle. I am sure the king's army has restored the peace within the walls. The king and queen will be gracious toward you for your hospitality and, of course, your discretion."

Astrid's father, Hagen, lets out a strangled noise that is a mixture of a grunt and a choke from his spot in front of the fire. Sybbyl, casting her eyes away from Magdalena, returns to the simmering pot on the worn wood stove.

"Well then"—her voice betrays her as it shakes— "I must ready myself for my return. Everyone must be quite worried by now. I must . . ."

"You *must* do no such thing," Hagen growls. Magdalena recoils. The man rises from his chair. He is thin and gray, but under the loose skin on his arms, she can see what remains of ropy muscles and strong tendons. He moves toward her on slightly bowed legs, swaying left and right as he goes. She instinctively leans further back into her chair. "My Astrid sent you here for our protection, and that is what we aim to do. My girl is strong and smart, and the fact that she isn't here right now tells me that she is most likely dead or has been taken. Now, if you are who you say you are, then you know that one foot outside this house could mean the end for you, the end for us all. You will not move a muscle until I say so. My Astrid's final wish will be honored."

Magdalena can do nothing but stare. She has never been spoken to in such a manner in her life. Her mouth opens and shuts. Her full lips quiver slightly. Her brain tells her to scream at this peasant of a man, but her heart is too broken for the act. Behind the sharp tongue, the words he spoke ring loudly. *Likely dead.* She shakes her head side to side. Trying to reassure him? Trying to dislodge his words from her ears? She isn't sure. All she knows is she wants to run from this place and the guilty stares and the words being said and the ones unsaid.

Several loud bangs at the front door cause all the occupants within to jump. Liri grabs hold of Magdalena and buries her face into her shoulder. *The men of the mountain are here.* Magdalena's heart begins to race at the thought as she looks around the room, finding no other exit.

Hagen holds a single finger to his lips as he turns to answer the insistent bang. He has barely cracked the door when it is pushed open abruptly and a tall, broad man with dark hair cut short storms in. The man shuts the door behind him and brings his hands to his lips, where he blows warm breath into red fingers. A few stomps of his boots to remove the accumulated snow, and he drops the thick, black furs from his shoulders and into a heap on the floor.

"Brom. You look frozen." Sybbyl rushes toward him as Hagen backs away. Magdalena watches. This is the tavern owner. She sees the evidence of his profession in the broad chest and strong arms capable of carrying barrels of port. He is here to tell what he has seen. Sybbyl is trying to delay the news by offering food and drink, while Hagen is retreating as if this man is the very reaper of death. The man is shaking his head and muttering gratitude and apologies combined to Sybbyl. His eyes look up, and he sees Magdalena for the first time. His face is a flood of shock, fear, and confusion.

"Brom? I am Magdalena, I am—" she hesitates only slightly "—the daughter of the king and queen. What did you see? What of my family and the people that serve us?" Magdalena's voice sounds strong. She has always been a good pretender. She has had to be in order to survive.

"A daughter," he breathes and lets out a short, cynical laugh. "You are not Haluk then? You are not the serious boy we have all watched grow up? The one who was to be our king?"

"No." Magdalena forces herself to hold her chin high. "I am afraid my parents had only one son, my little brother Niklaus."

Brom shakes his head slowly and whispers into the room, "What have they done?"

"Please. Can you please tell me what you saw at the castle? What happened there?"

The man crumples his face. His lips and brows fold toward the center line. He looks to be in physical pain. He rubs his face over and over, trying to ready himself, perhaps. He is silent for what seems like an eternity. Slowly, he begins to shake his head as a sob catches in his throat. Sybbyl lets out a blood-curdling scream and slumps to the floor. Hagen reaches out a shaking hand, searching for the chair at the opposite head of the table. Locating its back, he lowers his body weakly to its surface. Magdalena stares, mouth open, heartbroken. The room knows before any word can be spoken.

"They are all dead. They are all dead," Brom cries out at last. The words escape him in a rush of relief from the torturous all-consuming nature of them. "There were bodies, so many bodies. All of them gone. Women, children. They were all piled atop one another. A big mass of them like they weren't human. Legs and arms intertwined and knotted together. The snow was red from their blood."

"Astrid? Did you see my daughter?" Hagen asks weakly.

"No. Don't make me tell ya, Hagen. I've known you my whole life. Don't make me do this," Brom cries through gritted teeth.

Hagen slams his fist down hard on the table before them, causing Liri to squeal and bury her head further into Magdalena's arms. "You will tell me, Brom. I deserve to know."

"Hagen, those bodies were of my friends. Those faces were from the village. I will never be able to get that out of my mind."

"Was one of them Astrid?" Hagen speaks slowly and sternly, but his eyes don't rise from the grain of the wood on the table before him.

Brom rubs his hands over his face and looks down to his boots. "She looked just as beautiful as last I saw her. She looked like she had gone quick." Hagen nods his head as if this confirms what he already knew, but the tears drop from the tip of his nose and land on his hands, now folded neatly in his lap. Sybbyl begins to wail and twist the fabric of her apron in her hands over and over again.

This can't be right. This can't be happening. Magdalena's eyes pass to everyone in the room and the brokenness before her. She wants to hide, to leave them in their grief before they realize she is to blame. Astrid removed Magdalena's robe and wrapped it around her own shoulders. When they reached the bridge and saw how guarded it was, Astrid knew that the only way to get Magdalena across was a diversion. She relinquished her garment, knowing what Astrid meant to do with it. She was going to draw the men out as if she was who they came for so that Liri and Magdalena could escape to this house. To safety. Brom must've seen that. He must have noticed the robe. The lush red-and-gold velvet could never have belonged to a maid. Is he looking at her now? Does he know what she did? She didn't argue with Astrid. She knew all along what Astrid was plotting, and she pretended

13

she didn't see what was happening. She pretended she didn't know how the story would end.

"I asked if the men said anything that you heard?" Brom says a bit harshly. She startles, not realizing he was talking to her. He is looking at her with what? Anger? Hatred? She can't tell.

"The men who attacked?" she asks.

Brom nods.

"No. I have never seen any man like that before. They were like animals. They didn't wear armor or carry a banner. They were wild. They came while we slept. There were so many of them. Astrid—" she chokes on her maid's name "—Astrid saved our lives. I am so sorry." The words sound pathetic to her own ears, but she doesn't know of any others to say.

Brom begins to pace the small room. "How many people knew about you?"

"Before this morning, only six. My parents, my brother, my two maids, and the doctor who birthed me."

"There has to be someone who knows what happened last night. Someone who escaped," Brom says wearily.

"Did you see your sister, Brom?" Hagen asks gently, and Magdalena hears Brom's words replay in her head. He hoped someone escaped, his sister.

"No. I didn't dare enter or call out to her though. She wasn't amongst the dead that I saw."

"There is hope then, dear son." Hagen sighs.

"Yeah. Well, I am not going to sit around and wait for those monsters to come to Kaelonoch. We have families to look after. Friends."

"Don't do anything foolish, Brom." Hagen rises on his unsteady legs and crosses the room to look into the reddened face before him. "We must be careful. We must be smart."

Brom takes a long and shaking breath before picking up the furs and placing them over his shoulders. "I know. Hagen, my friend, you can't trust anyone, you understand? Darkness has come to Masunbria."

With that, Brom Anker is gone, and all that remains in the room is the chill in the air, whether from his departure from the cottage or the look when his eyes met hers as he uttered his final words, Magdalena cannot tell.

2
Henrick

Henrick paces the polished stone floor of the great hall. His long legs seem to skip rather than stride as he passes by the floor-to-ceiling windows and the generations of his family's portraits that cover any available wall surface as they look down upon him in indifference. Their painted pupils have passed judgment on him since he was a small boy. Such vigorous pacing causes his wine to jump up one side of his goblet and down the other, the waves of red occasionally spilling over and drops falling to the ornate rugs below. Henrick stops suddenly and looks up to a grand portrait of his father. He is wielding a sword high in the air as he stands at the base of the Crask mountains. He appears bigger than life itself. Henrick snarls at the painting and then lifts his goblet in a mock toast before swallowing the last gulp and tossing the goblet across the room, where it shatters against the stone wall. He lets out a howl like that of a wolf.

"Please, Henrick, do you have to act like such an animal?" The woman at the table sighs while resting her head in the open palm of her hand. A sardonic smile plays across her lips, which betrays her amusement over her annoyance.

"Thea, my beautiful wife, don't you see? We have finally done it! My dreams. Our dreams. Thea, they have finally come true. The castle is ours. The kingdom, the people, the power. My darling, we can live the rest of our lives knowing that we will be remembered. Our names will spill from lips for generations to come. How can you sit there? Don't you feel it coursing through your veins, triumph and power and endless opportunity?"

"The only thing I feel is tired. Where are your men? I want to sleep."

Smiling softly at his dear wife, Henrick crosses the room to kneel before her. He pushes back a thick, chestnut-brown curl from her forehead as he looks into her deep brown eyes before gently placing a kiss on her lips.

One year, he sighs silently to himself. One year ago, he began planning in earnest how he would take over the castle and kill his brother. Of course, the thought was nestled in his mind for much longer than that, an itch never quite scratched, a nagging sore in his mouth that he couldn't talk or chew without re-opening. He and Thea were living in a small castle of their own in southern Masunbria. He had a title of some importance, a small staff, and an army for protection—all things so generously given to him by his brother. Or rather, they were all things given to him in an attempt to keep him content, quiet, to keep him from asking too many questions, to distract him from the terrible secret Hadrian was keeping.

Hadrian was older than Henrick by eight years. It was this fact, and this fact alone, that made Hadrian king over Henrick. As they were growing up, Henrick knew that he would always have been the better choice for King. His brother Hadrian was always so hesitant to make the big decisions in life. Magdalena was proof of that. When Niklaus had confided in Henrick that he did not have an older brother but an older sister, Henrick knew that this was his chance at last to make a name for himself.

"Thea," he says quietly, his lips moving against hers with the words, "you will make the most beautiful queen this kingdom has ever seen."

Thea wraps her arms around her husband's neck. Pulling him gently, she smiles into his dark eyes before bringing his lips to meet hers. They kiss long and slow, his dark beard scratching her chin. *I could live in her arms.* They are interrupted by a knock at the door to the great hall. Henrick nearly jumps in excitement. His sturdy hands rub together in anxious glee as he bellows his admittance to the caller on the other side.

"My Lord Henrick, the castle is yours," the man says upon entering, metal armor clanging with quick steps. "My men have finished clearing the grounds, and there is no one left that hasn't been executed or imprisoned. I believe now would be a fine time to gather your council and prepare for what dawn will bring."

"Dagen, my man. This is it. Do you feel it?" Henrick grabs the shorter, stockier man and embraces him in a fierce hug.

Dagen lets out a small laugh in response but returns the embrace willingly.

"Summon my council. I want Sigmund and his devious mind in working order, so make sure the old man is up for the challenge. I don't need my mood dampened by his frailty."

"Of course."

"Niklaus should be here as well. If we are going to convince him that he is ruling this kingdom, then he needs to think he is making decisions for it," Henrick says.

"As you wish," Dagen says dryly. "You know I still think we should have killed him too." Dagen's words and the lift of his thick eyebrows toward Henrick indicate that the offer to do just that is still on the table.

"Dagen, you have made that utterly clear. He has a purpose to serve. The people need to see that Niklaus was a victim in Hadrian's deceit. They need to feel his pain from that betrayal. He is likable, handsome, and charismatic, and the people of Masunbria will rally behind him. The neighboring kingdoms will pity him. The Typhans themselves will see a scorned son and hopefully be much more apt to hear our proposals for a future Masunbria. Like it or not, I can't do this next part without a puppet. Once he is no longer useful, we will dispose of him. In the end, Dagen, I will rule. I will create the greatest army ever seen, and together, you and I will conquer lands not yet dreamed of." Dagen nods as if he has heard all this before and still wishes Niklaus dead—all of which is true. Henrick lets out a laugh and claps Dagen on the back in dismissal. Smiling, he returns his attention to his wife.

They don't remain alone long, however. The massive, ornately carved doors of the great hall soon open wide, and through them come three distinctly different men. The returning Dagen, the head of Henrick's army, stands proud and strong, still wearing his breastplate and sword at the hip. He has a scar that runs from his hairline down the right side of his face to his chin. He is an intelligent man, and every move he makes, every word he speaks, is calculated. Henrick considers him his dearest friend, but he would never tell him that. Behind him comes Sigmund. He is an old man, and what remains of his hair is as white and airy as freshly fallen snow. He walks stooped over, and this gives him the appearance of being slow both mentally and physically, but anyone who thought that of Sigmund would soon find out how wrong they were. Last to enter the room is Prince Niklaus, heir to the throne of Masunbria. A handsome young man of nearly twenty, he wears his dark hair a little long for Henrick's liking, but it works on the boy, as it almost softens his strong jaw and solid build. He appears every bit the royalty he has had bred into him, and his transition to king will be with only minor adjustments.

Thea is in charge of those adjustments, and Henrick notices her eyeing the boy from her place at the table. Her hand plays lazily against her wine glass, poised to raise it to her lips but entirely forgotten for the moment. She is studying Niklaus as he and the rest of the men move into the room and begin to take their seats around the table, analyzing him. Perhaps she is creating a list in her mind.

Henrick is last to take his seat, and once there, he gives a quick nod to Dagen, permission to begin. Dagen, he notices, is attempting to conceal his pride in the swift victory he has commanded, but Henrick has known him a long time and can see through his calm façade. Its presence in his friend brings a small smile to Henrick's lips that he attempts to conceal with an itch of his nose.

"As the morning sun rose on this day, a new king awoke," begins Dagen with a nod to Niklaus. "Truly a dawning of a new era for the kingdom of Masunbria. This new reign cost us the lives of just twelve men, which, though tragic, is a number I am comfortable with. I think we should note how easily we were able to take control of the castle. The former king and queen had spent a considerable amount of energy limiting and controlling the number of people allowed to be near the castle at all. Their own personal coffers were all but depleted as they increased the generosity of their offerings, afraid, it appears, to ask the people to give more when they already had so little to give. Funds dissipated, their army had all but crumbled. Those that they could afford to employ were kept outside the walls. The king and queen had become easy targets.

"If it wasn't us, proud people of Masunbria, who had decided to overthrow them and instead had in fact been the Typhans who had come down the mountain and infiltrated the castle, we all would have awakened to a very different world. A world of death, no doubt. It is because of this that I truly believe we have saved our kingdom. We have the bodies of those who served the castle being loaded into carts to be returned to the villages for burial. Those tasked with this are my best men.

"They will have a very important role to play, and their success or failure will truly determine our fate. We must plant the seed of fear into every village across Masunbria. They must believe that our kingdom is under attack, that their homes and their lives are in grave danger. Fear should replace grief as the primary emotion in their hearts. Keeping them afraid will make them that much more compliant in replenishing and amplifying your coffers."

"Yes!" exclaims Henrick joyfully. "Your men, under your impeccable leadership, did us all proud. It was a delight from my vantage point, I must say, to watch your men dressed in bear skins, covered in mud, grunting and shrieking about." Henrick lets out a small laugh.

"We couldn't leave anything to chance. There of course was the fear that someone would escape, and we needed to ensure that if that happened, they would only have one version of the events, and that would be the one we created." Dagen drops his head and looks to his hands. Someone did escape. Not just someone, Prince Haluk, or rather, Princess Magdalena. The room is quiet for an unsettling moment.

"Where are we at with locating her, Dagen?" Henrick asks at last while picking at an invisible thread on the sleeve of his gray tunic.

"As you know, there was a slight deception on her part. She had given her robes to a maid, it appears. A maid named Astrid. We are working on more details about the woman. Once my men realized what had occurred, the princess and another maid, Liri, had already achieved a good head start through the woods. My men were able to follow their tracks for most of the night. However, between the winds and the snow falling steadier as the night progressed, the tracks were lost. I have ordered the men that are returning the bodies to the village to be on the lookout for either a male or female, of average height, lean build, with short pale blonde hair and bright blue eyes. There is still hope that

Magdalena will come forward as Haluk and attempt to regain control over the kingdom, at which time, we will reveal her true nature and let the people sentence her as they see fit."

Henrick nods though Dagen's answer does not please him. He doesn't like loose ends. "I need *her* back. Out there as Haluk, she is an obvious threat to our control. But my niece returned here can be a tool to gain us an audience with the Typhans. Once there, we can make an offering of Magdalena, a making right of what my brother made wrong. It is my hope that a bold move such as that will secure an alliance between us, an alliance that we can call upon when we are ready to expand our kingdom to the sea."

"I wouldn't count on her survival, dear uncle." Niklaus laughs dryly. "Maggie is not equipped to survive out there, not in the woods and the cold. Everyone has made it their mission in life to protect Maggie since the day she was born. Protecting her has been the beating pulse of this wretched castle. Our days revolved around her. Our nights. Our lives. My parents were fools, and I told them that. They cried and pleaded and tried to explain. They thought I would understand their decision to turn my sister into the heir instead of me. It should have been me. She should have been sent away just like all the princesses before her. I don't want to lay eyes on her ever again. I hope death comes slowly and painfully for the beloved Magdalena just as it did for my disloyal parents."

Henrick sits back in his chair. He can see the image so clearly in his mind of his own sister being taken. She wore white, and pale pink flowers were placed in her hair. A veil covered her face to hide her tears. She was twelve. He shakes the memory from his mind. His sister did her duty for her kingdom. She was brave. She made the sacrifice that so many before her made. Maggie was a coward, a selfish coward who would rather see her kingdom fall to war than to do the right and honorable thing. *What made her so much more special than my own sister that her life should have been spared, should have been protected?*

"Dagen, please continue to have your men search for Magdalena. Dead or alive, I want the girl found," Henrick says.

"We will find her, Your Grace."

The topic changes quickly to plans for the days to come. The next hour is spent with mental lists being made and strategies being discussed. Magdalena is not mentioned further. The meeting now concluded, Henrick and Thea silently, hand in hand, weave their way through the winding halls of the castle to their bedchamber. Henrick doesn't recall a time when he has ever felt so physically and mentally drained. Once they arrive in their rooms, Henrick heads directly for the large, four-poster bed and falls dramatically back into it.

He feels the bed dip next to him. He slowly peels his eyes open to find his beautiful wife stretched out, head cradled in her hand, and looking down at him. He reaches out and coils a curl of her hair around his index finger, a gesture he has done thousands of times over the years they have been together, a gesture so automatic now he doesn't even recall making the choice to do it.

"Henrick?" Thea's voice is full of worry. "Do you really think this plan will work? Do you believe we can convince the villagers that we had no part in Hadrian's and Katherine's deaths? What if even in our farce we are still blamed? They could believe we were the ones that told the Typhans the true identity of Prince Haluk?"

"Thea, I have found that people choose to believe whatever is easiest on their soul. If they hope what we are saying is true and we work just a little bit to convince them of its validity, they will happily accept it. It will be important to give them a cause to rally behind. Something for them to do other than think of their dead. Niklaus will be that rallying point. We will tell the people that the young prince, hurt and betrayed by his now-dead mother and father, needs the strength and love of his people in order to be the king they deserve. They will need to protect the boy, and themselves, if they want to live."

Thea pushes herself from the bed and begins moving restlessly around the room, absently touching items as she walks: the wood arm of a cushioned high-back chair near the hearth, the worn leather books on the table, the scarlet drapes pulled tight across the perpetually gray winter sky. Her index finger lightly traces the shape and texture of each item, testing it. Henrick watches.

"I think I had better go work on planning a funeral."

"What's wrong, Thea? It is our first night in the castle. We have been up all night. Why are you so restless? You can work on the funeral tomorrow, or the next day even. They are dead; they are not going anywhere. When the people hear what crime the king and queen committed, they will surely not care if we leave them to rot and be picked apart by vultures."

"It all just feels too fragile right now for me to enjoy it. There are too many loose ends that need tightening. If Haluk had just been captured like we had planned, this would truly be a night of celebration. We would have our evidence and our means to strike a bargain. I can't stand knowing she is out there somewhere," Thea parts the thick drapes and peers out into the darkness. "Perhaps some time alone will allow me to invoke a solution."

Henrick throws his hands up in the air to signal his defeat. There is no point in arguing with Thea. "Go on then, head to your library and make your plans. Just don't be gone all night."

Thea moves to the bed and plants a kiss on his lips before turning and heading purposefully out the door. Henrick sighs as the door closes. This, he knows, is the way Thea deals with circumstances she is unable to control. She picks ones she can control and obsesses over every detail. She will spend all night in the library planning the funeral for the late king and queen. It will be a somber affair, and to the people, Henrick and Thea will look full of mercy when they offer a proper burial to such traitors. Henrick shakes his head slightly and smiles. He is lucky to have Thea, even if she is incomprehensible at times. He rises from the bed and opens the door to his chamber. A quick nod to the guard stationed outside, and he exhales fully as he closes the door and leans into the wood grain.

Not long after, there is a knock on the door at his back. Henrick smiles as he spins quickly around to fling it open. A woman on the other side curtsies low.

"You summoned me, my lord?"

An unintentional growl escapes Henrick's lips as he pulls the woman into the room, slamming the door behind them. His hands pull at her dress, and his lips kiss her neck as he walks backward, leading her to the bed.

3
Magdalena

Following Brom's departure, Magdalena retired to the loft, where she has remained, choosing only to join the family when they take their meals. She claims it is her sore skin that causes her to be bedridden. She did, after all, run all night through the snow in bare feet, and though her skin is a pitiful shade of pink and tender to the touch, it is not of a severity that would cause one to lie in bed all day.

No, she lies in bed under the scratchy brown covers for two reasons. One, she knows nothing else to do. Liri has found diversion in cooking and cleaning and helping with chickens or some other mammal destined for dinner, all things she is quite capable of assisting with. Magdalena has no such talents. She could learn, of course, but that would also mean admitting that where these women possess skill and talent, she does not. It would be awkward, would it not? A reminder of their difference in station? The second reason for feigning ill has more to do with her own guilt. And if she was being honest, which she is not, the first reason is just a poorly veiled attempt to mask this second, and therefore only, reason. Guilt. Guilt for Astrid. Guilt for her parents' betrayal of their kingdom.

Sybbyl and Hagen are open in their grief over the death of their beloved daughter. She never saw a man cry until Hagen, and she does find the sight makes her rather uncomfortable. Even as small children, her mother would not permit Magdalena nor Niklaus to cry in the company of others. What on earth would two healthy princes have to cry about, anyway? It appears, though, that Sybbyl and Hagen are comfortable with their tears and anyone who cares to look upon them. No, Magdalena would rather not experience all those messy feelings, whether belonging to herself or others in the house. Instead, she has chosen to hide both figuratively and literally. To remain here. In these rooms. Staring up at the canopy of dried lavender and sage and their more mysterious brethren. Therefore, it comes as a rather unsettling surprise when that very afternoon Hagen appears at the top of the ladder.

"Good afternoon, sir." Magdalena jumps from the bed. Hagen's emotions toward Astrid have been the most frightening. He is angry one moment and saddened the next. Unpredictable. She doesn't like unpredictability in men. Even at his advanced age, he alarms her. She holds her breath, waiting for him to yell at her, curse her, blame her.

"Hagen. I've asked you before to call me Hagen," he says sternly as he enters the room and hobbles across to the bed that lies opposite Magdalena's. He sits and motions for her to do the same. She reluctantly lowers herself to the edge of her worn cot and levels her chin, trying to appear calm. Here it comes, she thinks. He will keep Liri here. He will keep her safe. She works hard, after all, and she isn't the one to blame. Magdalena will be cast out today. She understands why he would choose to do so. Magdalena in his presence is a danger to him and his wife.

"Sybbyl and Liri are outside tending to the chickens. They will be a while yet. I came up to talk."

Magdalena nods in response. He holds up a book and waves it slightly in the air before them. Its hard cover is a dark shade of blue, and the words on the spine are in gold lettering she can't decipher from this distance.

"I brought you something. To pass the time. I don't know if it is any good or what it is even about." He lets out an embarrassed chuckle. "Astrid used to do all our reading for us when she would come to visit. Had you met me as a younger man, I would have been ashamed to admit to you that I wasn't able to read much. But alas, I am old, and my sense of pride isn't what it used to be."

Magdalena smiles. "Astrid was very smart. She attended all my studies with me and eagerly absorbed history, reading, mathematics. She couldn't get enough. I was a terrible student. I bored easily." She smiles weakly. "Not Astrid though."

"We thought she served your mother. That is what she told us. She was happy; we could see that plainly enough." Hagen nods, a tear trailing down his lined cheek. "As her father, you must understand that I was protective of her. Sybbyl and I married young and tried for many years to have children. Each time the child was lost before we could feel its first kick. We stopped thinking of children after a while. We were much too old by the time Sybbyl became pregnant with Astrid. It had been ten years since the last child that had been lost. Astrid was a fighter from the beginning though. She was determined to come into this world. Into our hearts. From day one, I knew she was unstoppable. When she approached us about joining your household, she already had her compelling argument drawn out. She told us of the education she would receive, the wages she would earn, and the marriage she could secure. When she left, her mother and I cried. We continued crying, too, each time we would walk up the ladder to see her empty bed, when we sat at the table for meals and her spot was bare. Then she came home to visit. She was absolutely happy. It was radiating from her. She had made a good choice, and Sybbyl and I stopped crying after that. Instead, we waited anxiously for her next visit so we could experience life through her for just a little bit."

"I am so sorry," Magdalena chokes out, her throat strangled in a coat of guilt and her tongue heavy with the burden of it.

"I didn't come up here for you to apologize. I came up here to apologize to you. I have been around the cold long enough to know that you aren't bedridden by that bit of frostbite. You are hiding. From me, I presume. I have been harsh in my grief. Astrid sent you to us. I must continue to remind myself of that. She trusted us to keep you safe. To protect you. It is evident to me that my daughter cared enough for you to take your secret to her grave. If she knew I was harsh to you, she would be disappointed in me. But you are going to have to help out around here. Two more mouths to feed are a lot to ask any family, but Sybbyl and I struggle already. There is a lot to be done if the four of us will survive the winter."

"Once I get back to the castle, though, I will be able to provide for you both for the rest of your lives. We don't know why the Typhans attacked. As far as we know, I am still heir to this throne," Magdalena interjects.

Hagen raises his hand to silence her. "We will take this one day at a time. It matters not if you are here for a week, a month, or a year; you and Liri are a burden. A welcomed one, one that Astrid gave her life for, but still a burden. Do you understand?" His voice is not gentle, though it isn't unkind either. He is merely stating facts.

"Yes, of course."

"Good. You start tomorrow." Hagen rises and reaches out his long, crooked fingers containing the book—an offering of peace. She takes it gratefully, hugging it to her chest.

"You will tell me if it's any good?"

"How about I read aloud to you?" she asks hesitantly. "At night, after the chores, of course. I could read a little. If you'd like."

Hagen nods his head. "That'll do. That'll do."

She watches until he has cleared the ladder before falling back onto the bed. Tears flow and pool in her ears as she brings the book seam to her nose to inhale the musty scent of it and place a light kiss on its cover. He has released her from her burden.

"Magdalena!"

She hadn't realized she had drifted off to sleep, but Liri's voice awakens her, and she sees her friend bounding over the edge of the ladder with excitement. Magdalena tries to lighten her face, put on her mask.

"What is it, Liri? You are absolutely bursting!"

"My lady, they have the most interesting chickens here! Well, I am sure all chickens are interesting in their own way, but these are spectacular."

Magdalena can't help but let out a genuine laugh as Liri holds out her apron to reveal all her treasured eggs in various shades of brown and white. Magdalena takes great interest in each one, much to Liri's delight.

A series of swift bangs vibrates from the cottage door, through the home, up the ladder, and to the loft where Liri startles and drops one of her eggs to the floor where it splatters. Magdalena jerks her head to Liri, eyes wide as she waits for Liri's assurance that a visitor is expected. Liri shakes her head from side to side.

Magdalena hears Hagen's chair creak as he raises himself from the table. Each step he takes to the door feels as if it is reverberating through her body. The door opens, and a waft of cold air rushes through the cottage. It smells damp and lifeless. She strains to hear Hagen's words against the wind. He must have invited the person in because just as suddenly as the door is opened, it is closed. She inhales and holds her breath.

"Thank you. It is very brisk out there indeed. Woooo, I'd hate to be caught out there with nowhere to go. Oh my, sorry, where are my manners at? My name is Samalt Aslund. I come from the castle. Sadly, I am bringing news of a travesty that occurred there two nights ago."

"Yes, sir. The whole countryside is talking about it. Typhans, they say. Any news on the king and queen? Our daughter has served the queen for many years. We have been waiting for her to come home. We have been waiting to hear if she is alive. Did you come with news, sir?" Hagen asks all this in a rush.

"I am unsure about your daughter. Coming to your house today, I was unaware that you had a daughter employed at the castle, or I certainly would have done my very best to gather as much information as I could prior to knocking. Sadly, though, the king and queen did die in the attack."

Magdalena inhales sharply as this final statement pierces her heart. Dead. The air in the small cottage has shifted. Magdalena can feel it. There is a darkness seeping in around them. It is thick and smells of wet metal. It is the smell of death. Her parents are dead. Dead. Dead. She says the word over and over in her mind, but she can't seem to give it meaning, give it purchase. It is as if she is trying to convince herself that her parents are now a tree.

"Oh my," Sybbyl exclaims in a small voice. "That is a tragedy. The poor children. What of the princes?"

"That is why I am here, actually. Prince Haluk is missing. As you can assume, there is a growing sense of urgency in locating the missing prince. Masunbria needs their king."

"Yes, yes, absolutely," says Hagen distractedly. Magdalena can almost feel him weighing his options.

"Well now. Let's see what you fine folk are up to, shall we? Is there anyone else in this house that I should know about? Are you harboring any Typhans in your barn, perhaps? Is there any member of the royal family hidden under your beds?" There is something about the way Samalt speaks. The tone of his voice is mocking as if he is playing a game, a menacing tone that sounds light and airy on the surface, but beneath it there is something unsettling to the ears.

"My wife, you've already met, and my niece lives here as well." Magdalena notes the lie and wonders if Hagen, too, senses something sinister in this man.

"Niece? Where might she be?"

"Oh, yes, of course. Eliza, can you please come down, dear?" Hagen calls up the ladder. The false name assures Magdalena and Liri that Hagen suspects this man is dangerous. Liri looks at Magdalena, her eyes frantic as she shakes her head rapidly back and forth.

"Eliza, dear, did you hear me?" Hagen calls again, his voice high and melodic. Magdalena mouths to Liri to respond. She urges her. Pleads with her eyes.

"I'll be right down, Uncle." Liri's voice trembles. Magdalena nods and pushes her forward toward the opening, but Liri won't move.

"You have to pretend, Liri," Magdalena whispers in her ear. "You just have to pretend for a while, okay? It will all be okay, I promise."

Liri only stares back at Magdalena, but she moves of her own accord toward the ladder.

She turns to descend and locks her eyes on Magdalena's. Magdalena tries to smile, to reassure her it's okay, but she knows what Liri is thinking. Liri is thinking that Magdalena is sending yet another maid to her death. Maybe she is. Perhaps Samalt will recognize her. Of course, no painting of Liri was ever cast, but a surviving maid could have attempted to describe her to him. Still, maybe Samalt will take her and torture her for information. Maybe Samalt will kill them all.

"There she is. Eliza, please meet Sir Samalt Aslund," Hagen introduces.

"What do you have there? Eggs? Now why on earth would you have your eggs up there?" Samalt laughs.

"Making sure they aren't fertile. Better light up there for it," says Hagen. "Now, sir, I appreciate you coming all the way out here, but I can assure you that there is no one here but the three of us. We've been all over this farm doing chores, and I am sure if there was a band of ruthless killers around here, we would know about it, let alone a prince hiding under our covers."

"I think it best you let a trained huntsman search the grounds. You wouldn't want people thinking you have something to hide. That wouldn't go well for you and your family. And you really can't put a cost on the life of your family, can you, Mr. Greene? You have already probably lost Astrid; it would be a shame to have something happen to Sybbyl or your lovely niece."

Magdalena raises her hand to cover her mouth, afraid that even her small breathing will be heard by the man down below. From somewhere deep inside, a roaring begins. It starts small, just a trickle. Her breathing quickens, and her eyes cease to blink. Soon, though, it is no longer a trickle, but a mighty rush. Fear.

"How did you know our daughter's name was Astrid? I thought you said you didn't know we had a daughter employed at the castle?" Sybbyl says in a voice that does nothing to hide the tremble in her tone.

"Oh, Sybbyl." Hagen laughs. "When I asked Sir Aslund about our daughter, I spoke her name. You must not have been paying attention. I think all the events of the past two days have you shaken. You should sit while I show the good man around."

"Yes, your mistake, I am sure. The whole of Masunbria is gravely shaken. Now then, Mr. Greene, let's begin, shall we? I would like to start inside this nice, warm home before making our way out to the cold of the barns," announces Samalt.

His words seem to spread from his lips, coil around the rungs of the ladder, and slither their way up to her ear where the forked tongue of them lick and taste the fear and trepidation that grows inside her. She imagines him a serpent. His long, slick body filling up the entire room as he circles the three below, hunting for a fourth. She knows it is only a matter of time before he is able to sniff her out. That thought frightens her, but not nearly as much as the fear of what this man will do to the three people below who have helped to hide her. She has to try to save them.

Hagen clears his throat. "Certainly you can see that this is merely a small cottage, but what you can't see is that we have a cellar below where we keep goods throughout the winter. I am rather proud of it, really. I dug it out myself when I was a much younger man. What makes this cellar so clever and unique is that you can access it from inside the home rather than going outdoors. I built a door right here in the floor under the rug. Now, I tell you this because I do believe this is the only part of the house that my family and I haven't entered in the last day or so. I also believe that if we were all out doing chores, it would have been easy for someone to come in and hide themselves below. There would be warmth and plenty of food. It is where I would go if I was scared and on the run."

Magdalena can hear the sound of shoes crossing the floor and a scraping sound as furniture is moved aside.

"Yep, there it is. Sybbyl, a couple candles please."

"I want you two ladies to join us in the cellar," Magdalena hears Samalt say. More shuffling sounds, and then a moment later, she hears that the voices have become more and more indistinguishable.

This, she sees, is her only chance. If she can get away, she can save them. She has to. If she doesn't, then what was the point of Astrid's sacrifice? She knows there is no time for her to make it down the ladder and out the door. She scans the room for a place to hide but finds nothing suitable. She dashes quickly from the room she and Liri share to the adjoining room that belongs to Hagen and Sybbyl. The family has only sparse furnishings and nothing capable of hiding a grown woman. She is out of options and soon out of time. She carefully eases the door to Hagen and Sybbyl's room closed, separating herself from the loft entrance on the other side. Standing in the center of the room, she closes her eyes and takes a deep breath and hopes that when she opens her eyes again, she will have a plan.

But when her lids part, the room remains as barren as it was when she shut its view from her mind. There is a bed pushed up against the wall, a small chest under the only window, a wardrobe, open to reveal the few pieces of simple clothing Hagen and Sybbyl own, and scatterings of small pieces of their life piled neatly on any available surface. A pipe, some pressed flowers, a few candles, the start of some weaving.

The window. One small circle of a window. If she can fit through, she can jump to the ground below and hope the snow will break her fall. She runs to the window and tries to open it, only to discover that the window is hinged in the middle so that the top rotates one way while the bottom another. The opening of the window that would allow her exit is half the size she anticipated. *I have to try.* She runs her hands over her borrowed dress. Made for winter, it is warm and thick. She strips it off and lays it neatly on the bed.

She hears wafts of conversation as the occupants of the cottage emerge from the depths of the cellar and back to the main floor. *Time is running out.*

She clambers up the chest that sits under the small window and pushes the bottom half of the window outward. The cold winter wind enters the small opening, whipping her hair and causing her to shiver in her shift. She looks down and tries to gauge the fall. Below is where the pen lies for the pigs, and to her dismay, there is much less snow than there is mud. There is nothing to break her fall, not that she was certain snow would have helped anyway. Magdalena inclines her ear toward the door. She can hear the wood of the ladder squeak under the weight of the person ascending it. They are climbing.

Spinning so her back is to the window, Magdalena lowers her hands to the chest and walks her bare feet up the wall toward the window. Her foot reaches the edge, and she begins to nudge the window open. The hinges creak from their near-frozen state. Her arms shake from supporting her weight, and sweat begins to form on her back and neck. Once more she raises her foot to the window and pushes. The hinges groan, and finally, they give. One foot and then the other escape. She pushes hard on her hands against the chest, straightening her arms, and the fronts of her legs scrape against the wood grain of the window ledge as they free themselves from the room and dangle out the window. She can hear the men in the first bedroom.

Her heart is beating hard in her chest. The ledge of the window is digging into her bare upper thighs. She has to move, now. She begins to rock her body, trying to get enough momentum to tilt her lower half out the window. On the third attempt she succeeds, and her body falls a few inches before her middle catches hard between the window and the ledge. Gravity is pulling her out and down, but she can't move. She is stuck. She pulls in her stomach and tries to stop her lungs from expanding. She can hear them now, at the door. She wiggles and pushes her palms against the window ledge. Tears are streaming down her face. The wind is whipping her linen shift around her bare legs. She bites down hard on her teeth, using every ounce of strength she has left, and she pushes. Then, she falls.

4
Henrick

Henrick awakes to find the bed next to him empty. Thea didn't return again last night. This is not unusual behavior, but still there is a twinge of disappointment in the realization. Henrick hoped that with the promise of a new life, Thea would leave the old one behind. Her demons would remain back at their old home, where they would haunt the empty halls without her there to nurture and feed them. He is slightly angry at Thea for not giving this new life a chance.

They have occupied the castle for several nights now, of which she has turned to her inner torment for comfort and abandoned him. He will not let her deter his ambition, his vitality, his exuberance. He will find her and set her straight. He dresses quickly in a dark green linen shirt with three buttons at the neck, and black trousers, laced at the waist. He affixes his gold broach to the right breast of his shirt. It is the symbol of Masunbria—an old tree with twisting branches, like arms outstretched, and on one of those branches, a small dove, an offering. Pausing at the looking glass, he admires the way he looks in these rooms, the way he feels lighter than ever before. More handsome even, he notices. His dark eyes seem exuberant. His black hair, combed straight back, shines in the candlelight. He runs his hands over the stubble of a beard that lines his jaw. *It is good to be back within these walls.* He travels to the lady's library, playing a game as he goes. He touches everything he passes and declares them his. He informs the inanimate objects within the halls that he is their new master. It seems that the candlesticks and paintings take the news well, and he is delighted in his own humor when he arrives outside the library doors. Thea informed him the day prior that she claimed this space as her own, and he didn't object. Now, though, his hand hovers over the knob.

The room beyond is where his mother spent her days hiding from his father. His father was a terrible parent and an even worse husband. As a boy, Henrick recalls seeing the marks his father left on his mother's arms, across her neck, or under her eyes. He saw the way she wore her hair to cover a swollen cheek. Henrick was not yet ten years old when his mother decided she would rather die than live another day. Her only daughter was gifted to the Typhans; she saw her firstborn son become a man. She couldn't be bothered with how Henrick would survive until manhood or whether or not he needed her, loved her.

It was in this library that he found her. His father laughed at the news. They buried her under a tree in the garden. His father never got around to marking the grave, and now, so many years later, Henrick can't recall which tree she is even under. The people of Masunbria believed she died of fever. She didn't leave a letter or a message of any kind to comfort her remaining child. *I hate this room.*

Taking a breath, he turns the knob and pushes the door open. The light of the room blinds him for a moment as he steps from the dark hallway. Thea is seated at the desk in the center of the room. The dull sunlight is spilling in from the floor-to-ceiling windows that overlook the gardens. Her gardens. A chill runs through his spine as the image of his mother's body being taken by the earth floods his vision, roots rising to circle her wrists and ankles, pulling from her whatever life remained to feed itself. He crosses the room quickly and draws the curtains closed.

"Henrick, are you okay?" asks Thea, looking at her husband curiously. "You look pale."

"Fine. You didn't return to bed last night."

"No, I am sorry. I was up late and didn't want to disturb you. I think I have a plan, Henrick."

Henrick stares blankly at his wife.

"A plan for it all. The funeral, the coronation, the Typhans. Your niece."

Henrick continues to stare.

"You know, Prince Haluk, who wasn't a prince, the one missing."

"I know who she is, Thea. Samalt was out all day yesterday looking for her. He will find her. The guy is absolutely terrifying and bizarre, but he is effective. Dagen has no doubt in him, and, therefore, neither do I." Henrick turns his chin up at this last statement to signal to Thea that he has said all there is to say on the matter of Maggie. He watches Thea from the corner of his eye, daring her to speak of it again. She opens her mouth but decides to close it. *Good for her.*

"Regarding your absence last night, though, we do need to speak of that."

"It is not the same, Henrick. It isn't like at home, I promise. I just was too excited to sleep. Too anxious. I will be joining you tonight. I promise, darling." Thea smiles up at him. He studies her face a moment, looking to see what lives there, behind her eyes. What is she not telling him? He finds nothing, which isn't a surprise. Thea is a master of masking her emotions. He sighs wearily, abandoning his frustration entirely. There is no point. He can only hope that things will be different now, but it is up to Thea to make it so.

"Let's go to breakfast." Henrick sighs as he holds out his hand to Thea.

Henrick and Thea walk into the dining room. The smell of smoked pig and honeyed bowls of porridge welcomes them. The thick curtains have been cast open, and the daylight, dim as it is, streams into the room and across the long, planked wood of the dining table. Henrick is surprised to find Niklaus already seated there. He looks like hell, his face pale and his eyes red. His hair is disheveled, and his clothes are the ones from the day prior. He sits hunched over his plate and makes no effort to raise his head at their approach. He has a look Henrick is familiar with, the one that says that he has been up the entire night drinking to rid himself of something.

"Good morning, my dear nephew," bellows Henrick, slapping the boy on his back.

Niklaus flinches and brings his palms to his forehead, where he squeezes the skin there. Henrick masks his laughter as best he can.

"Good morning, Uncle." Niklaus groans from behind his hands.

Thea slaps Henrick's arm playfully as they take their seats and begin their meal. It isn't long before the three are interrupted by a knock at the door. Unable to resist, Henrick shouts his approval for the person to enter and sees Niklaus fold into himself once more.

"Oh, yes, I am so sorry, Niklaus," says Henrick with mock concern dripping from his lips.

Dagen and Samalt enter the room, and to Henrick's pure delight, they are still wearing their metal armor, which clanks with each step the men take. Niklaus, having had enough, pushes away from the table in agony and rises to leave.

"Sir Niklaus, this matter concerns you. Won't you stay?" asks Dagen, holding a hand up to pause the boy and his departure.

"Dagen, I am unwell this morning. I will refer you to my uncle on whatever your matter. I trust that Henrick will speak on my behalf with the best interest for us and the kingdom." Niklaus gives a quick bow to the room before hurrying out.

Henrick roars with laughter once the door is shut behind the boy. It will be easier than he thought to rule this kingdom the way he sees fit so long as the boy continues to drink like a fish. Dagen laughs as well and takes the seat Niklaus has just vacated. He picks up a fork and begins to eat the untouched slice of pork. Samalt stands awkwardly near the door, looking around the room and smiling. Henrick wishes he could do away with Samalt. A tall and lanky man with a nose too large and a jaw too small, his face appears like it was patched together from many different men to create a single awkward representation of the male species. He has dark hair that covers his forehead like curtains on a window and tickles the tops of his ears. When nervous, he constantly smooths his hair flat to his head in long, methodical strokes. He is unsettling.

"Alright, Dagen, what do you have for us this fine morning?"

"Well," says Dagen, mouth full of food, "it's about that damn girl."

"Oh, sir Dagen, please don't speak that way of her. She is just a little lost pearl hiding in a sea of grass," says Samalt with a wistful smile.

"What in the hell is he talking about?" Henrick asks Dagen, thumb pointing to Samalt.

"Maggie, of course," replies Dagen, rolling his eyes.

This girl again, Henrick thinks. "What could it possibly be now? You told me that he would find her. You told me that it was all taken care of, Dagen." Henrick sees Thea out of the corner of his eye dab at her mouth with her napkin to hide the smile playing at the edges of her lips.

"Samalt has been all over the countryside and hasn't had any luck finding her. The kitchen hand that was spared from Hadrian's household has proven helpful in giving us the names of Magdalena's maids and the farm which one maid, Astrid, grew up on. The other maid, Liri, has no family left, as her parents died of the outbreak many years ago. Samalt has visited the maid's farm and spent hours there combing the land and questioning the family. Nothing. My men have searched the forest for her body and, again, have come up empty-handed. We are going to have to release a statement soon. If Magdalena chooses to assert her claim as Haluk and we don't have possession of her, or evidence to prove that she is a woman, Niklaus will lose control. Worse yet, if the girl knows Niklaus was involved, she could, as Haluk, order his arrest or worse. She could raise up an army, and it would be our word on her nature against hers. Henrick, we are going to have to tread carefully."

Thea makes a noise as she clears her throat. Henrick glances at his wife. She is sitting with her hands resting gently in her lap. She is waiting. She is gloating. Henrick keeps his mouth pinched tightly shut. He sees Dagen look to Thea, back to Henrick, and then to Thea once more, a look of confusion across his face. Henrick picks up his fork and grips it in his fist so tightly that it begins to bend. The silence in the room spreads. Henrick grows annoyed.

"Out with it, Thea," Henrick demands at last, throwing the bent silver to the table.

Thea situates herself further in her chair and takes a sip of her tea before placing the cup gently back on the table. She looks at the three men in the room and smiles. "I have found the physician, the one who birthed her. I found records in Katherine's library indicating his identity and where, now retired and very well compensated for his silence, he lives. It is a small village in the north. My plan is to keep the Typhans alive in Masunbria. Your men must continue to ravage the land. Nothing too brutal, just enough to create fear. That will be the spark that starts the fire. We will devise a leader of the Typhan people, and that leader and his band of barbarians will attack the funeral where all the sweet villagers have congregated to mourn with our dear Niklaus. It is there that our Typhans will present this physician who will reveal Hadrian's lie. Niklaus will appear shocked; he had no idea. Henrick will be outraged and ashamed his brother would do such a thing. Niklaus, overcome with emotion and tormented over the news, will weep. The Typhan leader, face full of fury, will look straight into Henrick's eyes and give him a fortnight to bring the princess forward before war is waged on all of Masunbria and every woman is taken to what lies beyond Crask as payment for Hadrian's deception. The funeral will turn to chaos. Men will shout, and women will hug their babes close. There won't be a soul around who won't be looking for Haluk after a speech like that." At her final words, Thea throws her arms up in a shrug. The men stare.

Thea rolls her eyes at the looks of confusion and shock the three men are sending her direction. "You can take it or leave it," she says dismissively as she rises to leave, but Dagen reaches out his arm to stop her. He settles his large hand on her thin forearm.

"It's good, Thea. It is really good." Dagen smiles up at her.

Henrick stares at Dagen's hand on his wife's skin, and a fire rages inside of him, burning, rolling, and thick smoke seeps into his eyes. Dagen, having looked from Thea to Henrick, notices the look on his face and promptly pulls his hand from Thea's arm. The two men stare at one another, anger on the face of one, dismay on the face of the other.

***

Henrick finds Niklaus at the end of a narrow hall, forehead pressed to the cool glass of a second-story window. Henrick stands back awhile and watches the boy. He is drinking and watching someone or something out the window. The sky beyond has resumed its typical shade of depressing gray, just as it was the day before and shall be all the days to come until winter finally breaks. Henrick envies Niklaus. He wishes someone would have helped him kill his father the way he has helped Niklaus. Instead, he had to live and wait for age or illness to finally take him. Niklaus doesn't realize the gift Henrick has given him. It was Hadrian's fault anyway. He didn't understand Niklaus. Hadrian took for granted the fact that he was a father. He didn't take the job seriously enough, or things would have never ended up like this. Henrick knows that if he could have ever been a father, his own son would never turn against him because he would know that boy's worth and that boy would know Henrick's love. Henrick's eyes sting with the tears brimming there, and he wipes furiously before shouting a greeting to Niklaus.

"Do you have any for me?"

Niklaus reaches to the ground and pulls up a jug of wine but no cup. Henrick lifts the half-full jug to his lips and takes a long swallow. The warmth travels past his tongue and down his throat, and he feels better already. He shifts so he can look out the window so he can see what the boy has been watching. Below, men are loading up carts with the bodies of the dead to be brought into town. The snow is lightly falling, and the pale faces look up at Henrick in the second-story window. Flakes of snow land on open, unblinking eyes. They stand side by side, uncle and nephew, as men, women, and children are loaded one on top of another. The men aren't careful, but why should they be? They grab arms and legs and swing and release, swing and release. Henrick looks to Niklaus out of the corner of his eye and sees that the boy is mouthing something with each toss.

"What's that? What are you saying, Niklaus?" Henrick asks, his tone soft.

"Huh? Oh, um, their names, Uncle. I am saying their names as they are loaded. Well, the ones I know, anyway. It was those younger men down there that gave me my first sip of wine when my father wasn't looking. Those women would run to my side when I was little and had fallen out of a tree. They would look closely at my knee, all scraped and red. They would blow on it very gently. Those children below would ask me for candy or to play a game with them. Some of them I can recall as babies in their mother's arms. They gave their life so that I could live mine the way I was destined to. Free to rule Masunbria like her true first-born son. I see that, Uncle. I just want to pay them the respect they deserve."

Henrick nods his head in agreement and reaches an arm to wrap around the boy's shoulder while they both look out the window as the next body is loaded. They sip and they watch.

"Tell me, why did your parents bother to give your sister a girl's name at all?"

Niklaus lets out a small laugh before tipping the jug of wine to his lips. "They really thought someday she could be free. Each full moon, they held their breath to see if the doors to the mountain

49

pass would remain closed, if the monsters on the other side had finally forgotten, moved on, died, given up. Anything to signal that the end was here at last. They gave her a girl's name because they had hope. Pitiful, don't you think?"

"What was it like, to look at her and live here with her knowing that it should have been you?" Henrick can't help but think of his feelings toward Hadrian. At least Hadrian was legitimate, unlike what poor Niklaus has had to endure.

Niklaus sips more wine, and Henrick can see he is wrestling with something as he considers his questions.

"Haluk was a good brother," Niklaus sighs. "I know how that sounds, but it is true. I didn't know Haluk was Magdalena until I was seventeen years old. My parents kept the entire castle away from Haluk. Everyone thought they were just very protective of their eldest son and heir. They even tried to keep us apart, but Maggie would always find a way to escape."

"You should know that we have a plan for her. Thea has devised it. This story will only end one way, and that is with your sister gone from your life forever."

Niklaus doesn't speak but continues to look out the window. He raises his jug to his lips and takes a long pull. "Felton," he says as the last body is loaded. He turns then to look at Henrick.

"I don't care what you say about Maggie or what happens to her. She is nothing to me. If you think Aunt Thea's plan will work, then I support it."

"Good. We attack the seven larger villages of Masunbria tomorrow night. We will need to make the people afraid that the Typhans are here if this plan is going to work."

"Do what has to be done."

"More will die," Henrick says.

"Death is inevitable in the rebirth of Masunbria. Many more will die when I begin to conquer our neighboring lands. The greatness of our empire will be built on their bodies, and I will never forget their sacrifice. I will watch them all be buried and look upon each face just as I have today. With greatness comes sacrifice, Uncle. I understand that fully. Now, let's get to work."

5
Magdalena

Magdalena tries to open her eyes, but she finds that her lashes, top and bottom, are stuck together. She begins to lift her arm in an attempt to rub the matted lids, but the pain that courses through her shoulder prevents the action. It is a sharp, stabbing pain, that makes her dizzy even though she is lying down and has nowhere to fall. She lies quiet, listens. Where is she? Back at the castle, perhaps? She remembers the jump. She remembers how she had landed hard on the frozen, trampled mud. The unforgiving and unmoving peaks of hardened earth tore into flesh and hammered against bones deep within. She remembers crawling to a nearby pig enclosure. The pain on the right side of her body screamed as she moved faster and faster.

She can see herself as if she is floating above the scene. She is curled up in the small shelter, her white nightshift wet and covered in filth, sticking to her body. She can still hear the wind whistling as it blows between the cracks in the slats of the hut. She tried to cover herself with the straw that was scattered on the ground, keep herself warm. Then all she remembers is darkness. She must have fallen asleep. *Shock from the pain? But then what? Did Samalt find me? What happened next?*

She is so very thirsty that her mind can think of nothing else, and she decides that she must make an attempt to face whatever may lie on the other side of her closed eyes, for she feels that death is knocking regardless. Raising her left arm this time, she rubs at her eyelids, opening them. Blinking several times, she clears her blurred vision, and a breath of relief escapes her aching ribs as she takes in the worn beams above her. The sight of them relaxes her body, and her other senses, having seemed to lie dormant in her state of shock, begin to return to her as well. She can smell herbs seeping on a stove and the musky smell of wood in the hearth. Safe. She is with Hagen and Sybbyl. She is safe. Tears come, and she lets them fall, unworried about who may look upon them. She tries to open her mouth to call out, but it is so dry and her throat so raw she can't make a single sound. She slaps her left hand on the ground, raises it, and brings it down again. Soon she feels rather than hears the quick steps, and she knows she has been heard.

"Magdalena!" Liri is peering over her, touching her face, her hair, her arms as if ensuring that it really is her moving and awake. She bends down and plants kisses on Magdalena's forehead. Liri's tears fall to Magdalena's face and mix with her own. They form streaks as they trickle to the rug below. Roadways of pale skin under dried blood and dirt. Liri rises quickly and runs to the front door, where she swings it open wide. Cold air forces itself inside the cottage.

"Sybbyl, she is awake. Hurry."

Out of breath, Sybbyl kneels down and helps Liri bring Magdalena to a sitting position, back resting against the legs of the worn chair near the fire. Together they bring her blankets up and around her chin, tucking her into a cocoon. Magdalena closes her eyes, grateful to be alive.

Sybbyl returns with a cup of steaming liquid, and Magdalena gratefully accepts the offering. Inside she can see the hot water and herbs dancing together. She takes a long, slow sip. Her throat burns from the action, but she does it again and again. She breathes heavily with each tilt of the cup, drawing the heady scent of the herbs into her nose, hoping that they possess within them some earthly powers that will heal her mind and body.

Sybbyl reaches out and places her palm gently on Magdalena's cheek. "You, my dear, sweet girl, are so very brave." She leans forward and kisses Magdalena in the center of her forehead. Her lips leave a warmth behind, and Magdalena once again feels relief enter her sore body. She is here. They are here. She did it.

Her peace doesn't last long, for there is a single knock which vibrates the door and causes Magdalena's heart to plummet to her stomach. She gasps for air, but it is as if that single knock has collapsed her lungs into her chest and no air can inflate them. Sybbyl hurries to place a calming hand on Magdalena's arm.

"Shhhh, shhhhh. There, there. It is okay, my dear. It is Brom. We didn't know who else to send for. It is alright. He is a friend, remember? He is one you can trust."

Without invitation, the door swings open, and Brom Anker fills the doorway with his large statute. His face does nothing to hide the shock and worry etched within his features. He moves swiftly to Magdalena and kneels before her.

"Tell me," he says to the room.

"We know she is hurt; we are just uncertain how badly," says Sybbyl, pushing a strand of hair from Magdalena's forehead as if she were a small child.

"I fell from up there," Magdalena speaks weakly, using her left hand to point upward.

"I know. Hagen came and got me. Aside from the fall, my lady, you were in the pig hut yesterday for over three hours, barely dressed, in temperatures cold enough to freeze one's spit midair. Do you remember anything at all?"

"We brought you in as soon we found you," Liri says apologetically. "You've been asleep here by the fire all day and through the night. I haven't left your side. I've been so worried."

Magdalena shakes her head. The fall was yesterday? Did she really sleep that long? Why is she still so tired?

"The man from the castle, Samalt, he was here for so long searching the property," Sybbyl continued. "He entered mine and Hagen's room shortly after you jumped, we assume. He noticed how cold the room was. Hagen said something about bad craftsmanship, but that Samalt, he knew better. He knew by the chill and the smell of winter hanging heavy in the air that the window had been opened. He had moved quickly to the window to peer down, but he never saw you. After that, we believe he was just buying time. He searched the entire property, inside and out. The pig huts are tiny and ill built, and I think that's the only thing that saved you." Sybbyl laughs weakly. "Hagen has been meaning to fix 'em up, you see. Samalt took one look and knew if anyone was crazy enough to hide in there in weather like this, they'd be all but dead. If the weather didn't kill, the pigs surely would. The man is cunning. I think he would have stayed forever had a dispatch not come by horseback that drove him away. As he rode off, he gave one final look over his shoulder to where Hagen, Liri, and I stood. Brom, the look in his eyes was dangerous. Frightening. He called himself a huntsman, and if that's the case, then we were certainly his prey."

Brom shakes his head and drags his hand down and over his chin, which hadn't been shaved in a day or two. He tries to smile at Magdalena, but the effort falls flat, and he knows it. "Well, let's take a look at the damage." His eyes look at her expectantly.

What? she thinks. *He can't be serious.* She looks from Brom to Sybbyl and pulls the blankets up higher to her chin with her one good arm as she glares at them. She has spent her entire life hiding her body, knowing that what lies below her clothes is dangerous. The sight of her pale pink flesh by the wrong person wouldn't just start a war; it would fall a kingdom. Sybbyl begins muttering reassurances and patting Magdalena, but she isn't listening. Her body, her scandalous, dangerous, traitorous body. She is not going to show anyone, let alone this man, that which is her greatest curse and heaviest burden.

"I am not afraid of you," says Brom, arching an eyebrow.

"You should be," replies Magdalena dryly looking down to her hands folded in her lap. She shakes slightly and feels the pain of a headache develop behind her eyes. She is so tired. *Everyone should be afraid that I yet live*, she thinks. She pictures the four tapestries that line the walls of her father's den back at the castle. Each tapestry depicts a key moment in Masunbrian history. The first shows the fires that spread down the mountains and engulfed the forest below—the forest which was, and still is, their livelihood. Summer doesn't last long in Masunbria, but when it arrives, it is warm and dry. It is said that one torch is all it took for the Typhans to set the kingdom ablaze.

The second tapestry depicts the bloody aftermath as the hoard descended Crask mountains and slaughtered anyone who dared try to stop them. The Typhan men are shown with long blonde hair and full beards. The tapestry depicts one such man biting into a human heart, blood in red stitching dripping down his chin. The castle, as it was before, can be seen stitched in the upper right corner. It looks peaceful, in that state, aside from the stitched figure of her beheaded great-great-grandfather King Simeon.

The scene of the third tapestry, one that is said to depict the aftermath of a decades-long war with the Typhans, takes place near one of the hundreds of open pits used as graves for all those dead from so many years of fighting. The villagers not appearing in pits are depicted as frail ghosts of the people they once were. Many of them are chained together. Without clothes, they have skin of gray with bones visible along their chest. In this tapestry, her great-grandfather is seen down on his knees before a Typhan warlord. Standing next to his kneeling figure is that of a small girl, one delicate hand resting on the king's slumped shoulder. The other hand extends toward the Typhan leader, palm up. She is dressed all in white with a crown of flowers on her head. A white dove flies above the scene, a spark of light in the dark sky. The final tapestry is of the men of Masunbria erecting a massive wooded gate across the mountain pass, while the women are seen bringing baskets of goods and gold to place at the door. This is the only scene in which the sun appears to be shining on the land. The trees are seen to be growing new foliage after their burning. The people are plumper, and their faces are bright. They've been saved.

"Why is it that I should fear you?" Brom asks, awakening her from her unpleasant memories.

"Alive and here in Masunbria, I am capable of bringing disease, slavery, war, and famine to our land once again. You've heard the tales. You know that this body you are asking to see is a cursed thing for Masunbria." Her voice is cold and void of emotion, but she holds her chin high and meets his gaze.

Brom rakes his eyes over Magdalena's lean body with its long, toned muscles pulled tight under pale skin. He looks at her watery blue eyes, defiant as they peer into his. He studies her full pink lips and her short, pale blonde hair that is sticking up at odd angles and caked with dried mud and blood. He smiles down at her long fingers subtly twisting the blankets in nervousness. A crack in her armor.

"I'll take my chances," he says with a smile.

Brom is tender but thorough as he prods the tight muscles of her abdomen to watch her response. He lifts her shoulder and rotates it one way and then the other. He drums his fingers under her breast and across her ribcage. After he has finished, he eases her nightshift back in place and brings the blankets up to her chin. He rises and moves to the door to call for Hagen. He is there in seconds, apparently waiting outside. He stomps the snow from his boots and pulls the wool hat from his head swiftly, causing the thin wisps of gray to stick up in all directions.

"Well," Hagen says, smiling down at Magdalena, "what's the damage with our girl?"

"I am no physician, but I have seen plenty to believe that she has three, maybe more, broken ribs, a dislocated shoulder, plenty of cuts and scrapes that will need to be cleaned out in a hurry. None appear to need stitching up, but if they don't get clean, they will be a problem."

"Can you help her?"

"I know someone who can, someone who can be trusted. I do have news to share. My sister, Sabina, is alive. I got word from her just last night. She hid herself away during the attacks inside a kitchen cupboard. She is well. I also have news regarding Astrid for you both. Members of the castle will be delivering the dead by cart for burial this evening. They will also be speaking about the events that surrounded their deaths and the deaths of the king and queen. I know the thought of leaving home after what happened here is frightful, but you both should be there. Liri and Magdalena should remain here, of course. No fire, though, no candlelight. They must remain hidden in the event men like Samalt take advantage of empty houses to continue their search."

A shiver runs down Magdalena's spine at the thought of sitting in the dark and quiet wondering if Samalt is out there. Lurking. Looking. She knows, however, that what Brom says is true. Hagen and Sybbyl must go to town and collect Astrid. They must bring their daughter home for burial, and Magdalena owes it to them to be strong enough to allow them this small mercy without the slightest hesitation.

***

An uncountable number of hours have passed since Magdalena and Liri descended the stairs to the cellar below. With the darkness of the cellar enveloping them, there has been nothing to do but sleep. Leaned into one another, the women have drifted in and out of consciousness, awaking only occasionally to try to focus their eyes in the dark and listen for the breathing of the snake returned for his prey. With no firelight above casting veiled warmth through the slats in the floorboards, the cellar is darker than any night Magdalena has ever experienced. She can bring her hand to just before her nose and still not see her fingers wave. The cellar is a void. It allows the imagination to run wild. While the silence and darkness have overcome them, her mind has begun filling in details her ears and eyes can't. Samalt staring at her from across the dirt floor. His hand reaching for her ankle. A rat smelling her hair. It is unnerving. She thought nothing could be worse than the darkness and the silence until that very moment when she hears the door to the cottage open and boots creak on the floor above. She shakes Liri lightly to wake her. She hears it too, confirmation it isn't Magdalena's imagination this time. They interweave their fingers together and stare up.

"Sybbyl, I am going to grab some wine."

Relief fills Magdalena's heart at the sound of Hagen's voice. The light from the cellar door opening causes streaks of welcomed candlelight to permeate the space.

Once up the ladder stairs, Magdalena and Liri move toward the fire Sybbyl is prodding to flame. They are damp and cold from the earth they were huddled in. Hagen brings each a cup of wine. Magdalena gratefully accepts and takes a long, slow swallow. The warmth of the wine travels down her throat and takes residence in her belly. Both Hagen and Sybbyl collapse into the chairs near the hearth, their faces weary and their bodies seemingly unable to stand any longer. The weight of the day is a burden they can no longer carry.

"Astrid has returned home," Hagen says at last. "She will be buried tomorrow morning under the large tree down the lane. She used to climb that tree as a girl, and she would have loved that to be her resting place. Brom will be coming to help, as the ground is far too frozen for me to dig alone." Hagen laughs a short, false laugh and takes a slow drink of his wine.

"Who is ruling Masunbria now? What exactly happened?" Liri asks.

Sybbyl takes a sip of her wine. "Men came to town with their carts as we were told would happen. With them, though, was a stately man on horseback with a large scar across his face. Dagen Horne. He said he was the head of the army your uncle brought after the attacks. He told us what happened that night. He said that an attack came while the castle slept. They are certain it was the Typhans. They came as silent as the night and slaughtered ruthlessly, his words, not mine. Those that survived the attack say the men were looking for something, or someone, in particular. We were told that though the men of the castle had fought for their lives and the lives of the people within the walls, they were no match for these monsters. The time of peace we were all accustomed to under the reign of King Hadrian and Queen Katherine had made our men soft and unprepared. We were told that your brother fought them off the best he could as he made his way to your parents' chambers to protect them. He is singlehandedly responsible for the killing of several assailants. When he arrived, though, it was already too late. Your parents were gone. Enraged, your brother ran through the castle looking for any last one to kill. They had already gone though. He found a stable boy hiding behind some feed and sent him with haste to retrieve your uncle Henrick from his bed."

"What do they say of Haluk?" asks Liri, eyes darting to Magdalena.

"They say Haluk was a coward who fled in the night. Abandoned his family," Hagen replies quietly without looking up from the fire.

"Well," Magdalena says frankly, "they aren't wrong."

6
Henrick

Smoke billows from the twine-wrapped herbs Thea has lit. The smell awakens Henrick, and he rolls to his side to look at his wife's back. She is kneeling near the hearth, bundle in hand and whispering her chants to a god he doesn't know or understand. Henrick doesn't make a sound, doesn't move, barely breathes; he just watches. When Thea began performing her rituals several years back, Henrick was afraid to ask her about them. In many ways, he still is. He doesn't want to know whom she speaks to and what she asks. It is his fault anyway, this obsession of hers. He was the one who invited the seer into their home.

Thea was not able to conceive a child despite their best efforts. Several years ago, Thea became convinced that she was, at last, with child. Henrick believed she would soon rid herself of the fantasy, but it only grew stronger. Month after month, her faith in the unborn child she believed she carried only grew. She walked around their home cradling her flat stomach, already a protective mother. She would speak of being tired and sore, but she wasn't complaining. She was marveling at the ways in which her body was changing. She would describe for Henrick the feeling of muscles and ligaments being pulled and loosened. She would tell him about the miracle of her body as it begged her to rest so that her energy might be used to create a being. She had her ladies knit blankets for the baby bed she had commissioned to be built. At night, she would talk for hours with Henrick about names for the baby and what the child might look like. She hoped the child would have her curls and his sharp nose.

Henrick was at such a loss during this time of their marriage. He adored his wife and he wished the things she spoke were true, but as time passed, her stomach remained as it always was. Henrick couldn't comprehend what was happening to her, mentally or physically. No one countered her though. The ladies went on knitting, and the cooks continued to accommodate to her cravings. Henrick rubbed her feet. Carpenters built cradles. No one wanted to be the one to break her heart.

Several months passed and still Thea did not bleed. Henrick had her ladies reporting to him any sign of her monthly course. At first, he assumed she was hiding the evidence from them, somehow outsmarting the ladies, as she deduced that they were spies for Henrick. No matter how much he questioned them though, their story never changed. They bathed her and dressed her morning and night, and they took her clothes to be washed. There was no sign of blood. It was then that Henrick himself began to wonder if it wasn't true after all. He even let himself get excited about the prospect. He was more eager to talk to Thea about names and noses.

One morning, over breakfast, Thea jumped from the table and moved to Henrick in one swift motion. Her face was aglow. She grabbed his hand and placed his palm on her still-flat stomach. She exclaimed that the baby was kicking. He spread his fingers and held his breath. He waited, excitement rising. Nothing happened. He looked at Thea curiously. She insisted it was there and that she could feel it with her own hand and it was strong and steady. He again held his hand in place, where she instructed but felt nothing, not a twitch. He looked up to tell her there wasn't anything there, but he was met with shining eyes and a smile that broke his heart.

His wife wasn't well. He knew that for sure now. Whatever was going on inside her mind or body, a baby was not it. Heartbroken as he was, he was afraid for Thea. He summoned for a doctor, but Thea wouldn't let him touch her. Henrick tried to explain that the doctor was there to check on the baby, but still she refused to be seen. At a loss, Henrick sent Dagen out to find a seer. He didn't believe in that sort of thing, but he was out of options and thought perhaps a woman, better than any man, could convince Thea there was no child.

When the old woman arrived, Henrick led her upstairs where Thea sat, bathed in soft daylight, with her knitting. The old woman spoke not a word but lowered her thin, bone-white body to the chair across from Thea. Henrick stayed near the door of the nursery trying to hide with the shadows there. He knew this was his last chance to free his wife's mind from the cruel and torturous place it was currently residing in. They sat there, the two women, young and old, for a long while, not saying a word. Thea continued to focus on her knitting, and the woman watched, bony fingers knotted together in her lap. At last, the woman reached one of those bone-white hands over and placed it on Thea's stomach. Thea didn't move it away, nor did she look up at the woman's face. She simply paused her knitting midstitch, wooden needles crossing one another at the point.

"My darling, you are not with child," the old woman began. "You are intended for greatness beyond which you can imagine, but sadly, that greatness will come at a price. You will never bear children, but you will one day rule over many. You will stand tall while men, women, and children fall to the ground at your feet. You will not have a child of your own, as you will instead be the mother of a great kingdom. Your name will be spoken from mountain to sea. You will be celebrated all the days of your life and those beyond. You will never die, because mothers will tell their daughters of you, and those daughters will tell their sons. You, Thea, shall live forever on the lips of your people."

Thea spoke not a word in return. She slowly sat her knitting down on her lap and turned to look at Henrick. There were tears in her eyes and streaming down her cheeks as she looked across the room to her husband. Henrick met her sorrowful gaze with his own face distorted by pain and sadness and his own eyes swimming in the tears of despair. It was on that day that the knitting and baby bed were removed from the house. It was on that day that Thea and Henrick began planning to overthrow his brother, certain that was the path the seer had foretold. It was on that day that Thea adopted a new religion from the old woman and Henrick abandoned any remaining hope for a child. It was on that day that Thea began to bleed once more.

***

Henrick silently raises his hand and wipes the tears forming in his eyes at the memories he has spent the past few moments reliving. He silently chastises himself for allowing his thoughts to go there, to that place of dark, to that time when he lost his wife, never to be fully found again. She always had a piece of her that died with the hope of that child. Henrick lost a piece of himself too. A piece of his morality died with the thought of him never becoming a father. Before, he tried with some difficulty to be a good man. He practiced what that looked like and felt like, so he would become nothing like his father when he, too, bore a son. Once that option of a child was off the table, he no longer had a reason to be a good man.

It was within the pit of that moral abandonment that he found her: Catrain. She was understanding and comforting, and she made him laugh when all the world was so very sad and serious. Though to this day there is guilt that washes over him and drowns out his soul, he still can't shake Catrain from his life. She saved him from despair. Thea was drowning and pulling Henrick down with her, and Catrain reached out her arm, and he took it. He wrapped his hand around hers and felt the warmth and softness of her skin. His life has never been the same since.

Henrick stirs loudly to alert his wife that he is awake. He has to move, shake himself free of these thoughts. Thea turns and smiles warmly at him.

"What are you whispering about this morning, my love?" asks Henrick.

"All the moving pieces, my darling. There is so much that must align, and it is my job to orchestrate it all. You had better run along, Henrick. Dagen will surely want to fill you in on the raids last night. Let me do my work here, and I will find you later."

Henrick can't believe that the raids slipped his mind. He hops from the bed and pulls on brown trousers, leaving his ivory shirt untucked and unbuttoned. Kissing Thea atop her head, he leaves her with her smoke and heads down the hall, humming a tuneless song as he goes. Arriving at the dining hall, he sees that Dagen is already halfway through his meal, and he scolds himself silently for lying in bed and wasting time on his terrible thoughts.

"Tell me, Dagen. Tell me it all!" Henrick says as he takes up a seat near the head of his army.

Dagen smiles and tries to chew his food faster. He grabs a cup and adds some wine to the food mixture in his mouth to force it down earlier than suitable. His throat protests the mass of swollen bread and wine, and Dagen beats on his chest twice in an effort to help nudge the food further down.

"Brother, it was brilliant," Dagen wheezes, still trying to clear his throat. He takes another long swallow and wipes his mouth as he rises from his chair, a wide grin on his scarred face. He comes to stand next to the seated Henrick and begins to push aside plates and cups as he unrolls a map. Henrick looks at the drawing before him.

It is a rough sketch of Masunbria, the largest occupied land mass from the mountains to the sea. The forest is thick and covers much of the kingdom. As a result, the villages are small and spread throughout the land. In some instances, it can take more than a day to travel on horseback from one village to the other, the road between littered with treacherous trails of fallen trees. There are seven larger villages, Kaelonoch being the largest, followed by Cale to the south. Dagen has these and the other five indicated with thick, black circles. To call these *villages* would be a stretch compared to the cities that occupy territory in neighboring kingdoms such as More and Ezers. While those kingdoms are relatively small compared to Masunbria, the sea seems to birth people and deposit them in clusters upon the land and near the great water. No, Masunbria doesn't have the large cities, or the exotic wares to trade, nor does it have the sheer number of people dwelling within. What it does have is the land and all it provides: food, water, and protection.

The people of Masunbria have adopted a relationship with the animals, soil, and trees. They are farmers and hunters, and they take from the land and worship it at the same time. It has become their religion: the elements of dirt and plant, sun and wind. It was, after all, the great forest of Masunbria that saved many of them during the raids. It served as shelter to remain unseen. Men once built houses high within the trees to hide their family from the Typhans. Still to this day, one can look up and see their remains, covered in a tangle of moss and vines or occupied with the nests of small animals, as if the earth is attempting to reclaim what was once hers.

"My men were deliberate about the houses and barns they targeted. They had paid close attention, when delivering the dead, to which ones housed the elderly or widowed women and their children. There are still plenty of men in the villages that would take up sword to protect their homes, and we tried our best to stay clear of them. They worked quickly as the people slept, wanting

69

to keep the element of surprise. The horses they took were loaded down with the stores of food, wood, grain, feed, anything that would make life a bit harder for the people of the villages, especially during this hard winter with which we have found ourselves gifted. They moved quietly until they were ready. Once pleased with their loot, they began the real fun. They woke the villagers with war cries and set fire to several homes and barns. Just as we predicted, several men came out prepared to defend their home and families. It was a good show, but it came too late. My men were already riding off in victory with horses strategically stolen from the homes of those very men ready to defend and fight."

Henrick smiles at Dagen. He loves war and strategy, but not as much as Dagen. Dagen thrives on it. Dagen used to be a soldier of Hadrian's. He was assigned to Henrick after an altercation with the husband of the woman Dagen had been sleeping with, which left him with the massive scar through half his face. It was a jagged and brutal-looking line of hate that, just one hair to the left, would have taken out his eye. When he arrived at Henrick's door with orders from Hadrian in hand, Henrick was furious. He thought Dagen a spy planted by his brother more than a servant to him. He ignored Dagen for the first few months he lived with them, and Dagen ignored Henrick in return. Both men were unhappy with the assignment. It was out of that unhappiness that their friendship began to form, little by little, day by day. To say that Dagen was supportive of the decision to overthrow Hadrian would be an understatement. It was personal with Dagen.

Dagen takes one last spoonful of porridge and, mouth still full of food, asks Henrick if he is ready to go. *Time to play hero*, Henrick thinks as he wipes his mouth and follows Dagen out of the room. The excitement is growing as he mounts his horse and breathes in the crisp morning air.

***

Pulling the horses to a stop at the center of Kaelonoch, Henrick looks around in disbelief, actual disbelief, not the mask he was prepared to don once there for the benefit of the storyline. The village is all but destroyed. Windows have been smashed. The contents of entire homes seem to have been regurgitated through their front doors to now lie broken and lifeless in the dirt road. Shards of glass glitter in the sunlight from the smashed jars of preserved food meant to last the winter. Barrels of stored water have been tipped, and a river of mud covers bits of clothing and children's toys. People are milling about, talking to one another frantically or picking up bits of their life sprinkled throughout the grounds in a solemn state. Children sit crying in the dirt. Old men wring their hands as they watch their wives poke through the rubble.

Henrick looks at Dagen, a look of shock on his face. Dagen leans in close and whispers to Henrick, "I thought it best to downplay it a bit over breakfast so that your expression would be genuine when you saw it." Henrick simply nods back, unable to form words. Though Dagen's men didn't raise a sword last night, the damage done here will surely cause death from starvation or exposure.

A crowd has begun forming of its own volition around Henrick and Dagen. Dagen lowers himself from his horse and begins to walk from man to man, shaking hands as he goes. He stops and greets the women with a comforting hand and pats the top of little children's heads as he goes. Henrick bites the inside of his cheek to keep from smiling. Dagen is a master. His face is sympathetic yet angry, heartbroken yet resolute. Dagen nears the still-intact Sordusten Inn. Serving as the tavern in Kaelonoch, it is a two-story stone building with two large, currently shuttered windows on either side of a worn red door. Above the door is a hand-painted sign, the black letters having been painstakingly drawn on with a careful, steady hand. Dagen climbs atop one of the several empty barrels that line the outside of the establishment.

A hush overtakes the crowd as they move closer to form a half circle around Dagen. Henrick remains on his horse, preferring to watch the theatrics from the back row in the event he can't control his face. Dagen raises a hand to calm the crowd. More people see the activity and move to join.

"My dear citizens, I have come to you today a discouraged man, a man who failed to protect you, a man who thought he understood the motives of his enemy but was proven incorrect. You see, I assumed that they were here for a specific purpose, perhaps gold, jewels, or treasures. I thought they were well-provisioned men who had no need for the things taken from you here last night. That is why I failed to protect you. I didn't know you were in need of it."

"Why would Typhans attack without provocation? Did our offerings not reach them?" a man from the crowd shouts.

"We can confirm that the last offering was made by Hadrian, and was made on time," Dagen replies. "It was generous, and it should have satiated the barbarians. My friends, we are in a great time of fear and uncertainty. The treaty with the Typhans has clearly been broken. How? We can't say. We do know that the same men who destroyed your homes are the ones responsible for the deaths of your king and queen. We also know that Prince Haluk, heir to the throne, has abandoned you all. He fled in the night, and though we have searched tirelessly, there is no sign of him.

"There is hope, though, my friends. His name is Prince Niklaus, and unlike his brother, he remained. He fought. And he shall be your king. He shall defeat the enemy. The prince has ordered food and provisions to be given to every last one of you from his own supply. You are Niklaus's people now, and he will do all he can to ensure you are cared for. In return, I ask that you attend the funeral of the late king and queen tomorrow. Niklaus needs the love of his people when he lays his parents to rest. We need to be a united Masunbria. We know that times were hard before these attacks, but together we will find a way. I, myself, will be posting guards in town day and night to ensure your safety. These things, these promises I speak, they are not just empty words. With me today is the very brother to the late king, my Lord Henrick. Please, it is his guidance and Niklaus's grace that will save Masunbria. There he is, friends . . ."

The applause from the crowd travels like a whirling wind, up through the dirt and destruction, and lands at the heart of Henrick. Their faces upturned to him mounted proud on his horse are his undoing. He smiles warmly and waves to the crowd. He gives a nod to Dagen, still on his barrel, and offers a salute, his praise for a performance well done.

7

Magdalena

Her parents are to be buried today. The thought leaves her feeling hollow. Their death didn't seem real until now. She didn't see them pass and didn't gaze upon their closed eyes and still form. She has mourned since learning of their death seven days ago, but she also has found it easy to ignore. Now, though . . . now that there was an event specifically to mark their death, she couldn't ignore it any longer. The grief she felt as she rose that morning washed over her body and wrapped her in its dark embrace. She spent most the previous night convincing Hagan and Sybbyl to allow her to attend the funeral today.

News traveled fast about attacks throughout the kingdom. Typhans were in Masunbria and raiding villages as they slept. While Hagen argued her attendance would be a risk they shouldn't take, eventually he succumbed to her pleading. She will go in place of Liri, and she will disguise herself the best she can. The castle will be looking for a thin blond man, one who walks tall and full of pride, with his strong jaw and steady gaze. They will be looking for Haluk.

Her hands shake as she does up the laces on the borrowed gray dress with its long sleeves and full skirt. She stuffs the dress with bits of hay to make her body appear plumper, rounder, fuller. She pulls on a winter bonnet and stuffs the stray pale blonde hairs under it. Bending, she picks up a piece of charred wood from last night's fire. The black of it transfers to her fingers instantly. She walks into Hagen and Sybbyl's room, where there is a small mirror, a gift from Astrid, she was told.

She kneels before it, knees digging into the uneven floorboards, and looks at her reflection. She doesn't recognize the woman looking back at her. She has not seen herself since she left the castle, and the sight is alarming. Her face is still marked with welts yet to fully heal, and her eyes are two sunken orbs surrounded by dark circles. Her lips are dry and cracked, and the bones of her cheeks are more visible than before thanks to her lack of appetite. She wills herself not to cry at the sight of it all. Raising the charred wood, she begins to rub it back and forth on the hairs that remain visible from the edges of the bonnet.

It is mid-morning when they begin walking. One large mass of people, dressed in what was certainly the best they owned, making their way to bear witness to the burial of a king and queen. The winter wind cuts through the thin fabric of Magdalena's dress. She pulls the shawl tighter around her neck and the lower half of her face. The shawl is to aid in disguising her but now has become a necessity. Magdalena walks with her head down, matching the steps of Hagen and Sybbyl through the trampled snow. She focuses on appearing both meek and weak, the opposite of Haluk. A hand on her elbow jolts her from her trance-like walk. She swallows back the scream that is threatening to escape her lips and risks a glance at the person who has detected her. She is met with a stern-faced Brom.

"What in the bloody hell are you doing here?" he hisses in her ear.

She lets out a sigh. "I am attending a funeral, same as everyone else." She lifts her chin slightly, daring Brom to make a scene now. He doesn't. He is too smart for that. He knows the throng of people are being watched. He repositions her arm so it is linked under his own—trapped, rather. The pressure he places on the hold is his way of silently reprimanding her. She could pull away, push him, kick him, but she doesn't. That, too, would draw unwanted attention. It best to act as all the other mourners, walking solemnly on this cold morning. She can see he is muttering to himself, and she can't help but grin. She finds Brom both irritating and amusing.

They begin to near the castle, and Magdalena can feel her pulse quicken. She hears it from those around as well, the sharp inhale as the massive stone structure comes to view. The sight of the castle has that effect on people. There are four turrets, one on each corner, stretching high to the clouds, small windows dotting the edifice. Beautiful as they are, it is what is below holding them up to the sky that is both alarming and enchanting. Each tower appears to be growing out of the backs of the four stone carved men below. Each man is in a bowed position of submission, and before each man is a stone child—a girl dressed as a bride with a carved crown of flowers in her hair and the roundness of youth in her chiseled cheeks.

The male effigy in the north corner represents war, and you can see the armor he wears, carved to look like slabs of metal welded together. The man's sword lies useless at his feet. His face has been marred with battle, and below his bended knees is a pond that in the gray of winter looks like a puddle of blood. The child bride before him holds a dove in her outstretched hand, a symbol of peace. To the east there is the man of famine. The substantial stone sculpture here wears no shirt, and every chiseled rib is visible. His hunched body shows each line of his spine, and his stomach has been made dramatically concave. Near his feet lies what appears to be a plate, with only crumbs dotting its flat stone surface. The small feminine figure before him is holding stalks of wheat like they are part of her bridal bouquet.

To the south kneels the shackled form of slavery. Chains wrap around his wrist and ankles, and his stone back is crisscrossed with marks left from cracking whips. The eyes of this man are more haunting than those of any other. They look as if all hope has been abandoned. They look defeated, like a bird made to live in a cage. The child bride set to save him stands baring a ring of keys in her small fist. The final man, the one to the west, is of disease. His stone skin is full of pustules, and his mouth is twisted into an agonized scream as he stares at the girl before him holding a chalice close to her heart, her eyes cast down into whatever potion swims inside.

Magdalena moves with the rest of the people through the iron gate and under the carved stone slab. As she passes through, she looks up and reads the words chiseled there almost one hundred years ago: "We give the flesh of our body, the beauty of our land, so we may be free. She is our liberator and our protector." Pain and guilt wrap her in its tight embrace. The castle is a constant reminder of what the Typhans brought with them when they descended the mountains: the death, the war, the hunger; the devastation. It also is a reminder of the weapon used to defeat them. Woman. Princesses given on their twelfth birthday to become brides, to birth a new generation of Typhan warriors and prevent the Masunbrians or any of the neighboring kingdoms from raising arms against them, lest we kill one of our own. One of our beloved, beautiful, girls.

Her home, once a place of comfort and security, now seems more like a cold, chilling reminder of death. The throng of people makes its way into the courtyard, which has been decorated for the occasion. Large bolts of red silk are secured from high windows and drape down the castle walls. With the end unattached, the wind whips them freely, and it is as if they are dancing together, wind and snow and silk. There are hundreds of candles lit on any surface that would support them. The glow gives the illusion that the courtyard holds warmth and security where beyond the gates does not.

The people with her feel it too. There is almost a collective exhale, a relief, as if they have just arrived home from a long journey. The dais is another calculated design. The chairs have been covered in red-and-white velvet, and the awning above them, protecting them from the now steady falling snow, is made of gold silks. It is beautiful.

The blaring of trumpets silences the crowd, and they turn to face the dais. It is then that she sees him: Niklaus. He is leading the processional from the castle doors. He is dressed in black from his shirt and pants to boots and gloves, and on his broad shoulders sits the black fur of a bear wrapped stately over his chest and down his back. Her eyes burn with tears as her stomach churns. She wants nothing more than to call out to him, to push past all the other spectators and run, climb the steps, wrap him in her arms, and weep. Her little brother, if she could only get him alone, explain to him that it was never her idea. Brom's arm tightens her own further into his chest. She turns to look at him, ready to push him away. She will not tolerate being silently scolded while she watches her parents' burial. Once her eyes meet his, though, she stops herself. In his eyes, she can see understanding. Sorrow. Sympathy.

"Don't," Brom whispers in her ear. "I know you are smart. You can feel just as I can that we are treading on dangerous ground here. You are either a woman and a betrayer or a man and a coward. This is not the time or place to see which one of those gets you hung. We shall watch and listen. Together." She doesn't acknowledge his words. She just stares straight ahead. Her mind and heart swim in an ocean of rage, embarrassment, grief, and longing as she watches her uncle Henrick and aunt Thea take their seats next to Niklaus.

She looks back at her brother. She wills him to meet her gaze. She watches him for any sign that he is sad, lonely, or afraid. She watches to see if he is looking for her in the crowd. He doesn't even blink. The trumpets cease, and her uncle rises from his seat to the center of the dais. He clears his throat and smiles down on the mass of people below.

"My dear friends, you have come from near and far, from every corner of Masunbria. You have come to remember a king and queen who served us well. I am Sir Henrick, brother to the late King Hadrian. I ask for grace from you all. I never imagined that the day I spoke about my older brother would come this soon. My brother was a great man. He was brave but never boastful, clever but not cunning, proud but never conceited, smart but not condescending, and cautious but never cowardly. I learned a lot from him about life, honor, and pride. I learned from him the importance of family. My wife, Thea, is here with us, and together we pledge our unyielding support to my dear nephew, Niklaus. Over the last few days, I have seen with my own eyes that my brother raised at least one of his sons to be an honorable man. I hope you all can find solace as I have in knowing that our beloved Hadrian has given us hope in Niklaus."

Here, Henrick pauses and wipes his nose with a square of cloth he pulls from somewhere in the depths of his furs. He continues his eulogy, recounting tales of the king and queen. Some are poetic, some humorous, and some sound more fictional than factual. Above each tale told, like hawks circling the sky, looking down upon their prey, all of her uncle's stories lead back to Niklaus. Henrick never once mentions Haluk by name, but each compliment of Niklaus is laced with an unspoken defamation of the cowardly heir.

Her parents are carried out and each placed on beautifully decorated pyres. Niklaus lights the fire, and her parents are burned before her eyes. Magdalena wishes she hadn't come. Her bound arm is throbbing, and her ribs and hip are screaming in pain from standing in one spot for so long. Her heart is breaking along with her body. She has grown weak and is now thankful for Brom's arm trapping her own, as that is the only reason she remains upright. The sight of her younger brother rising and moving to the front of the dais gives her the fortitude she was lacking, and she stands a bit straighter. Expectant. Nervous.

"My people, today we have said goodbye to our past and we have set into motion our future. My parents have departed this world. They suffered an untimely death at the hands of savages . . ."

His words are cut off sharply by the whiz of an arrow that flies past his head to lodge itself into the skull of the late king's burning corpse. Screams rise up from the crowd. Men rush to surround the dais, swords drawn, eyes scanning the turrets and high walkways that connect them. There is shouting of orders, and a man with a scarred face tries to move Niklaus behind him for protection. Niklaus refuses and stands his ground.

"Show yourselves!" Niklaus yells.

At his words, fifty men, covered in furs and filth, storm through the iron gates. The crowd begins to panic. Screams rise up as those assembled start to push and shove one another to the periphery of the courtyard. Hagen grabs Sybbyl's hand as the crowd threatens to separate the two. Brom, pulling Magdalena with him, pushes his way toward them. Once there, he positions his large frame to try to protect the frail couple from the hysteria circling them. Magdalena can feel the vibrations of the men marching into the courtyard, and she can smell the earth and metal rising off their bodies. She stands on her toes and peers over the mass of panicked people. She sees her brother: he stands firmly at the top of stairs, chin jutted forward, hand on the hilt of his sword, still sheathed. A man appearing to lead the Typhans raises his fist, and the army behind him comes to an abrupt stop. The man, tall with long, dark hair tied at the base of his neck and wearing a patchwork of furs, takes measured steps toward the dais. Toward Niklaus.

"Why have you come to our land? Why have you broken our treaty of peace?" Niklaus demands.

The man doesn't respond but slowly climbs the stairs until he and Niklaus are face-to-face. The Typhan is large, much taller and much broader than Niklaus even. He looks down at Niklaus and cocks his head to one side. His smile is sickening as it spreads across his face. He begins to laugh. He looks to his men, and they, too, begin to laugh. The crowd is silent as they stare, fear rising with each heckle. Just as suddenly as it begins, the laughter stops. The Typhan leader looks harder at Niklaus, puzzlement playing across his face.

"You know why we are here. Your father and mother broke the treaty, not us." The man's voice is a deep growl.

"The offerings came with the moon. I saw them myself. You lie," Niklaus barks back, pointing a finger to the man's chest.

"I am not talking about the offerings." The man smiles. "I am talking about your sister. I am talking about the one who was to be mine. Where is she?" the man yells. "I know the truth, dear boy. I know Haluk isn't a man after all. I know your parents deceived us and kept a girl for themselves."

"No," Niklaus says, shaking his head. The look on his face, though, is one of confusion, not resolution. "I don't believe you. My parents would never do that."

The man motions to his army, and a small, frail, old man in a brown tunic is thrust forward from somewhere in the depths of the pack. His dark hair is dotted with fallen snow, and the deep lines of his face are twisted in despair. Magdalena draws her hand over her mouth to prevent any noise of recognition from escaping. Niklaus pauses and looks down at the man. Comprehension soon registers across his face.

"Stantham, what is this? What is the meaning of this?" he looks back at the Typhan leader. "Why do you have the court physician in your possession? What have you done to him?"

The Typhan lord only smiles and motions to the old physician.

"It's true, my lord," the old man squeaks out. "I have delivered from your mother only one son, and that is you. I am so sorry, Your Grace. I knew it was wrong. Your parents, though, they couldn't do it. They couldn't part with her. So they decided to raise her a boy. They thought they could hide her forever. Please, Your Grace, have mercy. I only did as I was ordered. Please." His words mix with his sputtering sobs, and he falls to his knees. The people, who have been silently watching until now, begin to register what has just been said. Gasps and wails of fear begin to rise up all around Magdalena. She moves in closer to Brom, her mind reeling.

Niklaus begins to take several steps back from the Typhan leader, his hand covering his mouth. He stumbles and falls to one knee. Henrick storms before the fallen Niklaus and draws his sword.

"The king is dead. We had nothing to do with this. Their betrayal should not rest on our heads," Henrick shouts.

"Oh, but it does." The leader smiles. "You see, I want my bride." One of his soldiers hands him a rolled canvas, and he slowly, carefully, unrolls it. It is a painting of Haluk, something they must have taken from the castle walls during their raid. "Here she is. She belongs to me." He shows the crowd the painting before turning back to Henrick. "You have a fortnight to deliver her, or I will wage war on Masunbria, and every woman we find will be taken over the mountains as payment. You decide: one girl, or thousands."

Magdalena's blood runs cold, and the people around her begin to talk at once. Men grab their wives, mothers their young daughters, as the Typhans withdraw from the courtyard. Once safe from the barbarians, the crowd turns its attention back to the royal family. Fists are raised and men shout. Magdalena doesn't move. She doesn't turn her head. She barely breathes. She stares at the scene before her in horror and disbelief. She watches her uncle drag her brother back inside the castle walls. The man, Dagen, yells for everyone to return to their homes and lock their doors.

***

The walk back to the village of Kaelonoch is a blur. Magdalena wills herself not to think, but rather just put one foot in front of the other. As they approach the point in the journey where their paths are to split, Hagen, Sybbyl, and herself back to the farm and Brom back to the village, Brom grabs Hagen's shoulder and gives it a squeeze. "How about a drink, friends? We are not open for business today due to the funeral, but I think we all could use a drink. The place will be empty. It will be safe enough."

Hagen looks to Magdalena for a decision. She wants nothing more than to return to the house and crawl into the small bed and not get up. A drink or two could perhaps make that slip into numbness a little quicker, she reckons. She nods in agreement. They make their way to the Sordusten Inn.

Once situated inside the clean but dark tavern, Brom places cups of wine in front of Magdalena and Sybbyl and pours ale for himself and Hagen. Magdalena raises the cup to her lips and breathes in the scent of it before taking a large swallow. Her body is sore, her heart broken, and as she feels the warm wine travel down her throat and spread throughout her middle, she prays that it contains some form of magic to make it all go away for a time.

Sitting the cup back down on the surface of the bar, she scoots it around until it is perfectly covering a stain on the bar top. She has been taught her entire life to cover what shouldn't be seen, to conceal and obscure the image so that what remains is only of your choosing.

Brom reaches his hand over and, without moving her perfectly placed cup, refills the wine. Magdalena picks up the cup and takes another long swallow before placing it back in its spot. She raises her head for the first time since she sat down and looks at the faces of the three.

"The entire kingdom will be looking for me now. I know what I must do." Magdalena takes up her wine and spills the warm liquid into her mouth. She holds it there a moment, letting the rich wine swim along with her thoughts. She swallows. "Tonight I drink, for tomorrow I am to be wed."

8
Henrick

The seed firmly planted, the search for Magdalena begins to spread throughout the kingdom. Immediately following the funeral, Dagen and his men departed from the castle to spread word of the Typhan attack and the threat made to any that weren't in attendance. With the testimony of the court physician, any doubt as to the validity of the once-loved king's act of betrayal against his people will surely vanish. Sketches were made of Magdalena from the most recent portrait that lined the wall of the great hall. Her face will appear in every village throughout the kingdom. The girl won't be able to hide now. Once she is delivered on his doorstep, Henrick will take her into the mountains. She will serve as a great offering to the true Typhans, and he will descend Crask with the greatest alliance ever forged. He will give the Typhans their prized bride and all of Masunbria to call their own, and in exchange, they will help him take the kingdoms to the sea.

Henrick is supposed to appear to be in mourning for his lost brother. As such, it was not advised that he accompany Dagen to spread the tale of Hadrian's deceit and the threat the invading

Typhans had declared. Instead, Thea had given Henrick the menial job of writing to each kingdom in the surrounding lands. Masunbria, residing in the west, in a basin at the bottom of the mountains, is the only thing standing between the Typhan hoard and the neighboring kingdoms. If an attack is brought down the mountain, it won't stop at the border. As such, all four surrounding kingdoms give to the monthly offering. Their contributions have historically been minimal, however. Though all kingdoms have pledged their princesses-turned-saviors to the barbarians, it is Masunbria that has always borne the greatest burden in regard to keeping the Typhans at bay. Henrick's tale of impending peril should help increase the generosity of Masunbria's neighbors— resources for defense, horses, food, bribes, all things that will build Henrick's coffers under the guise of preventing another great war from spreading throughout the land.

Henrick longed to go with Dagen. He threw a fit, as it were, when he was told that he could not go. He needs to be free from this castle, even if just for a single day. He has become jittery. His skin feels wrong to him. He wishes he could remove it, simply slide it off of bone and muscle, shake it out and fit it back on again. Ever since that first night back within these walls, he has felt a great unease grow inside him, an itch that he can't seem to scratch. It is as if the castle is draining him, sucking what life remains in his bones to feed itself.

Henrick places a palm on the cold, rough, stone surface of the outer wall. *What is it you want from me?* Wearily he spins and, leaning his back against the wall, scans the room before him. He is in what was once his father's den and later became Hadrian's.

The tapestries of history cover the walls to the south, while the wall to the north is lined with shelves containing books— primarily handwritten diaries from the men of his family line. A separate row of shelving contains jars with herbs, and another has rolls of scrolls and various scraps of maps. The contents of these bookshelves are covered in a layer of dust—more proof that Hadrian was so consumed with his daughter's safety that progress for Masunbria was far from his mind. The wall to the east is made up of a large, floor-to-ceiling window, and sitting before it is a wood desk and yellow velvet chair. Pushing wearily away from the stone, Henrick pulls out the chair and plops himself down, elbows resting on the desk surface as his fingers massage his temples.

Thea has written Henrick a script for him to use in his correspondences, but grasping the quill, he suddenly feels the impulse of creativity and quickly disposes of her instructions. Rummaging through the drawers in the desk, Henrick comes up with a stack of good paper. The first priority, of course, is mastering his stately signature. Henrick spends the next hour scribbling his name all over the sheets. He studies the rise and fall of each letter. He stands back and looks at it from a distance. He folds the sheet and pretends to be just receiving the missive as he opens it to see whom it is from. He feigns a look of shock, drawing his hand to his open mouth. *A man of great importance if the height and curve of the strong lines that create his H is any indication.* He burns the paper full of *Henrick*s and lays his head down on the desk.

He can feel the windows behind him allowing the winter sunlight to warm his curved back. He closes his eyes tightly, the skin wrinkling in the corners. This room is watching him, judging him. It doesn't think he is worthy to sit here. He is reminded of the portraits in the great hall, the men who have always looked down upon him, dismissed him. They must be talking amongst themselves—these rooms and those paintings.

"You alright, my love?"

Henrick jolts, whipping his head up from the desk. He blinks rapidly at the spots that dance in his vision—a result of his eyes having been so tightly closed. *It's Catrain.* She smiles at him shyly as she closes the door behind her and takes slow steps into the room. Her brilliant blue eyes pass over the tapestries. She winces as she notices the stitched blood, the headless king, the mass graves. She spins on the blue-and-gold carpet at her feet, her dark hair flying about her shoulders. She bites the bottom corner of her lower lip as she takes in the bookshelves before running her finger along the thick layer of dust that lives there. Henrick watches her, wishing the sight of her will ease the rawness he feels inside of him. Whatever these walls are doing to him, even Catrain can't cure it, he thinks as he lets out a heavy sigh. Noticing his discomfort, Catrain leaves the scrolls and walks toward the desk.

"What is it, my love?"

"I don't know, Catrain. It's this place. It is evil. Don't you feel it? It's cold in here. Forever cold, no matter how many fires are lit. The flames in the hearth are devoured by the stone. This place takes pleasure in my pain. It always has. That's why it took my mother from me. It created the monster that was my father. This castle allowed Hadrian to ruin my life. This place feeds off of my misery. Once we get Magdalena back and I make my deal with the Typhans, I can finally be rid of this place. I will ride east, and I will never look back. I will die an old man on the shores of More, and I will be happy. I will never again have to see the giant dying men and the small little girls this stone beast was built upon. I will never have to hear the way the wind moves through the winding halls sounding like my mother as she wept. Catrain, the day we leave can't come soon enough. I am afraid these walls will kill me."

Henrick lets out another breath. It feels like no matter how much air he draws into his lungs, they won't completely fill. Catrain walks slowly behind his chair. She brings her fingers into his hair and begins to massage his scalp.

Bending to his ear, she whispers, "You aren't the same man who used to live within these walls. The castle has no power over you anymore. You should show it who you are now—what kind of man you've become."

She moves around his chair and slowly, seductively climbs on top of the desk. Crawling on her hands and knees, she arrives at the center, directly in front of Henrick. Sitting back on her knees, she reaches her arms behind her to undo the small buttons that go down the back of her black mourning dress. Henrick watches as she lets one strap fall from one shoulder and then the other. He eyes the door over her shoulder. Anyone could come walking in, but she doesn't seem to care. The sun shines in from behind him, and her pale breasts seem to glow in the stream of light.

She is right. He will show these walls that he is no longer the pitiful failure of a second-born son. Henrick feels it now, this growing desire to show the castle a primal display of his masculinity. He is certain now that the castle has laughed at him and Catrain and their stolen kisses under the cover of darkness. These walls want danger. The risk of being caught. The men that line the wall of the great hall wouldn't tiptoe around their own house. They wouldn't be fearful of being caught with their mistresses. They would relish the display of their virility. They wouldn't deny themselves out of fear. They would take what they want. Standing, Henrick gives a smug smile as he begins to undo the laces of his pants.

***

Henrick wipes the sweat from his forehead and pours himself a glass of wine. He reaches to the floor to pick up the papers that were scattered there during his lovemaking with Catrain. In this very moment, he feels more alive than he has in days. The fear of someone walking in on them had been thrilling. He can sense it, too, the castle nodding its silent approval, aware now that the man who left this home so long ago isn't the same one who has returned. He smiles, his first genuine smile in what seems like days, as he grabs a sheet of paper before taking his seat. This letter-writing task, only an hour ago sounding so very dreadful, suddenly sounds regal and important. He sits a little straighter in the cushioned yellow chair.

He addresses his first letter to the kingdom of More. Lying to the east, More is full of dense forests and fertile plains, and the sea, the glorious sea and all the opportunities that she carries with it. More has what Henrick wants. The castle lies right against the sea, and the villages that dot the coastline are rich with fish and spices and silks from places Henrick can't even imagine. The same goods that are bought from More for an exorbitant cost are used and worn by the lower-class women shopping for fish in the markets. Their streets are clean, and their people are strong and healthy. The smell of salt and fish in the air, though nauseating, smells of wealth. More's king has been on his deathbed for nearly a year now. The crown will be passed to his insufferable son, Prince Mikhail, when the old bag of bones finally has the decency to die. Henrick has never had the displeasure of meeting Mikhail, but rumors tell of both his beauty and his arrogance. The castle in More will be his new home once the Typhans help him to take it. That castle will only know this new version of Henrick. It won't ever be able to mock him or think him weak. Finishing the letter to More with his flourished, practiced signature, Henrick places it on the corner of his desk.

The next to receive his fear-laden letter is the only other kingdom that borders the sea: the kingdom of Ezers. This kingdom is small and sits to the north of More. Their ladies do not wear the silks from afar like the ladies of More; the people here are more weatherworn and hardened. Their skin glows from the sun, and their arms are wired with muscle from pulling up huge nets of fish. Henrick hates Ezers. More to the point, Henrick hates the king of Ezers, Alden. Once, during Henrick's years of drunken debauchery, he inadvertently crossed the border and found himself surrounded by sword-yielding guards baring the crest of the blue fish. Henrick was taken prisoner, of all things, dragged to the castle, and thrown into a dungeon. The place stank from the overflowing bucket dedicated for human excrement. His cellmate, an elderly man who was missing his right hand, sat in the corner eating a cockroach that he triumphantly caught upon Henrick's arrival.

Henrick beat on the bars and shouted his explanation as to who he was and what would become of his captors once he was free. No response. He sat in that cold, damp cell for nearly half the day before King Alden ordered his release and for him to be brought to the great hall. He arrived there cold, tired, hungry, and craving a strong drink. Henrick could see from the large, high windows in the two-story hall that, while he arrived at the castle at first dawn, it was now dark. Irate at this revelation, Henrick asked where the king was, demanded to see him. The servants, dressed all in white, spoke not a single word. They just carried in plate after plate of food, meats, fruits, breads, and so much wine. The feast laid before Henrick was impressive, and he ate and drank greedily.

Belly full of wine and food and exhausted from being confined to the dungeon, Henrick made his way to the far corner of the room where several couches in dark green fabric were arranged. He collapsed on the first one he came to, stuffing a bright blue pillow under his head, before dozing off. The fire was hot, and the music playing from a harpist was soft. Unsure how long he slept, Henrick was abruptly awakened by the great doors opening wide and King Alden entering the hall. He was a shock to look upon, his black-as-night hair, the sharp lines of his whisker-covered jaw, and his eyes as blue as the sea outside. Henrick wasn't able to look away from those eyes. They weren't kind eyes, nor were they cruel.

They were mysterious, troublemaking eyes, and when they set upon you, they bore through your skin and bones and saw into your soul. Alden apologized for the confusion, hugged him as if he was an old friend, and sent him on his way. Just like that. Henrick stumbled out of the castle and walked on uneasy legs toward the border to Masunbria, looking over his shoulder continuously as he went. To this day he swears that somehow those eyes watched him the entire way home.

I wish you a slow and painful death, Henrick. Leaving out his amusing closing, he laughs and merely signs his name. Thea would make him write it all over again if he didn't do it correctly. Henrick adds this new missive to his slow-growing stack. He still has to write to Rekabia and Skogen, but he needs more wine first. Rising and spinning out of his chair, he takes up his empty goblet and stops for a moment to stare out the window. If Henrick's calculations are correct, Dagen should be arriving to spread Typhan fear in the southernmost villages of Masunbria now. Anything can happen on the road: a spooked horse throwing his rider off a cliff, a peasant with nothing to lose deciding today he will rob a caravan from the castle. For as many times as he has threatened to kill Dagen, and it has been more than he can count, he still considers him a dear friend. Henrick rubs his face in exasperation as he looks out the second-story window.

"Be safe, my brother," Henrick whispers into the wind.

"Uncle, there you are!"

Henrick jumps slightly at the sound of Niklaus shouting from the open door. He turns to see Niklaus jogging toward him, smile wide and eyes alive. *This, whatever it is, is going to irritate me, I know it.*

"What are you doing staring out the window?"

Henrick doesn't respond, just stares at his nephew.

"Never mind that. Uncle, I can't take this anymore. I am a newly crowned king, and I deserve a celebration. I didn't have a true coronation. I went along with Aunt Thea's plans and did this awful display of emotion over dead parents I hated to begin with. It is my time now. I don't want to sit around and do nothing for a fortnight until our next theatrical display. Don't try and stop me; I have made up my mind. I will keep it quiet so that it appears that we are still in mourning, but I want to drink and dance and make very poor choices." Niklaus lets out a breath and looks expectantly at his uncle.

Henrick considers. A party does sound like exactly what he needs, another way to demonstrate the power and influence he now possesses, a way for him to be seen and subsequently admired by others. He scratches his chin. "Thea isn't going to like this. Throwing a party while we just made a display of telling the citizens their women would be sent over the mountain if Magdalena isn't found would most definitely be in poor taste."

"That lie right there is exactly why we need to have a party now. The women all over the kingdom will be beating down the door for a chance to earn my favor. They will think that if only I would fall in love with them, then I will protect them if Maggie refuses to do the right thing. My bed will be full, dear uncle. It's brilliant. Also, Aunt Thea doesn't rule over you and me, Henrick.

If you tell your wife we are having a party, then she shall plan the party."

Yes, Henrick thinks. *I am the man of this castle, after all. What I say shall come to be.* He puts his arm around Niklaus's shoulder, and together they go in search of Thea.

Thea was furious about the party. Niklaus pleaded his case, but Thea wasn't moved. Niklaus begged, and Thea simply rolled her eyes. Niklaus asserted himself as king, and Thea laughed. He turned to Henrick then, his eyes pleading for Henrick to challenge his wife and her decision. Henrick searched for the words that would affirm his position and her submission. The ones he found were not effective. In the end, it took Henrick an embarrassing amount of beseeching and bargaining to get his wife to agree to the intimate affair. Her terms were firm. She refused to do a single bit of planning for the party, but she would allow it to occur. She would not answer any question about food or drink or which guests should be avoided at all costs. The men were on their own. Guards were sent on horseback to verbally extend invitations to the more privileged class of Masunbrian farmers. Wine and ale were ordered, along with a few of the more famous prostitutes. The staff was in chaos as they attempted to create this impromptu and ill-prepared-for event.

Henrick, recalling how weakly he withered under his wife's critical glares, storms through the castle, stomach sick from shame. He is looking for Catrain. He needs her. Rounding a corner, he almost hits his head on one of the candelabras that line the walls of the hall. It seems to smirk at him. The stone beast is laughing at him once again. The walls watched him beg Thea.

They watched as he was unable to faze his wife with his stern words or his authoritative tone. He remembers Thea's arched eyebrow and her sardonic smile. He pushes into Thea's room, where Catrain is neatly folding Thea's dresses. Her breath catches in her throat when she sees Henrick and the look in his eyes. He takes Catrain's hand and leads her to Thea's bed, where he pushes her down on the feather-stuffed mattress. His mouth greedily devours hers as he thinks of the pain Thea would feel if she walked in and witnessed this.

9
Magdalena

Liri's insistent shaking of Magdalena's shoulder the next morning brings her out of her comatose state. Last night at Sordusten Inn, she drank more wine than ever before and stumbled gratefully to bed when they arrived back to the little cottage. The quantity of wine was a success, and she slept a dreamless sleep, a blissful void of memory and pain wrapped in a cocoon of darkness and warmth. As soon as she wakes, though, the images return, the people screaming her false name in hatred, her brother's sneer as he cursed her, as if her name was now poison on his lips. She wishes she could return to the darkness, but Liri is persistent and she resigns herself to rising. Brom is already here and has brought with him someone to look after her wounds, as promised. Another man, a stranger, who will look upon her body. She again pulls on the borrowed dress that her body refuses to acclimate to and makes her way down the ladder.

The small cottage feels cramped with the two extra occupants. It was not built to house six grown adults, especially when two of them were of substantial stature. Magdalena studies the new arrival. He is as tall as Brom and as broad but much older. Where

Brom has dark, close-trimmed hair, the new guest has hardly any to speak of, aside from the thick, gray, bushy eyebrows that arch over his steady brown eyes. He appears old enough to be Brom's father, and, in reality, they could be mistaken for father and son if she didn't already know that Brom's father was long ago dead. Both men rise at her arrival.

"Good morning," she says without inflection in her voice.

"My lady. I would like to introduce you to Willem Falk," says Brom. He makes an unconscious pivot of his body, a backing away, a submitting to the man next to him. There is an unspoken hierarchy here, and Brom is, in the way both man and beast have since the dawn of time, signaling his submission to the alpha of the pack. The day prior, Brom conveyed that the man he was bringing was someone he respected greatly, and if this gesture is any indication, Magdalena can see his words ring true.

"Lady Magdalena, it is an honor to be in your presence," he begins with a smile. She bows her head slightly in return but doesn't speak.

"My name is Willem Falk, as Brom said. I had the honor of serving your father in his army from the time I was a young man. He was a good man, your father, and my years of service to him were the greatest of my life. I am deeply sorry for the loss of him and your mother. I am grateful that Hagen and Sybbyl, and Brom, have kept you safe."

"Well, relatively safe," apologizes Hagen with a small chuckle.

"Nonsense," says Magdalena. "I am beyond grateful, and any wounds I have incurred while here were not due to a lack of care on the part of my benefactors. I understand you are here to examine my injuries. Were you a physician in my father's army?"

"No, no. I simply have seen about all there is to see in regard to wounds and broken bodies. I'd be happy to take a look, if that's alright with you?" Magdalena nods her approval, and together they seek out the privacy of the loft.

Gratefully, Willem works quickly. A trained man of war, it is evident immediately that he has mended more than his fair share of wounds. He doesn't speak while he looks upon her body, and she doesn't meet his eyes. She feels exposed both in a literal sense and in a figurative one. Since the night she fled the castle, she has felt as if she inhabits the body of a stranger. Her breasts, for years having always been tightly bound for concealment, now feel too heavy, too visible. When changing, the air now brushes against her bare nipples and sends an odd sensation into her stomach. As Haluk, having clearly never worn a dress, she never felt her bare legs rubbing together as she walked. The feeling of the soft skin of her inner thighs brushing each other feels intimate. Her entire body feels sensual. As Haluk, she wasn't fully a man, nor could she be fully a woman. She just, was. Skin and bones and blood. These new feelings confuse and frighten her.

William finishes, pulling the scratchy brown blanket around her shoulders before turning and climbing down the ladder. Magdalena's body is stiff as she struggles to dress. The sounds of a heated argument float up from the ladder, and she quickly finishes doing up the buttons and heads down from the loft.

"What difference does it make? Two weeks ago you would have trusted her," Brom yells, face red.

"It is different and you know it," snaps Hagen as he stabs a shaky finger into Brom's heaving chest.

"What is going on?" Magdalena asks as she lowers her stiff body next to Liri on the bench at the table.

"Brom is wanting to start a war," hisses Hagen. He turns his back to Brom, who is pacing the small cottage from kitchen to sitting room and back again.

"I am not starting a war, Hagen. I am merely trying to protect our people from something that has already begun."

"The Typhans?" Magdalena asks. "I am sure that once I am delivered, they will not be a threat any longer. Niklaus will become king, and he will continue to keep you all safe."

"Your drunk of a brother?" laughs Brom. "I got an order this morning for twenty kegs of ale. My sister, Sabina, informed me that Your Grace is throwing a bloody party. A party. I was told to keep quiet, of course. Invitation only and all that. How can he think of throwing a party? His parents were just put to rest yesterday. The Typhans have attacked the castle, attacked many of our villages, stolen the horses and supplies we need to survive the winter, and they have made a threat against all of the women of Masunbria. Your brother decides now is a good time for a party?"

"He is young," Willem says cautiously. "He needs good council, and I am afraid he won't get that from Henrick. I knew Henrick when he was a young man. He was irritable and irrational even then. There is something Henrick sees that is lacking within himself, and he blames others for it. Niklaus is Hadrian's son though. We must remember that. Hadrian was smart and level-headed. I am confident that Niklaus has the capability to become the king we need."

"We have the king we need," Brom yells, pointing his finger at Magdalena.

"What?" Magdalena's face is full of confusion as she looks at the faces around the room. "Brom, look at me. I am not a king. I am not Haluk. It was all a lie. I am nothing more than a cowardly princess who hid for twenty years and refused to protect her people by honoring the treaty. Today I will make it right though. Today I will fulfill the destiny I should never have avoided to begin with."

"No. It was not all a lie. Yes, you as a man was obviously a lie. But the people of Masunbria saw Haluk and saw a king. You are smart, wickedly smart. We heard that in the way you spoke and in the way you wrote. You are fast with a sword, and we saw that at the summer games each year when you took home the prize against men from all over the kingdom. We watched you feed the hungry and comfort the sick. You have been bred for this since you were a child. We have watched you grow, and we have been proud of you, proud of our great son and future king."

"Brom, your words mean more to me than you will ever know, but everything has changed now."

"Not to me. Magdalena, the words of praise I spoke have nothing to do with being a man or a woman. You are still the leader I would follow into battle."

"If I don't turn myself in, a battle is exactly what will occur. You can't want that for your people, Brom. Even if you think

Niklaus unfit to rule, at least he can be unfit during a time of peace. I must turn myself in. You know there isn't another way."

"What if we can beat the Typhans once and for all?" Brom asks excitedly. "What if instead of living in constant fear, paying the offerings, giving our princesses to the barbarians, what if we could just be free? A free Masunbria. We don't hand you over, my lady. Instead, you raise an army and you fight back."

"Why would I take that risk? If we were to lose, I would have led hundreds, maybe more, into battle, and for what? The Typhans won't be merciful. If we fail, Masunbria will be crushed and all the people in it."

"Freedom, that's why you take the risk." Brom's tone is soft and pleading. "None of us are truly free as long as the Typhans have a hold on us. Not a single one of us walks outside without looking to Crask in trepidation. We gathered in the courtyard yesterday where we all were forced to look upon those stone statues. Those monuments were built to represent all that we have overcome, but in reality, nothing has changed since the Typhans were here. We are still hungry; we are still dying. The war now is between one neighbor and another over land and crop needed to feed their families. The monthly offerings are proof that we are still prisoners to the Typhans. Each year the Typhans have asked more and more from us, and we continue to give, and our people continue to starve. You had to have known, my lady. Did your parents really keep you blind to the plight of your people? We've been dying, Magdalena. Signing that treaty all those years ago just bought us time, nothing more. Let us fight to live. Just give me one day. Give me a chance to prove to you that there are people that want freedom, even if it comes at a cost."

"No one will follow me to battle, Brom," Magdalena sighs. "Not now. They maybe would have followed Haluk, but no one would follow a woman, and you know that."

"I am just asking for one day, Your Grace." Brom looks her in the eyes, his own pleading. Giving him this day is the least she can do. He lost so many friends. He has been kind to Magdalena, and in return she will give him what he asks. After that, though, she will go to Crask and do what should've been done eight years ago. Magdalena nods her head—she will give him one day.

"Thank you, my lady." Brom nearly jumps. He gives Liri a quick smile before running from the cottage. Willem smiles weakly and follows more slowly out the door. Magdalena sighs wearily as she stares for a moment after them. One more day.

She has a single day before she walks into Typhan land. She has heard rumors of what life is like over the mountains. Of course, no one has ever crossed over and returned to tell the tale themselves. That lack of firsthand knowledge doesn't seem relevant when it comes to stories told around the fire or cautionary tales whispered to small children.

The Typhans worship many gods, all of which are hungry for riches, battle, and blood. Unlike the monarchy in Masunbria and the neighboring kingdoms, with the Typhans, there are several families said to lead their own factions. The more wealth a faction has, the more power. The greater the army, the better chance a faction has of procuring wealth. Everyone of fighting age must earn their place or be cast out. As such, even the Typhan women are trained to be warriors—spending their childbearing years on raids earning their faction wealth. Pregnancy is an inconvenience that results in a depleted army and lost revenue. That is why the Typhans want the princesses.

The girls are to marry a faction leader and bear his many, many children. Which faction leader, and from which family will receive this bride, is said to be determined in a great physical contest that lasts many days. The winner will get the next princess, and, gods willing, through that princess he will bring forth the next generation of soldiers for his family. The princesses will be impregnated as many times as their bodies will allow. There are no tales about what happens to the princesses after they are no longer of use to the Typhans. Tomorrow, when Magdalena ascends the mountain, she will become a prisoner. She will marry the strongest, bravest, and best-trained faction leader, and she will bear his children. He will raise them to be warriors, and she will watch her babies become men and women and, one day, she will watch them die.

"Let's get outside," Liri whispers at Magdalena's ear. Her soft words draw Magdalena from the disturbing visions she has conjured up of her future. She smiles weakly and rises. She pulls on a pair of worn, brown boots and throws furs across her shoulder, a patchwork of animal skins with spots of missing hair from their years of use. Liri twists her long almond hair into a bun at the base of her neck. Pulling hoods over their head, they brace themselves against the cold wind as they crunch through the thick snow and make their way to the barn. Once inside, Liri begins gathering eggs in a small basket. She works quietly, and

Magdalena watches though her mind has once again returned to the life she must prepare herself for.

"Brom is attractive, don't you think?" Liri asks. It takes Magdalena a moment to register the question.

"I suppose so," Magdalena stammers. "I honestly haven't paid any attention to him in that way. You have?"

"Of course, silly." Liri laughs. "He's so strong and determined. He smiled at me when he was leaving. Perhaps he has noticed me as well?"

Magdalena kicks at a clump of frozen mud on the barn floor and sighs. "Liri, I would have no idea how to read the mind of a man. I maybe pretended to be one, but I am more clueless than you are."

Liri puts down her basket of eggs and walks over to Magdalena, shutting the pen door behind her. She grabs Magdalena's hand and guides her to a twine-wrapped bale of hay. The two sit, Liri still cradling Magdalena's hand in hers. Magdalena doesn't meet Liri's eyes. She is afraid that she will find pity there.

"Are you afraid?" Liri whispers into the dim and dusty air between them.

"Yes."

"I am too. I just hope we don't get stuck with someone very old."

Magdalena's head shoots up, and with wild eyes, she turns to face Liri. "You are not going with me." Her voice comes out a growl.

"Of course I am. I may not be a princess, but I can bear children. There is no reason they won't take me."

Magdalena suddenly pushes to her feet. Her face is red with anger. "It isn't about whether or not they will accept you. You will not resign yourself to that life. I am going alone. You will stay here. Hagen and Sybbyl will look after you. Liri, after tomorrow our paths won't ever cross again."

"Do I not get a say in this?" Liri's hazel eyes are defiant as they bore into Magdalena's icy blue gaze.

"No, as a matter of fact you don't. I have given you an order, and you shall obey." There is no kindness in Magdalena's words. Even to her own ears, she can recognize that voice—the voice of Haluk simmering under the surface.

It's a long moment before Liri speaks again. "Brom is right, you know. You going with the Typhans isn't going to save Masunbria. It will only buy us time to die a slower death. I thought that if I threatened to go with you, you would choose not to go; you would stay and fight. I should have known better. Your guilt will take you to the mountains even if in your heart you know it won't save your people."

"How dare you speak to me like this? I didn't ask for this life, Liri. I didn't ask for my parents to deceive everyone the day I was born. I didn't ask to be raised a man. Do you know what that was like? Hiding away in the wing my parents confined me to. You and Astrid sneaking from the secret chamber between my mother's room and mine so you could attend me. The feelings I have for my parents scare me. I don't know if I should love them for keeping me safe or hate them for forcing me to live in a body that was a prison. I am angry at them for setting all this in motion and then having the audacity to die and leave me to figure it all out. I am not afraid of going to the Typhans for the reasons you think. I know I will be a prisoner there, but in so many ways, I have been a prisoner my entire life. I am afraid to leave Haluk behind because I have no idea who Magdalena is, or if she can even survive without Haluk."

Liri's face softens as she rises from the bale of hay. She crosses the dirt floor between them and takes Magdalena into her arms. She grasps tightly, and Magdalena can't stop the flood of tears that flow down her cheeks to dampen the furs on Liri's small shoulder.

10
Henrick

The party is well underway in the grand hall. It isn't pretty. Nearly fifty guests are in attendance, and the proportion of women to men is dramatically unbalanced. One fight has already occurred, and another seems to be hanging heavy in the air. There is far too much drink and far too little food. The musicians themselves are mostly drunk. Thea made an appearance early on to see what colossal mess the men had dreamed up, but she has since departed for her rooms to gloat. Henrick is at the head table watching the chaos with a mixture of amusement and trepidation.

Goblets have been knocked over, and a pool of red wine covers the stone floor, dying the bottoms of the maidens' dresses as they walk. There is a cluster of men in the far corner throwing knives at the head of a giant bore mounted on the wall. The prostitutes that have been invited are scattered across the cluster of settees, young soldiers twirling their hair and peering down the tops of their dresses. A loud crash echoes through the room as the musician playing the harp keels over in a drunken stoop, his arms getting tangled within the strings of his instrument as he goes. Voices of those dancing ring out their complaint, and the man is promptly kicked aside while a well-dressed young man retrieves the harp and begins to poorly pick notes at random. Goblets are sent whirling in the air toward his head. Henrick swears he sees a knife thrown as well. He eyes Samalt making his way through the crowd and motions him over. Samalt bows low as he approaches Henrick. Henrick smiles and offers him the seat next to him, which Samalt accepts graciously.

"Samalt, I can't help but notice that you seem less inclined to enjoy yourself tonight than usual, and that is truly saying a lot, I am afraid."

"Well, sir, I am on duty tonight and not here as a man looking for an eligible maiden. Though, I would dare say that perhaps many of the women here tonight are not the marrying sort. In Dagen's absence, I am supposed to stay diligent in my pursuit of Magdalena and, well, look after you, sir. Dagen was very adamant that you remain safe while he is away."

Henrick lets out a small chuckle. *Well, well. The ole boy has a soft spot for me after all.* Here Henrick thought that Dagen was incapable of emotion.

"I admit that watching this debauchery all but made me forget the thorn in my side."

"Well, I have been tasked to not forget her, sir. Though it isn't hard to keep her on my mind. I have a small painting of her likeness that I keep right here with me." Samalt reaches into his breast pocket and pulls out a small, neatly rolled canvas which he carefully unravels. He hands the canvas to Henrick, who looks down and into her eyes. She stares back at him. Her icy blue eyes are cutting through his skin and muscle and entering his bone where they feast on his marrow. She is challenging him. "Come find me, Uncle," her lips say as one side of her smile is turned up just a hair more than the other. Her short, white-blonde hair is slicked back, and her long white neck is on display, daring him to wrap his hands around it and squeeze. She doesn't think he can do it. His grip on the painting is tight as he peers at the face of his past.

"She is lovely, isn't she, sir? Hard to believe we all mistook her for a boy." Samalt mumbles near Henrick's ear, startling him and causing him to jerk his head from the unwanted closeness of Dagen's creepy puppet.

"Yes," Henrick replies with grit in his voice. "She looks like her mother did at that age. The people love to hear stories of how Hadrian fell in love with a poor girl from the village with no title and no riches, but the truth is that he picked out the most beautiful girl from all the lands and from all the classes—a girl that I had seen first. I spent my years as a young man traveling around Masunbria drinking, occasionally fighting, and finding women to keep me warm at night. It was on one of those excursions that I saw Katherine. She was carrying jugs of water back to her family home. Her face was smudged with dirt as if she must have recently wiped her brow with a dirty palm. Her clothes were simple and plain and betrayed the many times they had been mended. But her smile. Those lips. Her smile was brighter than the hot sun beating down on me as I stood, drunkenly, outside the tavern taking a piss. I was mesmerized. She paid not a care to the tangles in her hair or the tear at her hem. Her skin was golden from the hours spent in the sun and not milky white like that of the privileged class. I wanted to know how her warm skin smelled, what it tasted like. I wanted her to be mine."

"Lady Thea is a catch above all the rest, sir. I am in awe of her brilliance and her beauty. You are a lucky man to have found her," Samalt stammers, unsure of how to respond to Henrick's reminiscing of his brother's wife. Henrick takes a long drink from his goblet, draining the entirety of the wine held within. Samalt reaches for the painting, but Henrick smacks his hand away. Hiccups. Continues.

"Enamored, I returned to the castle as quickly as I could to tell my father that I had met the girl I was to marry. She was invited the next evening to dine with my family. I was unable to sit still the entire day, awaiting the sun to set and her to arrive. Nothing prepared me for her arrival though. All that daydreaming and anticipation was still not adequate to temper the breathlessness that her arrival bestowed upon me. She was glorious. Her hair had been washed out and combed, and the pale blonde of it begged to be touched. Her skin looked soft and smooth under the simple dress. She smiled nervously at me. I won't forget that smile. That was the last moment I had with her that didn't involve my brother.

"By night's end, he fell in love with her too. He begged my father for her hand in marriage. I raged. I tackled Hadrian to the ground in one quick burst, fists flying to his face one after another. In the end, my father allowed the marriage between Hadrian and Katherine. I was forced to either accept his decision or leave. So I left. I was given no food, horse, or wealth. I spent the next five years making one terrible choice after another. That's when I met Thea. Or should I say, that's when a beautiful girl with chestnut curls and skin the color of cinnamon found me. I was lying in a heap outside a tavern. I had just had the literal shit kicked out of me by three men. I was drunk, bloody, and smelled awful. She spoke in a tongue I didn't understand, but I saw sympathy and kindness in her eyes. I was an unwelcome guest in the kingdom of Rekabia, and the people had made sure I knew that each night since my arrival. Thea saved me that night, and she has continued to save me every night since." Henrick reaches for more wine and lets go of the picture of Magdalena. It floats in the air a moment before beginning its lazy descent to the stone floor.

Samalt hurries to grab up his most prized possession and takes care to roll it neatly before placing it back in his pocket. "Sir, looking around tonight, I would say that you have fared far better than your brother in all ways."

Henrick looks at Samalt, but there is no smile on his face toward the compliment. Samalt grows uncomfortable and shifts in his chair.

"Find the girl, and when you do, Samalt, I want to be the one to deliver her across the mountain. I want to watch the blood drain from her face when she sees the fate she thought she could avoid. I want her to know my hatred for her, my hatred for her mother and her father."

"I won't let you down, my lord." Samalt bows before quickly taking his leave.

Henrick turns his attention back to the twirling men and women before him and refills his drink. The room is warm, and the dancing has become hypnotic as men in black trousers and white, well-laundered tunics twirl the women in their long dresses of royal blue, forest green, and burgundy. He must have fallen into a drunken trance while watching the laughter and the noise before him because he doesn't hear Thea approaching him until he feels her arms wrap around his chest from behind. He leans his head down and inhales the warmth of her skin, placing a soft kiss on the side of her wrist.

"What brings you down from your tower, my fair lady? Come down to see the depravity?" Henrick slurs.

Thea laughs and tilts her lips to his ears. "No," she whispers, her lips tickling his skin. "I came down to see how my matchmaking skills were going. You see, Henrick, I have found a queen for our dear Niklaus, a queen that can be controlled by me, a queen that has always served me." Her words are like a serpent in his ear, and the hairs on the back of his neck stand on end.

"Look," she whispers, "take a look at your nephew, Henrick."

Henrick squints his wine-drunk eyes to the room, seeking out Niklaus. It takes him a long moment to find him. He is spinning a maiden around the floor, a smile on his face. He pulls her into him, and Henrick sees him bend down to inhale the skin at her neck. He spins her once more, and that's when Henrick sees it. His heart drops to his stomach. Catrain. His Catrain.

"That's right, Henrick," Thea purrs in his ear. "Catrain was the perfect choice. She has been my loyal lady for so many years now. She shall make a lovely wife for Niklaus."

***

Henrick, eyes tightly shut, holds the small round table with one hand while draping the other over his throbbing forehead. He is lying on his back on the too-small-for-his-large-frame settee in his den. His ankles are spilling over the decorative arms, and his feet dangle limply. The room won't stop spinning. His grip on the table tightens. He tells himself that the table is not moving and, as long as he holds tight to that table, he will not move either. The visual doesn't work. He leaps from the couch, causing a blinding pain in his temples, and vomits into a nearby crystal vase. Feeling that he may prefer death to his current state, he stumbles to the thick, blood-colored velvet curtains to peek out. Blinding sunlight reflecting on the snow-covered ground assaults his eyes, and he closes the curtains and spins, putting his back against the shuttered window as if he must protect the room from the dreadful intrusion of day. He trudges back to the couch and falls dramatically to his knees on the ornate rugs and then flops his top half onto the firmly cushioned seat. His head tilted, his cheek being squished to where his lips part, a spot of drool begins to accumulate on the red fabric of the couch.

His eyes stare dead ahead as he recalls the night prior. He hears Thea whisper her name in his ear. He sees Niklaus pull her to him in a tight embrace. He pictures her laughing at something he must have whispered in her ear. A single tear falls from his eye and tracks down the bridge of his nose to pool with his drool stain forming on the couch. His heart feels empty in his chest. The sorrow is a weight that prevents him from taking a single full breath. Catrain will marry Niklaus. No matter how many times the phrase replays in his mind, the reality of it will not take hold. A knock sounds at the door.

"Go away," Henrick groans, face still pressed to the couch so the words become mostly unintelligible—at least, that's what he figures out once the knocking continues. He weakly picks up the closest item to him and tries to hurl it at the door. The blue silk pillow floats through the air and lands softly about three feet from its destined target. Henrick lets out a cry of annoyance.

The door opens, and Henrick closes his eyes. *Perhaps if I pretend to be asleep, they will leave.* He slows his breathing and makes small noises of snoring. Nothing. He doesn't hear a sound. *Perhaps it has worked.* He slowly begins to open a single eye.

"Ahhhhhh," yells Henrick as both eyes fly open. There, his face so close it could be touching his, is Dagen hovering over him with a smug smile on his face. Dagen laughs, and Henrick falls to the ground and covers his ears.

"What, no welcome-home parade? I thought the least you could do was have a smile and drink waiting for me. Ugh, you smell worse than I do. Come on, get up." Reaching under Henrick's arms, Dagen pulls him upright and plants him on the couch. Unsure what the wet stain is, he decides to sit Henrick right on top of it.

"Dagen, something terrible has happened since you left. I can't tell you about it, but it is beyond anything I could have expected. I am a broken man, Dagen."

Dagen lowers himself to the couch next to Henrick. Henrick doesn't look at him. Dagen rests his elbows on his knees and steeples his fingers between them. He takes a long, slow breath. "Catrain?" is all he says. It is said as a question, but one that he already knows the answer to. Henrick brings his hands to cradle his throbbing head.

"Thea is right, Henrick. I know you know that. Catrain is who should marry Niklaus. Catrain has been loyal to you both for many years. Her devotion to you alone shows me that, even with this marriage, she will rule in your best interest. I know that you love her, my brother, but I think you have to consider which is more important to you. Your kingdom and your legacy? Or Catrain? You can't have them both. That is the hell of this life, isn't it? There is always a flow. A rise and fall. A give and take. A balance. Every 'yes' spoken is a silent 'no' and every 'no' a silent 'yes' to something else.

"It is like the seas on the coast of More: in and out, in and out. Sediments rising from the ocean floor to be given to the land only to have them taken back a moment later, the waves switching in an instant between push and pull. Which one do you suppose would be most dangerous to get caught in? I have heard it is the pull. Not the loud and visible push of the wave, but the silent and hidden pull of the undercurrent. That's what kills you. You can ride this loud wave, Henrick. You can get up and take the beating that you are sure to take from it. Or you can stay here, in this dark room, and wait for the undercurrent to take you. Both are painful, but you must choose one." Dagen pats Henrick on the back and goes to rise from the couch. Henrick reaches out and grabs his arm.

"I ask you to dine with us tonight. I am glad you are home. It would have been a shame had someone else gotten to kill you before I could," Henrick says weakly.

"I missed you too, Henrick." Dagen walks silently from the room.

***

Later that evening, after having climbed into his brass bathing tub, so full of water it spilled over the edges, Henrick scrubbed his body clean with soaps made by Thea and infused with mint to clear his mind. He dressed in a clean, white tunic, and dark blue trousers. Before leaving his bedchamber, he affixed the crest of Masunbria to his breast, using a square of cloth to polish the gold surface of the great tree.

***

Henrick pauses to gather himself outside the dining hall doors. He uses his hand to once again slick his black, oiled hair back from his forehead, tentatively touching the locks with his fingertips to make sure not a strand is out of place. He is going to face the wave. He is going to walk into dinner and smile, and talk of Dagen's travels, and hope that he doesn't drown watching Niklaus and Catrain sit together. He takes a steadying breath before pushing open the wood doors. Entering, the first thing he registers is the rich scents of the ham, glazed with cinnamon and orange spice. The long table is covered with fruits and cheeses, the large ham occupies the center, and the platter it sits upon is decorated with egg halves that have been topped with various green herbs. A cast-iron pot steams with a thick soup, white with the heartiness of cream. He asked the kitchen staff to prepare a special meal for Dagen, and it appears they didn't disappoint.

"Ah, there he is. Uncle, that was some party last night! I haven't seen you all day. Was the fun too much for you, old man?" Niklaus, occupying the far head of the table, gives Catrain, who is sitting to his left, a wink.

Henrick bites the inside of his cheek to keep from screaming at Niklaus. He gives a laugh that, even to his ear, sounds a little psychotic as he takes his seat at the other head of the table. Niklaus is looking at him from across the expanse of food expectantly as if he is supposed to respond to his question.

"The events were a good distraction, Niklaus. I will give you that. But the time for fun is now over. A man does know the difference, don't you agree?" questions Henrick.

Niklaus looks embarrassed as he turns to the rest of the room. To Henrick's pleasure, the rest of the table doesn't disagree with him and instead looks at Niklaus with expectant smiles.

"Very well then," Henrick clears his throat. "It looks like we are ready to dine and move on. I want to begin dinner with a toast to Dagen. We are happy to have you back, and we are thrilled to see what your travels have produced. I had intended on a parade in your honor, but this great meal and this toast will have to suffice as we are, sadly, still in mourning."

Glasses are raised, and Dagen smiles warmly at Henrick. Several kitchen maids plate the food before retreating to the corners of the room to sit and await the needs of those at the table. Henrick stares at his plate. The flicker of candlelight from the chandelier overhead seems to cause the glazed ham to glisten in what looks like a sheen of sweat. He feels the threat of bile rise in his throat. He hasn't eaten all day, but the thought of chewing and swallowing is proving too much, and he slides his plate back and leans away from it in his chair, balancing on the back two wooden legs. He surveys the room. Catrain, he notices, is holding her fork with her left hand. *That's odd.* A smile plays coyly on the lips of

Niklaus, and Henrick watches as he casts his eyes discreetly to Catrain at his left. There is some silent message in that mischievous look, and Henrick's mind works to define it.

"Henrick, aren't you hungry?" Thea asks, breaking him free from his focus on the activities at the far end of the table.

"I fear I am too excited to hear what news Dagen has for us," Henrick stammers. "Tell us, Dagen. Did everything go as planned on your journey through Masunbria?" Henrick asks.

"Not quite, my lord. I actually come with what I think is bad news. There is something happening in Cale."

11
Magdalena

The dim light of dawn finds its way through the cracks in the thatch roof of the barn, causing small particles of suspended dust to float in the beams of light. The barn is silent but for the small sounds of life that surround Magdalena. The chickens are warbling and scraping their feet against the packed earth as they search for the pieces of corn thrown to them upon her arrival. She can hear the steady breath of the cow before her as each exhale sends the floating dust whirling through the rays of weak sunlight. Magdalena can feel the warmth of the animal on her face as she leans forward, close to the cow's side, and begins to gently pull warm milk from the gracious girl. The sound of the milk hitting the empty tin bucket becomes, Magdalena imagines, the loudest noise that can be heard from this little farm to Kaelonoch.

"I'd say you're getting the hang of this life," Brom says, startling Magdalena from her thoughts and causing her to kick her bucket and warm milk to spill from the lip. The cow before her moos in frustration and stamps her feet on the frozen ground.

"She doesn't trust easily." Magdalena sighs as she wipes a lock of hair from her eyes with the back of her hand.

"Well, I'd say she is in good company then," Brom replies dryly.

Magdalena lets out a snort of a laugh and returns to the impatient cow before her.

"My day is up," Brom remarks.

"So it is."

"I am not sure if you will be thrilled or disappointed in what the past twenty-four hours has produced," says Brom, kicking at a frozen clump of mud with the toe of his boot.

Magdalena remains silent as she continues to pull milk into the bucket.

"They came around yesterday to collect for this moon's offering. This moon they ask for more than they ever have before. The promise to replenish our stolen goods hasn't been kept. This winter is harsh, and after the attacks, the people of Masunbria have little to spare. Yet the castle keeps taking from its own people to give substantial amounts to those monsters in the mountain. The village has buried six of their own in just the past two weeks. There is no mercy though. Do you know what they have decided to do this moon to the families that can't pay? They announced that they'd take the families' eldest sons to work the mines. It matters not if the boys are fifteen or five. They will be taken until the debt is paid. A woman in Kaelonoch couldn't pay her share yesterday. They took her son, a four-year-old little boy. He was her only child, and she had lost her husband in the attacks on the castle. They found her this morning hanging by a rope. Spring will bring respite to some of the demons our people are battling, but it will exasperate others. Fields will need to be planted. Soil turned.

Seed dropped. With weakness, illness, and fewer hands, it is unlikely many in the village will see their crop planted in time to reap a bountiful harvest come autumn. If this winter doesn't kill your people, the next surely will."

Magdalena closes her eyes and focuses on her breath as she fights back the tears that threaten an escape. "Why are you telling me this?"

"Because I am done watching you milk cows. I know you don't know the people of Kaelonoch, but they are my family. They are good people. They don't deserve this. We have been slaves to the Typhans for too long. Things are getting so much worse. I know you know that. As Haluk, you saw with your own eyes how your people suffered under the demands the offering placed on them. The Typhans may no longer inhabit Masunbria, but they still bring death to this day. Magdalena, I was right. There are men willing to stand against the Typhans. The day you granted me was successful. Willem is here. He is in the house. We need to talk about what we will do next. Will you come in?"

Magdalena doesn't take her eyes from the udders before her. Squeeze and pull, squeeze and pull. *I can't do this.* She can't be the person that Brom and Willem expect her to be. Haluk could. Haluk had an advantage, but that was taken from her. It was easy to be him. To pretend. She doesn't know who she is now. She isn't a future king, but she has realized that she can't be a bride to a barbarian either. She is lost. It won't take long before they realize that themselves. She doesn't want to be there when their faces finally register the truth: that they have put their faith in someone so broken. She needs to get away. Run away. It is then that the seeds of a plan begin to sprout. She will tell Brom to meet her in the house. Then, she will leave her pail where it lies, and without a word, she will disappear. She will make her way out of Masunbria and head to More or Ezers. She has longed to see the sea anyway. She can find work once there. No one will recognize her. She didn't ask for any of this life. Her parents chose it for her, and now they are gone. She can just leave and hope that her brother figures out this mess. Or maybe Willem can lead Brom's army and Masunbria can be free. She closes her eyes and can almost smell the salt of the sea and the sweat on her arms. She can almost feel the sun baking her skin. Perhaps she can start a new life, create a new name. She could be a woman this time. Perhaps she can even find a kind, hardworking man, and they can have a family of their own. She could disappear into a life free from obligation. Free from judgment. Free from her past. Free from the lies.

"Head in, Brom. I will join you momentarily," she hears herself saying without thought behind the words. Brom silently turns and walks away. She is alone.

She rises, steers the cow back to her pen, and gives her a kind pat on her broad side. She looks to her right at the small cottage just as Brom disappears through the door. She then looks to the left, to the woods. She places her bucket on the stool and wipes her hands on her borrowed skirts. Without another thought, she turns and walks to the left, one foot in front of the other. She doesn't look back. Her feet crunch and sink into the snow as she moves purposefully toward the woods. Reaching the tree line, she stops abruptly. The toes of her borrowed boots touch the start of a forest floor while her heels are planted firmly on Hagen's farm. She looks into the dense woods beyond. She can almost see it: her future. If she squints hard enough, it is right there for the taking. She just needs to take one more step and then another and another. It is as easy and as hard as that. She closes her eyes, and she can see the farm and the children beyond. She can smell the bread she will bake with her own hands. She can hear the laughter of children running in the warm days of summer. Tears push free and fall down her cheek.

"You are missing the reunion." Hagen's voice startles her, and she wipes at the fallen tears.

"So I am," she chokes out.

"You thinking of heading out?"

"What? Of course not. I have a responsibility here. I have an obligation."

"Yeah, I suppose you do," Hagen replies wearily. "You could go, you know? From the moment you were born, you had no free will. You have it now. You could just disappear and hope for the best."

"You make it sound like I'd be a fool to choose anything else."

"Well, that's the thing, isn't it? Nothing in this world that's worth it comes easy. The hard right or the easy wrong. Those are your two options in this life."

"You think abandoning these people would be easy for me?" Magdalena asks incredulously. "Walking through those woods would be the hardest decision I would ever have to make."

"I don't buy that. The hardest decision you would ever have to make will come once you walk through that front door. Then it will come again when you face the men Brom wants you to lead. When you look into their eyes and vow to stand by them. Then it will come once more when you stare upon Crask mountain, arm raised at the ready, knowing the men to your right and those to your left won't all make it. Again, and again, and again, it will come looking for you. If you decide now that your future and the future of your people are inseparable, there will never again be a day free from hard decisions. It's your choice, my lady. For once in your life, it is your choice. I'll leave you to make it."

Without another word, Hagen turns and walks back to the house. Magdalena remains motionless as she stares into the forest before her. Wiping tears furiously from her eyes, she takes one last longing look at the path ahead of her, then turns on her heels, mutters all the swear words she knows under her breath, and makes her way to the cottage.

"What took you so long?" smiles Brom at her entrance. Hagen hadn't told them. He had kept secret her taste of betrayal. Brom and Willem are seated at the table while Liri and Sybbyl are busying themselves in the tiny kitchen. Liri's hands are covered in flour as she works on a mound of dough. Sybbyl is washing up the plates from their morning meal with water warmed over the fire and deposited into her metal basin. Hagen is working to warm his hands at the hearth. Magdalena has noticed that Hagen's frail body seems perpetually cold, as if the winter wind has settled deep within the marrow of his bones.

"Stubborn cow," replies Magdalena. Hagen smiles at her response and lets out a little chuckle of his own. Magdalena moves toward the stove in the kitchen to warm her hands over the iron belly of it. "Willem," she offers in greeting, displaying for him the only smile she can force. Above the stove hangs various implements for stirring or scooping—all hand carved by Hagen and hanging on small hooks. Magdalena tries to steady her pulse as she studies the wood grain of each of them.

"I must say, my lady, it looks like you are keeping busy and are healing well."

"I am healing well, thank you. As far as the work, I have grown to find farm life therapeutic."

"She spends all day out there." Liri rolls her eyes as she wipes her hands on the faded green apron tied around her waist. "I am starting to think she prefers the dirt and the animals to people."

"It's the quiet I like, Liri. It has nothing to do with your company," Magdalena retorts, turning away from the stove. "With that said, I have a lot still to do before night falls. Let's hear it." Magdalena leans her lower back against the warmth of the stove and crosses her arms over chest while looking expectantly to Brom.

"I have the men, Magdalena. A start, anyways." He rises from the table and takes a few steps toward the kitchen. He holds a folded piece of paper between his index and middle finger. The note hovers in the air between them. She doesn't move to take it.

"They will follow a woman to battle? A woman whose very existence beyond her twelfth year is a danger to them?" She looks him steadily in the eyes. She can see Liri out of the corner of her eye look back and forth between Magdalena and Brom. Cocking her head, Liri turns to fully face Brom, silently awaiting his answer.

Brom doesn't respond, but she sees him worry his lower lip before looking away. *There it is, the truth.*

"You didn't tell them their leader would be me." She snorts out a laugh. "What did you say, Brom? Tell them tales of freedom and leave out the part where I was to command them? Or perhaps you've changed your mind on that account and Willem will do it instead? Or, let me guess, I can lead them to battle, but I can't rule them after, is that it? You think I'm stupid? Do you think that I don't see how no matter what path I take—to the barbarians to be a wife or remaining here to do your bidding—I am a slave now that I am a woman. I could run your battles and you'd still put me aside and a man on the throne in my place. You are using me, Brom Anker, just as everyone has used me all my life. You should be ashamed of yourself." Magdalena spits out these last words and turns her back on the room. Her hands are shaking as she holds them over the stove and rubs them together to mask their betrayal.

"Your people need you, Your Grace," Willem speaks softly to her turned back. "We can't let the Typhans continue to rule our lives. Your brother has no solution aside from turning you over. From what we can tell, he has been too busy drinking and womanizing to find a way out of this mess. You are cunning, you are well educated, you are battle ready. The people would have laid down their lives for Haluk; give them a chance to offer the same for Magdalena." The entire cottage is so quiet you could hear a pin drop. Everyone is holding their collective breaths.

"Then what?" It is Sybbyl who breaks the silence. Her voice is small, and she is wringing her hands. "You use her sharp mind and her body that has been trained for battle, and she leads you to war, and let's say she wins. Then what? You men won't let her be queen. She will have risked life and limb, and you all will put her in skirts and tell her to sit down and look pretty." Sybbyl spits out the final words, anger building as she continues, "I won't stand for it. You want her to lead this uprising, then you and your army must prove, in writing, that you will make her queen. Everyone must, in ink, pledge fealty to Magdalena, and they must honor her as the only heir to the throne." Sybbyl's face is red and her breathing is sporadic. Hagen moves to comfort his wife, but her darted glare sends him back. "Hagen, you'd better be with me on this." She arches a gray brow in his direction.

Hagen nods his head reassuringly, eyes wide in surprise or terror, Magdalena isn't sure which. He doesn't make a move toward her though. There the six occupants stand. Three women in the kitchen, three men near the table. A thousand years of history between them. A thousand years of tradition, custom, convention, conduct. It is Willem who makes the first move, two long and purposeful steps forward. His body is positioned between the two factions, man and woman. Willem pulls his sword from his sheath and lowers himself to one knee, head bowed, arms holding the steel before him in offering.

"This is the oath of knight and guardian of the kingdom. I pledge my fealty to you, Magdalena, on this very blade. I vow this blade will be used to defend you and keep your counsel, and if I shall fall, this blade shall fall with me. I shall give my life freely for yours. I shall yield to you and your commands. I shall take no action against you. I swear this oath before you and the witnesses before us."

The words swarm Magdalena as the memory comes of so many men taking the same vow before her, before Haluk. She knows the reply by heart. She wills herself to speak the words, this time as Magdalena, as the first woman in all of Masunbria to speak her vow to a knight and accept his vow in return. She takes a shaking breath, not sure if what she is doing is brave or foolish, or if there is even a difference anymore.

"Sir Willem Falk, I accept your vows, and I make these vows to you. You will always have a place near my fire and food on your table. I vow never to ask a service of you that would be a dishonor to you or your family. I vow that I will speak nothing but truth to your ears even if it leads to my death. I swear this oath before you and the witnesses before us." Magdalena's voice shakes as she finishes. She walks the short distance between her and Willem. She takes his sword from his hands and runs the blade across her palm, across the hundreds of scars that live there already. Fresh red blood pools instantly. She reaches down her hand in offering, and Willem rises to face her. His own hand, now smeared with her shed blood, is placed over his heart. It is done. They are forever tied as brothers in arms. *So it begins.*

12
Henrick

Henrick looks out the window in the den. He can see down into the castle gardens below. The statues and water fountains are suspended in the death that is a Masunbrian winter. Beyond the garden gates is nothing but dense forest, the heartbeat of this kingdom. Over the tops of the trees he spots the rising sun. The sun, he notices without a trace of irony, touches the land of More before arriving at Masunbria. That, he believes, is an omen. He can see himself now, feet planted in sand, nothing but a vast sea before him and the sun touching his face before it reaches anyone else's. He has resigned himself to rising early and working hard. The distraction has helped thus far.

The engagement of Catrain and Niklaus, though an ever-present sore in his heart, has been dulled these past two days by endless work to secure the kingdom and future that is rightfully his. Henrick lets a chill travel down his spine. The fireplace is cold. The stone castle seems to embrace the cold, soaking it up into the very pores of its structure. The servants have yet to make it to this room, early as it is. The goblets of yesterday's wine still litter the desk. Since killing most of the staff, there has not been nearly enough help for a manner of this size. Infuriating.

The sound of the wooden door creaking open brings his attention from the window to greet his early morning companion. Sigmund begins shuffling in. He has known Sigmund since Henrick was just a small boy. Sigmund had served on his father's council and now serves on Henrick's. He had hated Henrick's father, a sentiment they both share, and the foundation of their friendship, odd as that friendship is.

"Good morning, Sigmund."

"Good morning, Your Grace." Sigmund drags his feet across the red-and-blue carpets and eases himself weakly into a high-backed chair. Henrick watches him move. *He looks weaker*, he notices with a twinge of sadness.

"Glad to see you are alive today. Say, just how old are you anyway? I have a bet running with Dagen on what day you will finally die. He chose yesterday. So again, I say good morning to you and, I guess, good morning to me as well since here you are. Dagen will be so disappointed."

Sigmund lets out a short laugh. "I am pleased that I could make you so happy so early in the morning just by being alive. Maybe we should meet more often, get your day off to the right start?"

"Well now, that wouldn't work. For example, if we met up tomorrow, I would be angry at seeing you and losing a day I picked."

Both men laugh. There were not many people that responded well to Henrick's playful banter, but Sigmund always did. He was a most interesting specimen. He was comfortable in his skin, his old, saggy skin. Henrick liked that about the man, most days. Some days the brave old man would speak frankly about matters he shouldn't, and on those days Henrick would dream about ending the game with Dagen right then and there.

Henrick, noticing that Sigmund was shivering slightly, rises and moves to the cold fireplace. He kneels at the hearth and begins to align the sticks and wood to heat the belly of the stone beast.

"Okay, old man, tell me as I light this fire about what Niklaus has been up to. When I asked you to follow him, I hoped you would discover something useful, something I could use against him if need be. Please tell me he is not as boring as he appears and that you have some leverage for me."

"Oh yes, I do. He is not boring at all, it turns out. He is enamored with a kitchen maid. Her name is Sabina. Shortly after you commissioned me for this mission, I began to notice the stolen glances and the tension in the air whenever they were in the same room. I began to follow Niklaus a bit, and that is when I saw the two of them in a lovers' embrace down a darkened hall. It was then I knew I must befriend the girl, for if she shares his bed, he may surely share what is in his head." Sigmund lets out a laugh at his own rhyme. Henrick turns his head from the fireplace and rolls his eyes at the old man.

Sigmund lets out a grunt and then continues, "Sabina is one of the lowest servants employed here, and as such, she is assigned the least pleasing duties around the castle. She is frequently cleaning out chamber pots and hauling in wood for fires. I would venture to say that she is the hardest-working person here. Since all her friends are dead, she is doing the job of at least six girls. I am surprised she even has time for young Niklaus. Anyway, I decided that I wasn't going to run into this type of girl in the sitting room, so I went to where I knew I would find her."

"You went to take a shit?" Henrick asks, back still turned to Sigmund as he blows on the small flames.

"Precisely!" chuckles Sigmund. "Actually, I was rather ill. I hoped you would notice I didn't dine with you for several days and that you would send someone to check on me. But you didn't. Must have been a whole week you had picked in your game with Dagen."

Henrick lets out a laugh. "I am far too selfish to notice things like that."

Sigmund scoffs. "Well, so you know, I was in my chambers, about dead, when the girl came in. She was startled to see me sitting there on the floor, bedclothes soaked in sweat and the room stinking of the sickness that lay in the bottom of the chamber pot. It was a sight that I am sure would have sent most ladies hurrying from the room, face white with disgust and terror. Not Sabina though. She apologized for her intrusion and went to the pitcher to pour me a glass of water and wet a rag for my forehead. She sat with me then, took care of me, got me cleaned up and into bed. I must say, Henrick, it was such simple, quiet kindness; it was like a mother with a young child. It was how your Thea would have been had she been able to bring babies into this world."

"Sigmund," Henrick sighs, "you shouldn't talk about that. If Thea heard, she would be right back there. I can't have that happen again."

"Henrick, you are a fool to think that your wife doesn't live in that pain every single day. Your wife mourns in silence for those babies she never had. Then she wipes her eyes, stands back up, and helps you conquer the world. Truly, she is a most amazing woman, whom I respect and admire. Still, I know there won't be a day that goes by that she will not mourn those children that could have been."

Henrick, back still to Sigmund, bites the inside of his cheek in frustration. Of course he knows that Thea mourns still. He doesn't need this old man to remind him of that. There are nights when he awakes to see her sitting quietly, staring into the dance of the fire in the hearth. He doesn't move, doesn't make a sound; he just watches. She sits and rocks her body slightly forward and back, both hands resting gently on her forever-flat stomach. Silent tears stream down her cheeks as she sways into and out of the light. Henrick never rises, never makes a sound or an attempt to comfort her. He never mourns with her. He pretends to sleep.

"Get back to your story, old man," Henrick says wearily.

"Yes, of course, Your Grace. So there I sat—did I mention I very well could have been dying? Anyway, she returned, just as she said she would. She helped me into bed and talked with me while she worked to get a warm fire going. I learned of her parents' tragic death in a fire when she was twelve and her older brother who thought it his duty to parent her after they were gone. That's why she left to come to the castle. She wanted out from under his disapproving, critical gaze. A good man, she assured me, but she couldn't love him as a brother if he continued to act as a father. She didn't fit in much here at the castle though. She is a lovely girl with beautiful long auburn hair that she ties back and away from her face. When I mentioned her hair, she laughed. She said she must tie it back that way so it didn't fall into the chamber pots as she carried them around. She had learned that the hard way, she admitted. A girl with a sense of humor. An easy way about her. She doesn't take life too seriously. I can see why Niklaus was drawn to her. Of course, she is pretty, in a different sort of way. She has a tender, round face dotted with freckles, with soft green eyes and a gentle smile. But it is her heart that he loves, I do think. Anyway, from that early day in the castle, we have become fast friends. So I seek her out and chat with her while she works."

"Have you confronted her about the affair?" Henrick asks, moving back to the chair opposite Sigmund. The room is already beginning to warm, and he is pleased to see that Sigmund has begun to shiver less.

"I didn't have to. She brought it up herself. She came in this morning, and that sweet, gentle face was gone. Fallen. In its place was worry and sadness, and neither emotion suited this bright young girl. I pressed her for an explanation. Finally, after much coaxing, she broke. Tears began pouring down her cheeks as she told me that the boy she loved had recently accepted an engagement with another. She said that when he had told her, he had promised he would find a way out of the marriage. He wanted her, a life and family with Sabina. He explained that the marriage was being forced upon him and that there was no sliver of love between the two. They were pawns in a game, was how he had put it. She believed him. That was until this morning. She was doing her rounds and was focused on her work and hoping to get some fresh air, as the day promised sun instead of the perpetual gray. Her mind was on the sun and the winter birds, and that is why she didn't hear them before opening the door to his chamber. She was anticipating an empty room, arms loaded down with rags, and there, in the bed, was the man she loved with his future wife engaged in passionate acts best left for after the marriage vows have been spoken. Her eyes locked with his, and his face changed from one of pleasure to shock and horror. Sabina said she had opened her mouth as if to scream, but nothing had come out. She had turned and silently shut the door behind her before running to the servants' stairs and screaming into her open palms."

Henrick sits still as stone. If he moves, he will betray the emotions coursing through his body. Catrain. His Catrain. Rage, humiliation, and sorrow rise in his throat as if a demon he swallowed is now looking for escape. He is going to drown now. He thought he was riding the waves, but, no, the waves were going to crush his bones beneath their force. His lungs were going to fill with water so no air could enter.

Sigmund, clearing his throat, continues, "It seems our Niklaus has taken a shining to Catrain after all. In such a short time too. Thea was so certain that the girl would win him over, no matter what hesitation he showed. I am sure Thea will be happy to hear that the two will have no problem consummating the marriage when the time comes. She might even think it best to move up the wedding date in the event Catrain becomes with child earlier than anticipated."

Henrick steadies his breathing before speaking. "Thea is a wonder, isn't she? Thank you, Sigmund. You have done well. I ask that you continue your friendship with Sabina. Now, I really must get back to work. You can show yourself out."

Once the door closes behind Sigmund, Henrick leans his head back to rest against the tall back of the chair, inhaling gulping breaths and trying to slow his racing heart. He grabs fistfuls of his dark hair and squeezes until pain courses through his scalp, and he stifles a yell. How could she do this to him? She couldn't. That's the answer. There is no way Catrain would betray her love for him, especially for a sniveling imbecile like Niklaus. No, Niklaus coerced her somehow; Henrick is sure of it. Perhaps Niklaus discovered that Catrain loved him and threatened to bring the news to Thea if Catrain didn't agree to his advances. Yes, he is certain that no matter what, Niklaus is to blame, and he is also certain that Niklaus will pay dearly for it.

His thoughts are interrupted by a knock. Henrick barks permission to whomever is on the other side to enter. He prays it isn't Thea or Niklaus. Both would be a blow that he isn't prepared to take.

"Good morning, sir," Dagen greets as he enters, with Samalt following uncomfortably close behind him.

"Is it though?" groans Henrick. He motions wildly with an arm in what he thinks is the general direction of the chairs in the room while still clutching his head with the other hand. He hears the men sit, and then he hears nothing, just their breathing. After some time, he decides to open one eye and peer at the men. Dagen is smiling annoyingly at him while Samalt is sitting straight as a board, hands pressing his hair flat against the side of his head.

"What is it?" Henrick yells.

"My lord, it's Cale. Immediately upon my return to the castle, I sent Samalt to Cale to see what he could discover. I was unsure what he would find. As I stated at dinner, I just had a strong feeling that something was off with the little village. Samalt returned first thing this morning with reports confirming my suspicion and, unfortunately, with proof that things in Cale have gotten even worse."

Henrick rubs his hands down his face dramatically. He didn't think this day could get any worse, but here he sits. He motions his permission to talk to Samalt, who has been nervously petting his own hair since he sat down. He stops and folds his hand in his lap.

"Thank you," Samalt smiles. "I agree with Dagen. There is something brewing in that small village; I could smell it in the air. It was the smell of a people with nothing to lose, which, I am sure you will agree, is the most dangerous smell. Everywhere I went seeking answers about Haluk or signs of the Typhans, my questions were met with sly smiles and wild eyes. They would whisper amongst themselves as I walked past. Then, last night, after I dined in the small tavern, I made my way upstairs to the rooms I rented. The small door was open as I approached. When I entered, the smell hit me before my eyes could even begin to register. The smell of iron. Blood. The bed had been covered in it, and scrawled on the wall above the headboard dripped a single word, written in dark, thick blood: 'Liar.'"

"Something, or someone, has gotten to them," says Dagen.

Henrick leans forward, resting his elbows on his knees and his chin on steepled fingers. He taps his index fingers together near his mouth while staring at an invisible spot on the floor. He thinks of Catrain and her betrayal, the seizure that wasn't successful as Haluk had managed escape, Thea growing distant still. Nothing seems to be going his way. Now there is a poison in his kingdom, a poison that could spread. He is losing control, and he knows he must regain it, and quickly. He leans back in his chair and looks from Dagen to Samalt.

"When Thea and I lived at the manor, we had a small lot of chickens on the property. One day, I decided I wanted to learn and observe the birds, so I had the hand show me around a bit. They were interesting to watch as they pecked the ground or bathed themselves in dirt and dust. I started throwing them bits of food when I would come, which was every morning now. I liked the way they would scamper around trying to race each other. Sometimes they would fight over one piece when another lay mere steps away. As the days wore on, I noticed that they would see me coming before I even approached the fence and start clucking and moving about in excitement. They knew I meant to feed them. They recognized me. It was fascinating.

"My favorite was a hen with dark burnt-red feathers who would come right up to my feet and crouch down and let me pet her. She was the friendliest of the bunch. I was most excited to see her because it was almost as if she was more excited to see me and interact with me than she was the food I was throwing. Of course, because of how friendly she was, I always gave her the best of whatever I had. So perhaps she was just the smartest chicken and had found a way to get the best food without having to fight for it. Anyway, one day I walked out there and didn't see the little red hen. I made some noise so she could hear my voice, and still nothing. I popped my head into the coop, and there she was, sitting there, not moving, not acknowledging my presence, not wanting the food I was offering her. I moved to find the farm hand and tell him what I had seen.

"After looking her over, he walked out of the coop shaking his head and told me she was very ill. I asked if she would be alright, if she would recover. He wearily hung his head and told me that she might recover and she might be just fine and back out lying at my feet. Or, he said, she might die from this, but before she did, she would likely infect the entire flock and they would die as well. Then, he said, we would have no eggs and no chickens. I understood. Spare one and either we hope for the best or, by sparing that one, we put them all at risk. Those were our choices. I killed her myself; one swift snap of the neck, and my little red hen was gone. If Cale is an infection, we need to take care of the problem before it spreads to the rest of my flock."

13
Magdalena

Magdalena lies staring at the beams above her head. She knows she should get up, but she finds it difficult to summon the energy to do so. It has been five days since her parents' funeral. Time is quickly running out. Today she meets the men Brom has been busy recruiting. Today she, as Magdalena and not Haluk, attempts to raise an army. After Willem pledged his fealty, he and Brom departed to make plans for this day, and Magdalena threw her furs over her shoulders and left the stifling cottage. She walked purposefully to the barn, where she dug through the wood pile to find one of suitable length and heft. Throwing her furs onto the pile of hay, she began. Feet spread, weight balanced on the balls of her feet, she performed the deadly dance she had been taught since a young child.

She lunged and bounded, ducked and pivoted. She punished her body for the days spent hiding in the loft. She punished her body for the injuries that still ached. She punished her body for revealing all of her weaknesses. Her shoulders and forearms throbbed, but she pushed harder and faster. As a child, she had learned quickly while sparring with the other boys that her reach was shorter than theirs and her ability to swing the sword as hard or as often as her male combatant was improbable. No, speed and endurance were all she had to work with. She had to train to be quick on her feet, to be able to outsmart and outlast her enemy. She was taught that she must move twice as fast and swing twice as often. Make him chase her around and around. Exhaust him from his efforts to chop her head from her neck just long enough that she can take one well-timed, well-aimed plunge into the soft of his belly.

Her lungs burned, her head spun, and still she pushed herself further and further. She was many things, and stubborn was absolutely one of them. That night, she sat at the table as Sybbyl rubbed a yellow, sticky, warm mixture into Magdalena's hands. The earthy smell burnt her nose and stung the angry red gash from her oath with Willem and the dirt and wood debris that made its way inside from her personal torture in the barn.

Hands bandaged in pieces of torn cloth, Magdalena took up the book that Hagen gave her and found her place near the fire. There she read aloud about a great knight who was on a quest across the unforgiving land for a stone said to heal his maiden from her cursed sleep. Liri, seated on the floor at Magdalena's feet, lazily plaited her long hair as she watched the fire dance. Hagen sat at the table and listened while he made little animals out of wood, a hobby that Magdalena found endearing. Sybbyl remained in the kitchen, busying herself with tinctures or salves from the dried herbs she collected when the weather was warmer and the earth was alive. The little cottage, with its soft noises of an ordinary life and smells of herbs and burning wood, felt like a home.

When the fire began to die, they each made their way to the loft. As she lay still on her small bed, her mind refused to be silenced. It reminded her of her parents, her brother, the feelings she felt in the warm cottage as she read and listened to knife scrape wood and smelled the sweet and spicy scents of herbs being brought to boil. It was then that Magdalena cried. She let the tears fall freely, back turned to Liri, hand over her mouth to silence her despair. Liri didn't say a word; she just let her have her sorrow, and for that, Magdalena was grateful.

"Magdalena! Your oats are cold now. Get up!" Liri's shrill scream travels up the ladder and breaks Magdalena from her musings. Irritation drips from each word out of Liri's mouth, possibly because she has called her at least three times before this last summons. Magdalena lets out a groan and rolls out of bed and onto the floor. The sound of her landing vibrates through the tiny cottage as the indicator that she is making progress toward greeting the day. *That should satisfy Liri for a while.* She crawls on her hands and knees to the chest that sits in the corner and lifts the heavy wooden lid to peer at the pile of dull clothes inside. Men's clothes.

Gratefully, she has traded in the dresses and can once again wear the clothes she is most comfortable in. What lies within the wardrobe is the result of a sixteen-year-old boy who spoke up against a member of the royal guard at the offering day and was made an example of in the center of Kaelonoch. His mother, distraught over losing her only son but well aware that she must see the children remaining through the winter, sold her son's clothes to Brom. Magdalena pulls out the trousers and a thin, dirt-brown shirt with buttons down the front. She slips them both on, rolling the sleeves of the shirt to her elbows. She relishes the way her legs feel, now covered and separated by fabric. She feels so much less vulnerable, and she notices her confidence in what today will bring elevate slightly, thanks to the pants. She stops at the little mirror in Sybbyl's room and sees a version of Haluk before her—not actually Haluk. Her hair has begun to grow out a bit, and there is nothing to bind her chest with. She fingers the scented oils and the simple yet delicate hairpin on the small table, and her thoughts go to her mother.

Her mother was beautiful. She had hair like Magdalena's, so blonde it was nearly white. Hers was long and wavy, and she would braid it in an elaborate design with ribbons weaved within the locks. She would dab her pale checks with beet powder, and her lips would be glossy and red from her stain made of berries. When Magdalena was little, she would sit and watch her mother at her mirror, and Magdalena would imagine what it would be like to be beautiful, what it would be like to have hair flowing down her back and eyes lined with charcoal. Closing her eyes, she can smell her mother's skin—cinnamon and rose with a hint of clove. Tears spring to her eyes at the memory.

"Magdalena!" Liri screams up the ladder, and Magdalena is grateful this time. She can't seem to get control of her thoughts this morning. She turns her back on the little items of femininity and walks resolutely down the ladder and into the belly of the cottage.

***

The day passes in a slow silence as the four occupants await the sun to fall and night to cast its shadows upon the land. At last, it is time to depart. The four hooded figures make their way through brush and mud to Sordusten Inn using the light of the moon and Hagen's knowledge of the land as their only guides. Once inside the cellar, the blinding light of the candles burning are such a contrast to the dark of night that Magdalena has to blink several times to get herself adjusted. She looks around the room before her. The low ceiling is crisscrossed with beams that are blanketed in a thin veil of cobwebs. The floor is made of packed earth, and along the walls are stacks of crates and wood barrels. Some of the barrels are being used as chairs by those scattered throughout the damp and dank cellar.

The four make their way to the back of the room where a large shelving unit is full of jars of pickled vegetables and canned meats. Magdalena keeps her head down and her hood up as she goes. Just beyond the edge of the fabric, though, she can make out the crowd gathered. She counts twenty or so men and one woman. The men are of varying ages, and they look typical of all men of Masunbria—well-built arms, broad backs and chest from working the land, the skin around the eyes etched with thin lines from days spent squinting against the wind that comes down from the mountains.

They are huddled in little groups, and they whisper as Hagen, Sybbyl, Liri, and Magdalena walk past. They don't recognize Magdalena; she can see that in their curious faces. Brom had assured her that most people, unless they saw her hair, wouldn't be able to pick her out from a crowd. It was meant to be reassuring, she knows that, but the words stung a little. As Haluk, she had been determined to be a prince *for* the people. Known by the people and trusted. Loved by them, even.

Using his hand to brush off the wood dust, Hagen sits four crates purposefully down on the dirt floor, far away from the others in the room. He sits them down two by two and instructs Sybbyl to join him at one of the crates in the front. Liri and Magdalena are made to sit behind them. Magdalena rolls her eyes. She is going to spend the entire evening staring at the back of their heads. She sits down on the low crate and tries to quietly slide it to one side. Hagen, apparently having eyes in the back of his skull, turns and gives her a stern look. She sits still.

She is being treated like a child, and her irritation is rising. She has begun to sweat, and whether that is from the stupid hood that Hagen insisted she never remove or the childish manner in which she is being treated, she doesn't know. She is grateful when Brom brings her a cup of wine. Brom returns quickly to the front of the room where, bringing down a large beam across the seam, he seals the door from the inside before turning to look upon the occupants.

"Good evening, dear friends," he begins. "I am happy to see that you all are here tonight. I know the risk you took to arrive, the trust you have in the others with us tonight. These things are not unnoticed. Many of you lost someone very dear to you in the brutal attacks at the castle. As you know, my own sister, Sabina, works as a kitchen maid and survived only by hiding herself inside a cupboard large enough to hold her small frame. I was lucky. Many of you were not. I also know that many of you are afraid of what the Typhans have threatened in regard to our women. I want to begin this meeting by acknowledging that, but then I want to ask us to put that aside for the rest of the night. I want our discussions from here on out to be free from the weight of it. I want us to think logically and not out of fear. I hope that you can understand my aim here." Brom pauses and looks around the room. The heads bob up and down. Magdalena shifts uncomfortably on her crate to see past Hagen's head.

"Thank you for that." Brom nods in return. "We have seen with our own eyes King Niklaus challenged by the Typhans—war all but declared—only to fill his halls with drink and women in the days to follow. He has sent his legionnaire, Dagen Horne, to each village in Masunbria to demand more than we have to give. Our bellies grow empty, and the winter is still long, and Niklaus has not just the audacity but the means to throw elaborate dinners and parties? Fani has been inside the walls, and she will tell you tonight that their plates are full, their hearths are warm, and no one seems the least bit concerned about the Typhans. How is that so?"

"I don't know how he can be so callous. My family isn't going to outlast the winter," sighs a young man, eyes a watery brown and face full of worry. "It will either be the Typhans who will take my wife and my children in their sleep, or it will be starvation and the fever that comes with the relentless cold and no fire to ease it." The man places a shaky palm on his cup of ale. He can't be much older than Magdalena, and she thinks of his young family and struggles to swallow back the sadness as images of small children cold and still flood her imagination.

"Jonan is right," says Brom. "We have always looked out for one another in Kaelonoch, but as the date approaches when the

Typhans are to return, and the weight begins to settle on our little village due to the offerings imposed, there is a real threat that man could turn against man if it meant that his wife and children could survive one more night. That is why we are here. To prevent such things from occurring."

"Maybe Jonan should have done a better job preparing his family for hard times. I hope, Brom, that by saying we must look out for one another, that you aren't insinuating that we all take care of him and his just because he was too lazy or too stupid?" a gray-haired man with a hooked nose, small jaw, and mean glare says from the corner. "Jonan is not my problem. None of you are." The man parts his lips and pushes his jaw out so his lower teeth bare before the top.

"Go to hell, Segan," shouts Jonan as he rises to his full form. "Why is he even here? He cares nothing about Kaelonoch, never has."

Brom holds up his hands in an attempt to calm the crowd, and agitation vibrates through the dust-filled cellar. "Segan is here because he feels for the safety of his land. Not yours, or anyone else's, but his. Yes, we all know Segan doesn't care about Kaelonoch, but he does care about what is his, and he is willing to do anything he can to protect that. He is also a smart enough man to know that there is strength in numbers, and if he can join our group, he will have a better chance of not losing everything he has worked for. We aren't here to debate what each other's intentions are. We are here to talk about what is happening in our kingdom."

Voices, one talking over another, rise from all corners of the room.

A woman in a tattered red dress claps her hands together slowly. It is surprisingly effective. The men quiet down and stare.

"Fani, you want to add something to this madness?" Brom says, his heated tone from a moment ago all but vanishing as he smiles at the woman.

"Well, only if you boys are done wasting everyone's time. Time is money in my line of work, and I am not making any sitting here listening to you all argue," Fani drawls as she looks around the room with a smile.

A few groans come from some of the men around the room, but the arguing ceases. Magdalena is impressed. The woman before her appears more confident than any woman she has ever met. She holds her head as if she is balancing a crown and not a mop of dingy blonde straw for hair. She smiles as though all of her teeth are present and accounted for. Her skin is almost gray from a lack of proper diet, but something beyond the surface shines through even that pallor. A light. Her eyes, a warm golden color, are sympathetic as she looks around the room.

"As Brom said, I was invited to the castle to entertain some of the young soldiers. When I accepted the invitation, I thought perhaps I was to be the young men's last chance at fun before the war that would surely begin once Haluk, or whomever, didn't turn themselves in by the time the fortnight was over. I prepared myself for soldiers that would cling to me, tears in eyes, as they talked about their childhood and their sweet mother or loving wife, before doing vile things with me. I have been with men prepared to die before. I know how it goes. It's dreadful. That isn't what occurred though. These men were joyous, jubilant even. None of them had trepidation or fear in their eyes. When I returned to the village, I went straight to Brom. I had this growing fear roaring inside me. I knew upon leaving the castle that the Typhans were coming and that no one in that castle was going to do anything to stop it."

"You think they will just allow them in and not put up a fight? You are out of your mind," a man from the corner rolls his eyes at Fani.

"Or they will abandon the castle, and us with it," another remarks.

"Maybe they will take all the offerings they've collected and buy themselves safe passage as far away as they can get from here," states a stocky man with a thick black beard.

"We wouldn't even be talking about this if it wasn't for King Hadrian and Queen Katherine and their deceit," sneers Segan. "I don't know why we continue to pretend like there isn't an easy solution. We find Haluk. This group bands together to find her and bring that lying bitch to Crask, and all our problems go away." Spit flies from his teeth as he slams his cup of ale hard on the barrel top before him.

"Segan has a point, Brom, as much as I hate to admit it," the stocky, bearded man says. "We have less than ten days to find Haluk. Why would we waste them raising up an army when war could be avoided if we just find the girl?"

Several in the room make sounds of agreement. Magdalena catches Brom's eye. This isn't how he expected this evening to go. He looks panicked. He is losing control of this gathering, and fast.

Comments begin to flair wildly. Everyone is talking at once, and Magdalena can only catch some of what is being said.

"The king and queen were fools, but it is the girl I blame. She knows what she was obligated to do, and yet she hid. She put all our lives in danger. She is a coward."

"You know, learning that Haluk was a woman came as a comfort to me. I had always been oddly attracted to the prince—a thought that was most disturbing until this revelation."

Laughter erupts.

"That settles it then. We find Haluk and save our kingdom. She has brought nothing but shame to Masunbria. There is no reason for us to feel any level of guilt when we hand her over."

Heads nod in agreement.

"Perhaps we will be celebrated? A parade in our honor through the kingdom? Oh, my dear sweet mother will be so proud seeing me on a regal horse with a livery leading me past her home. Think of all the women I will attract. I may be married before the first crop!"

The laughter rises at this last statement and vibrates between her ears. Some are roaring, some chuckling, others choking on their ale.

Anger rises in Magdalena's cheeks. She looks to Brom, who is struggling to stop the discussion, his face progressively growing redder with each failed attempt. There is no stopping them. They are loving each moment of this. The insults and accusations they are hurling, making them feel superior, noble even. They are trying to outdo one another now. Adding layer upon layer to their tales. She can't take it anymore. She can't sit by and listen to it. No matter how true some of it is.

"Enough!" Magdalena yells, standing and removing her hood.

"Oh no," whispers Sybbyl.

"This is what you people do? Your people are dying today. Not nine days from now when the Typhans come, but today. They are starving, and they are freezing, and there is no end in sight as long as the offerings are being demanded—as long as Masunbria exists at the mercy of the Typhans. My parents betrayed you, and I deceived you, and I can understand if some of you want me dead for it. That's fine. Let me die on the battlefield with you by my side as we fight for a free Masunbria. Let me attempt to make up for my failures, and my parents' failures, by shedding my blood to try to give you a better tomorrow. You can take me to Crask, but even with me across the ridge, do you really think you can continue to live under these circumstances? Masunbria needs her freedom. It's time for a revolution. As Haluk, I proved more than capable of leading one. Can you say the same for Niklaus? Or will he just sit on this throne, with his women and wine, and allow you all your undignified suffering? You believed in me as your leader once before. Let me die with honor, serving you, to free you."

"Ladies and Gentlemen, I give you Princess Magdalena," states Brom with a sigh of resignation as the group stares silently, mouths agape.

14
Henrick

Henrick gently folds the paper in half and tosses it on the desk beside him. He massages the spot above his right eyebrow. The king of More has died, and the throne now belongs to his son Mikhail. Now is a very inconvenient time for the old king to have died. Henrick's coffers haven't been filling as quickly as he had hoped when he imposed the increased tax on the people of Masunbria. In addition, the aide from the neighboring kingdoms has been slow to arrive and, again, not as generous as he had hoped. Without substantial wealth to offer the Typhans in bribe, he knows that he needs Magdalena now, more than ever, and she still is nowhere to be found. The people of Masunbria are proving to be nothing but a disappointment.

In the case of Cale, disappointment is an understatement. Once Dagen and Samalt understood Henrick's intention of destroying Cale, they tried to talk him out of it. Dagen's concern was merely for the loss of men of fighting age, men they could use when they start their great war to obtain the lands that border the sea. They argued, but Henrick dismissed his general and his creepy sidekick without being swayed. He believed thoughts like those that lived and breathed in Cale to be dangerous if left unchallenged. No, he couldn't—wouldn't—let Cale infect the rest of Masunbria.

"Do you think it's Maggie that is stirring all the trouble in Cale?" wonders Thea aloud between bites later that evening during dinner. They have chosen to dine tonight in the great room. The coldness of the day has set into their bones, and unlike the dining room, the great room has the benefit of the massive hearth. The fire blazes beside the table, casting shadows throughout the room and over the portraits lining the walls. The brushed eyes stare down as Henrick, Thea, Niklaus, Catrain, Dagen, Samalt, and Sigmund partake in a feast of roasted lamb and red wine.

"Uhhhh," groans Niklaus. "No one cares about Maggie, Aunt Thea. There is not an idiot in the world who would follow her, let alone an entire village. She is a traitor and a coward. I want you all to stop talking about her. I really wish you, Samalt, would find her, like we have ordered you to do. You are proving to be utterly worthless. Maggie is a constant reminder of a life that I soon wish to forget entirely."

Henrick rubs his face in frustration. "We can stop talking about her when she is well over the mountains and we have our Typhan army at our side. The people have not worked hard enough to bring her forward. They are either lazy or they haven't taken this Typhan threat as seriously as we had hoped. Either way, they need a little motivation. Cale will be just that."

"And what will occur in Cale, Uncle?"

"Glad you asked." Henrick wipes his mouth and takes a long, dramatic breath. "We burn it. To the ground." The room stares silently at him.

"You are joking?" Thea asks.

"Of course not. We need something dramatic. We will use the slaughter at Cale to further our story about the Typhans. We have left the kingdom in relative peace in hopes that they would focus on locating Magdalena before the Typhans returned for their women. It seems that they need to be reminded of what they are up against. Cale can do that for them."

"You want to burn them alive? Aren't they paying into our coffers?" Niklaus says with confusion.

"Women and children as well?" Thea is looking at him as if at any moment he will surely burst out laughing at his twisted joke.

"Okay, what is this?" Henrick rolls his eyes. "None of you seemed to care about any of the people we killed taking this castle. All of a sudden, I am now some monster? Let me remind you that these people are not innocents. The people in Cale have been given ample opportunity to conform. They have chosen to rebel. They brought this on themselves. I am not killing them—they are killing each other. As far as the women go, well, they are just as culpable as the men. They could have reported to us who amongst them possesses a traitorous heart. Instead, these women, with no apparent regard for their lives or the lives of their children, have chosen to aid the rebels in concealment. Men perhaps wrote the death sentence, but the women did nothing to stop it."

"You are telling me that you have exhausted all means of discovering who the source of the rebellion is? Of finding out who left the bloody message scrawled on the wall in Samalt's rooms?" Thea's voice picks up as does her inquiry.

"Don't tell me how to do my job, Thea," barks Henrick.

"Don't you speak to me like that. If it wasn't for me, you'd still be sulking back home as you waited for Hadrian to throw you his scraps. I am just trying to ensure that you don't let your ego ruin everything I have created for you."

Henrick slams his fists on the table so hard that glasses topple over, and Catrain lets out a shriek. *Disrespect. First, I learn Catrain is sleeping with Niklaus. Now, Thea dares to speak this way to me in front of everyone.* "Get out, Thea. Get up and get out of here. You are no longer welcome at this table. I don't want to see your face again in matters of council." Spit flies from between Henrick's bared teeth as he stares Thea down.

Thea rises calmly, wipes the corners of her mouth with her white linen napkin, and walks silently from the room without looking back. The remaining dinner companions eat the rest of their meal in stunned silence.

After dinner that evening, Henrick decides he needs some air. Donning his thick black furs, he leaves the warmth of the castle to walk through the gardens. The night air is cold, and each breath that leaves his mouth sends a cloud of vapor before him. The garden is eerily silent as the stone statues appear as if they are men and women frozen in the winter wasteland—a male form holding a goblet to the sky, a woman kneeling to feed a small, frozen bird. Walking away from the castle, away from the suffering stone men and the small girls, he heads toward the outer stone walls. He wants nothing more than to put distance between him and that rotting house of death. He pauses slightly as he passes under an old tree with its tangle of roots protruding from the earth. His mother has been on his mind lately, and he has been trying to remember which tree she lies below. He thought that if he looked hard enough at the shape of the bark or the twist of the branches, he would have a vision. The tree itself would tell him. It would reveal that through her, it has grown strong and mighty. Henrick would then cut the tree down. In spite of his mother, he is strong and mighty, and to prove that he will remove from this earth that which her body has fed and nurtured all these years, that which replaced him.

***

Well before dawn, Henrick pulls his horse to a stop on top of a snow-covered hill that looks down upon the village of Cale. The town below is littered with small stone homes and little shops. He can see small dots of animals in pens as they root around in the dirt, eager for their morning meal. The village is silent, the people yet asleep. Henrick covers his nose with a gloved hand, the moisture inside his nostrils having begun to freeze. One by one, Henricks sees the flicker of torches being lit as the costumed men who hold them surround the village. Dagen pulls his horse up close to Henrick.

"Are you sure about this?" asks Dagen. "We can always capture and interrogate? It's been a while since we've let Samalt have some fun."

"Just do it," Henrick growls in response.

Dagen looks sideways at Henrick for just a moment's hesitation before he lights his own torch. Holding it high in the air, he gives three distinct passes with it over his head. That's all it takes. The men on horseback charge Cale from every angle, torches raised high over their heads. There are nearly sixty men coming down into the village from all directions, ensuring that no one escapes. The first to arrive light thatch roofs, which engulf in flames instantly. Next, shatters of glass echo through the trees as windows are broken open with the butts of the torch before being thrown inside. The men travel fast, lighting anything that will hold a spark. The people, awakened now, run out of their homes confused and scared. They aren't upright long. The men on horseback charge, trampling them to the ground or spearing them through the heart.

Their screams as they fall vibrate up the hilltop and settle into Henrick's ears. Smoke billows up from the tiny village as the roofs collapse and the furnishings within catch on fire. He can see flailing bodies as they are overcome with flames. They run in circles, disoriented, through the dirt streets, until finally collapsing in what he imagines to be a stinking heap of burnt hair and body fat. The quiet, sleepy village has been transformed in mere seconds to a ball of fire as the sounds of death and agony fill its streets. His costumed men are on foot now, driving blades into every body they encounter. One of the men finally silences the bleating squeal of a terrified sheep with one swift slice of the neck. Henrick feels bile rising in his throat as he watches the scene below. He tries to prevent its eruption, but the scene before him proves too much, and he turns his head and vomits off his horse.

***

Upon his return, he discovers that Thea still is refusing to speak to him after his outburst last night. It matters little to him at this point. She will come around, just as she always has. Until then, he will reside with one of his life's greatest companions, wine.

Henrick has been careful since the siege to not let himself rekindle that friendship too readily. Henrick tended to have what Thea called *spells*, which was a nice way of saying that he would drink himself into oblivion for days or even weeks on end and then emerge like some sort of handsome butterfly and resume his life of greatness. It was his reset. It was a time where he could feel things that, under sober circumstances, he either couldn't or shouldn't feel. The period of drink would allow him to face his darkest demons, and then, once they were slayed, he would be fine again. For a while, anyway.

Henrick, having ensconced himself in his den all day and all evening since his return, now finds himself properly intoxicated. He reaches for another bottle. The night is still and dark, but his mind is full of screams and the bright light of an inferno. *I have to get out of this room.* He rises and loads down his satchel with several more bottles of wine. He hurriedly stuffs into his mouth the cold, misshapen form of his dinner—duck with a cherry sauce, that has now formed a thick gelatin coat on the meat, stuffed with soggy bread crumbs and herbs. Lifting a bottle of wine to his lips to force the food down his throat, he catches an unpleasant smell arising from nearby. It is him. Sniffing under his arms, he is assaulted, more clearly now, by the smell of his own stink. Henrick lets out a laugh. It is as if he is a wild animal. Or barbarian, perhaps. He wonders if this is what a Typhan must smell like. He feels sorry for his sister at the thought.

He uncorks another bottle, ensures his satchel is packed with his reserves, and exits the room. Henrick slinks in the shadows as he moves down corridors. He avoids the light of the torches along the wall by hopping clumsily away as if the light would burn his skin if it were to touch him. He giggles and stumbles, enjoying the game. He occasionally pops his head into a room here or there as he goes. Once the first bottle is empty, he stops and relieves himself into a tall, decorative vase in the corner of the hall and opens a second bottle from his satchel. He realizes, with some shock, that he is standing in front of Thea's room. He wasn't conscious of his body leading him to this wing of the castle.

He pushes open the door silently and creeps inside to stand at the foot of her bed. He watches her sleep while he drinks. Her tight brown curls splay across the white cotton of her stuffed pillow. He sees her chest move up and down as she breathes slowly. He shakes his head slightly. She doesn't understand him. Never has. Not like Catrain. He misses Catrain. She would have understood why he had to do what he had to do in regard to Cale. She would have known the weight of his decision to burn it. She would have seen past his words of confidence. Catrain would have known that his current state of drunkenness was to ward off sleep for fear that his dreams would be haunted by ghosts—ghosts that would surround his bed, their skin burnt and peeling off to reveal the bone beneath and their clothes no more than charred strips of fabric hanging loose from their bodies. No, Thea would look at his empty bottles and see weakness. She wouldn't understand that those bottles kept the ghosts away, allowing him to face what he had done so she could sleep soundly here before him.

Enough is enough. He needs Catrain. He can and will forgive her, for he is certain she is a victim to whatever game Niklaus is playing. He leaves his wife and makes for the adjoining room.

Until wed, she would continue to sleep near and serve Thea. Henrick gives a slight knock but no answer. Peering back at Thea's sleeping form, he quietly enters the dark room. He feels his way to the bed, for no fire has been lit nor a single candle to burn. His fingers move silently across the blankets. Like little ants, they scurry and feel their way over bumps and ridges, seeking out her soft flesh. Empty. Rage begins boiling inside him. If she is not in her bed and she is not tending to Thea, that means only one thing. She is with him.

Running out her door to the corridor, he stumbles and slams his body into the stone wall. The bottles in his satchel break under the weight of him. Red liquid begins to pour from the seams of his bag, down his pants, and onto the stone floor beneath. Pushing off the wall, he moves forward, unsure at first where he is going but letting the anger lead him where it chooses to go. The winding staircase stretches up before him, and he climbs. Higher and higher. His rage guides his legs to rise and push and rise again. *Niklaus will feel my pain.* He repeats that phrase over and over as he climbs. He barrels down the hall until he finally reaches the closed door he has been searching for. *Niklaus will pay one way or another*, he thinks, and he slams open the door. A scream from inside. Henrick moves quickly even in his inebriated state and places his hand over her mouth. He smells of sweat and wine and betrayal and something else, something more dangerous. He pushes and lowers himself down, pinning her to the bed below, which creaks under their weight. Sabina screams into his palm, and tears fall from her face, but no one hears and no one comes.

15
Magdalena

Word spread quickly through Masunbria about the devastation that had befallen Cale. Her people, so she was told, were split. There were many who pleaded for protection from the castle. They were willing to pay whatever outrageous offering the castle requested as long as that guaranteed the royal army would protect them from the Typhans. They were frightened and anguished and ran to the outstretched arms of the castle as their only refuge. The other half of the Masunbrian citizens were equally as afraid, but their fear lay with the enemy seen. While the Typhans were a real threat to these men, they were not as great of a threat as the one immediately before them—starvation, exposure, death. These men, the ones whose eyes dart glances around dim taverns and whisper behind stone buildings, they are the ones Brom is seeking.

These whispering men are the first seeds of her army, and they are recruiting more and more by the minute. Their names adorn the lists that Magdalena has pored over in an attempt to memorize anything she can about them. Her outburst at Sordusten Inn secured her an army, but not a trusting one. It was evident in the way they looked upon her that they felt hurt and betrayed. Their trust would not be easy to win, and Magdalena had no intention of working hard to do so. It mattered not to her if they liked or trusted her, as long as they followed her.

***

The morning sun peeks through the tiny window, and Magdalena groans audibly and rolls to her side to stare at the room before her. She had dreams filled with images of men in furs with blackened teeth and blades as long as arms and as thick as thighs. She stretches her shoulders and her neck. Her muscles are tight from the work she has been doing on the farm combined with her training. Hagen encouraged her to take it easy. He offered for Sybbyl to teach her how to make bread and roast a leg of lamb. She couldn't think of anything she would like to do less, and she conveyed that message loud and clear. There was no time to allow her body to heal fully and still be prepared for the war quickly approaching. Rising, she winces at the pain still present in her ribs as she struggles to pull on black trousers and a faded green tunic too large for her frame.

A knock at the door hurries her dressing. *Someone is here.* There was nothing planned for today. *This can't be good.*

"Magdalena, Willem is here," Hagen calls up.

"Be right there," she calls down as she scampers and hops around the room, pulling her boots on. She rushes down the ladder, skipping rungs as she goes.

"Willem, what brings you here?" she says as she tries to push her hair back from her face and behind her ears. Its current length is longer than it has ever been, and she is struggling to understand how to keep it from her eyes.

"Others are close behind. There has been a development," Willem rushes his words from his lips.

"What?" Magdalena can feel her throat tighten. *My brother? Is he sick? Hurt? Dead?*

"It's okay," says Willem, holding up his palms to calm her. "Brom will explain it all when he arrives. Everything is fine."

Magdalena searches his face for any clue that he is lying. She finds none. She leans against the table and finishes the last button of her tunic just as the door swings open wide.

"Oh mercy, sweet mercy, there she is," screeches Fani, moving through the open door and making her way straight to Magdalena. Fani grabs Magdalena in an embrace, as if they are the oldest of friends, reunited at last. Magdalena smiles and hugs the woman tentatively in return.

"Good heavens, look at you. You gave me such a fright the other night that I admit I was afraid to even speak to you. You are beautiful, aren't you? I mean your body is as hard and muscled as if I am hugging a young soldier, but your face is just precious." Fani pulls away from Magdalena and looks her up and down.

"She is a better soldier than any of the young boys you've been hugging there, Fani." Brom smiles, giving Magdalena a wink.

The gesture is kind and meant as a joke, but Magdalena grows uncomfortable, and gently she pulls away from Fani, whose hands have begun rubbing up and down Magdalena's arms and over her shoulders appraisingly. She knows her body is different than Fani's, just as it is different than Liri's or Sybbyl's. Her life has been very different, growing up a boy. Her days were spent on a training ground just as much as they were spent at a desk. She was proud of her accomplishments as Haluk. She knew her body was powerful and so was her mind. She has never been embarrassed by that fact, until now. Offering a weak smile to Fani, she shifts back to the table and takes her seat. More seem to file in. She recognizes some of the men from the tavern. The man they called Jonan enters, and in his arms is a small boy—his son. As more enter, they crowd the tiny cottage using any surface as a seat, and once those are all taken, they lean against walls or the backs of chairs. Sybbyl paces in her small section of kitchen, unsure what to do. Hagen sits down next to Magdalena and pats the top of her hand with his.

"Hello, friends," begins Willem. "Thank you for joining us here. I know you all took great risk in coming, and for that I am sorry to have called you. Thank you, Hagen, Sybbyl, for allowing us here. For obvious reasons, we couldn't meet in Kaelonoch. You all have heard of the tragedy at Cale. What I have to reveal today is that Cale was not burned by Typhans but by Henrick himself."

A sharp and collective inhale vibrates throughout the room. Surprise. Disbelief. One thing is certain, though: everyone knows that the words spoken are truth if Willem is willing to speak them. He wouldn't make such a bold statement without proof.

The small crowd bombards him with questions. Willem raises his hand, and they grow silent. Magdalena looks upon the faces in the room. Confusion and fear dance across everyone's features. She notices Brom near the door. His usual smile has fallen into a furious scowl as he stares sideway glances at the man to his right. The man on the receiving end of Brom's fury is tall and solidly built, with skin betraying days after days spent in the sun. His dark blonde hair falls to touch just below his shoulders, with the exception of the portion tied up in a knot with a leather strip to keep it out of his face. He wears armor of hardened leather with no sleeves and leather strips that wrap around his wrists and forearms, seeming to threaten to break under the solid muscle found there. Handsome, but unlike anyone Magdalena has ever seen. Willem extends his palm and motions for the stranger to join him. The crowd watches as the man walks purposefully past Brom to the front of the room.

After a short nod at the man now at his side, Willem begins again. "Late in the morning after the attack on Cale, Brom was making his way to the castle with his cart of wine and spirits when he was attacked by this man looking to take his drink and any coin he had on his person."

Brom goes to open his mouth to protest the way the story is being told. Willem holds up his hand, and Brom closes his lips. Brom rolls his eyes.

"Brom fought most valiantly, but the odds were not in his favor," Willem says.

"That he did," the strange man next to Willem says, voice heavy with an accent Magdalena can't place.

Sounds of outrage on behalf of Brom are heard throughout the cottage.

"Now, before you all get carried away with vengeance for Brom, know that this man has come to us willingly, and we found it of the utmost importance that you hear his story with your own ears. We understand that he could have hurt our brother, our friend, and that some of you may have strong feelings about that.

I ask that you put those aside to hear what he has to say. With that, please, Warrick."

"Aye, yes, thank you. As Willem said, I am called Warrick. I think it best to start with how I came to be in Cale. I was traveling through Masunbria 'bout eight or so days ago, and I came upon Cale, and it was in a bad state. The people were weak, and they were hungry. I needed time to be able to hunt and restock my supplies before moving on, so I told 'em that I would help them in exchange for free room and board. I worked the fields, and in return I was given a nice barn to sleep. I kept to myself. I never thought to ask why the people suffered as they did. I am not from here, and so I just assumed this was how it was in Masunbria. One day, the town was visited by the castle guards, where they were told that the king and queen were dead. There had been an attack on the castle. Typhans, they said. Apparently the Typhans had known that your heir was not a man, but a woman, a woman who belonged to them. The people of Cale were told to pay more and more coin and give more and more of their supplies for the offerings. The castle was desperate to stave off a war and thought that if Haluk didn't return, bribery could buy them more time to find the disguised princess."

"We know all this. We've been living those days ourselves. What is the point of this, Willem?" Segan asks, casting dark eyes on Warrick.

"The point of it," Warrick snarls back, "is that it is all a lie. No Typhan army has come down that mountain in over a hundred years."

"Yeah, what do you know of it?" Segan retorts with a roll of his eyes.

"I know because I am a Typhan," Warrick states, chiseled chin held high.

The sounds of shock are heard first before men begin to finger swords or knives or look to the room for another form of weaponry.

"Okay, we were planning to build to that Warrick, not just blurt it out," Willem says nervously. "Let's just settle down, okay? You just heard him say that it wasn't Typhans who attacked, and you heard that he knows that for a fact because he is a Typhan. What we haven't heard from him yet is who it was that attacked Cale. Please, let's calm down and just listen."

The room vibrates with an unseen energy. It smells oddly earthlike, as if there is some primordial message being excreted from the skin of those who face an enemy that has taken so much from them. Magdalena notices that Warrick, too, can sense the change in the air. He doesn't appear nervous. He appears alert, like an animal knowing he is being tracked.

"In the early morning hours, when darkness still covered the land, I would go into the mountains to hunt for food for myself and for the old man who owned the barn I slept in. Two days ago, when I returned home from the hunt, I learned that the old man had been hung in the middle of Cale for refusing to give up any more of his wheat stores for the offering. He was a good man, a kind man. He had a family to feed and didn't deserve what the castle did to him. I knew it was time to tell the people they were being lied to. The castle was taking from them to stave off a war with Typhans that wasn't coming. I knew it was time to tell 'em where I came from. Who I was. Luckily for me, they believed me and didn't try to kill me.

"The truth helped the town to grow strong. The men looked the guards in the eye instead of casting them to the ground before them. The women held their chins high. They were starving, sick, and afraid, but they no longer let the guards see that. I set out the day before the fire for the kingdom of Skogen. I had done some dealings there when passing through, and I thought perhaps I could bring back some food, some weapons, something to keep these people alive a little longer. Skogen is a good place to trade for people like me. They don't ask too many questions. I left Skogen and traveled back in the night, not wanting to be caught crossing the border with what I was carrying. That put me outside of Cale at first dawn.

"I saw the men poorly disguised as Typhans burn it to the ground. I saw all those people die. There is no mistaking who did this. The leader of the army sat upon his horse at the top of the hill. There with him was the right hand of the king, the one called Henrick. I saw 'em with my own eyes. I left then. There was nothing left for me in Cale. I had tried to save them and had failed. I made my way through the forest. I was headed out of Masunbria, headed to the water, when I came across Brom. I just wanted his drink and his money."

"Why come with Brom back here?" asks the man with the thick black beard. Magdalena believes his name to be Simeon.

"Aye, well, Brom wasn't too keen on giving up his wine or his coin. He put up a good fight. During that fight, he said something that made me pause. He said, 'I will hunt you down. A great army is coming, and you will be first on the list.' I stopped then and asked him about this great army. He refused to say more. I then told him what happened in Cale. I don't know why I did it. I didn't know him. Didn't trust him. For all I knew, he worked for the hand of the king. But when I spoke of what I saw, well, I could see from his face the answer then, the one I was hoping for. I could see that this man and whatever army he was speaking of were not keen on what was being done to the people. I told him I wanted to see this army; I wanted to help."

"Yeah, what a noble story. Listen up, Warship . . ." growls Segan.

"Warrick. My name is Warrick Northman, sir."

"Yes, well, Warrick Northman, why would a Typhan fight on our behalf?"

"Well, that, sir, is none of your damn business. All you need to know is that Typhans didn't do this. Your own people did, disguised as my people. Today, your enemy is those in that castle, not me or my people. I pledge myself to your cause, that I will take up arms against the castle and its crooked rulers, and I will be willing to die for it. I don't think you need anything more beyond that, am I right?"

Segan sneers.

"He makes a valid point. Our enemy today isn't what lies beyond those gates," Willem says, motioning in the direction of the mountains. "There has been no attack by Typhans, there has been no threat for one thousand women to be taken, there hasn't even been a demand for a greater offering. Do you hear that, friends? It has all been a lie. Our people have died of starvation, they have been hung for refusal to pay, their sons have been taken captive to the mines—and it was all a lie. A massive lie full of men dressed in furs. Do you get that? This man, you may hate. That woman over there, you may not trust. But what Niklaus and his uncle are doing is greater than any of that. This is becoming a kingdom I don't want to live in. Not a kingdom I spent my entire life defending. Henrick and Niklaus must be removed from power. The real threat isn't beyond the mountains. It is right here at home."

"Who will rule Masunbria?" Jonan asks. He, Magdalena recalls, is the man from the cellar who was worried over his wife and children. He looks so frightened as he sits on the arm of one of the chairs near the hearth. His small son sits on the floor at his feet, a dirty thumb stuck in his mouth. Jonan's blonde hair is mopped with sweat at the forehead and sticking to his skin. His brown eyes seem to swim in sadness and fear as he glances to his son below.

"I have pledged my fealty to Lady Magdalena. You all have been brought here today to do the same, if you so choose."

"You have got to be kiddin' me," spits Segan.

"No, Segan, we aren't," sneers Brom. "What's changed from a fortnight ago when you thought she was a man? Not a single one of you can sit here and say that Haluk wasn't fit to be king."

"You will protect my family? You won't let anything happen to my wife and my two kids?" Jonan again, his voice shaking as he poses these questions to Magdalena while placing a palm on the boy's small head.

She looks from Jonan to Willem and to Brom. She knows she can't make that promise to him. She takes a steadying breath. "One day at a time, Jonan. I will do what I can to ensure that your family lives to see tomorrow. I have Willem and Brom to help me do that. I am devastated that my brother is conducting, or at least condoning, such hideous acts against our kingdom. He must be stopped. I hope you all can see that. I hope you can see that together, we are stronger than apart."

"The time to act is now," Willem nods. "I have a pledge here." He raises a paper in his hand and waves it slightly in the air. "All those wishing to pledge fealty to Lady Magdalena will sign this. Those names that fill this page will be the seeds of our army. You will go out from here and whisper and watch. You will gather names and bring them to us. You will serve as the first of many. You will be the hope this kingdom needs."

Brom is the first to sign. Jonan is second. Fani signs third. Other men begin to rise and follow. Magdalena sits at her spot at the table and waits and watches. No one glances her way. They are wary of this plan; she understands that. They are betting their lives on a woman and the words of a Typhan. She knows that isn't easy for most of them. She will just have to prove her worth on the battlefield. She watches the room empty—some having signed the pledge and others walking out without so much as a glance behind them.

"My lady," her thoughts are interrupted by Willem leaning palms down on the table, mouth poised near her ear. "I would like to introduce you to Warrick, the man from Cale."

Nodding, she stands. Carrying her cup of wine with her, she crosses the room to where the man sits alone in Hagen's chair near the hearth, studying a pint of ale—Brom's offering after all but the few had left the home. She lowers herself into Sybbyl's chair across from him.

"Do I bow then?"

"Excuse me?" Magdalena asks, raising an eyebrow.

"I'm not really keen on what to do here. Do I bow to ya? If so, do I get down on a knee here, or just a tip of my head to ya? Do I look at your face, or do I look at your shoes? I don't know much about these things, as surprising as it may be. I have not had the honor of being in the presence of a Masunbrian royal before."

"Well," the annoyance evident in that one little word, "you know then who I am, so that saves us from introductions and the awkward exchange of 'nice to meet yous' that aren't true anyway, as the only reason we are meeting is because of tragedy, and therefore, there is nothing nice about our meeting."

"Well, the wine's good, so there's that."

"You are not even drinking wine."

"Ya, I don't like the stuff."

Magdalena looks closely at the man before her. He is looking straight into her eyes. His face is passive, but there is a small glimmer of mischief that dances in the dark of his pupils.

She shakes her head in puzzlement and extends her hand across the carpets between them. "Magdalena."

He takes her small hand in his large, warm, calloused hand and holds it tight. "Warrick. It is nice to meet ya, Magdalena."

She can't help it; she lets out a small chuckle. He isn't terrible, much to her dismay.

"I have never met a Typhan before. I find your accent is strange. Why did you come here? Why leave your people?"

"Oh, ya know, just seeing the land."

"Won't you be missed? What if they come looking for you?"

"No one will come for me, my lady."

Magdalena stares at Warrick as her brow furrows slightly. "How is it that you have convinced Willem to trust you when he doesn't even know you?"

"He doesn't have to know who I was to know who I am," replies Warrick, taking a drink of his ale, his eyes never leaving hers.

"And who exactly are you?

"Nobody really. But I meant what I said. I am here to help. It doesn't matter the people I was born to. It doesn't matter why I left them. You just have to trust that tomorrow, I will be right by your side. The next day and the one after that too. I will give my life for your cause, but the reasons why, well, those are mine and mine alone. They aren't for you. If you can be okay with that, then I would be honored to stand by your side in battle."

Magdalena purses her lips as she thinks. She recalls the trail of men who recently vacated this room without a look in her direction. She needs visible support, and this man is offering it, a man battle hardened and a witness to the crimes against the people. He probably sees that as well. Sees the opportunity. For what, she doesn't know. She does know, though, that she would be a fool not to accept his offer.

"You are welcome here, Warrick," she says at last.

"Good. Now what?"

"Now we go to war not with barbarians, but with our own."

"Aye, I'll let that barbarian comment lie because I can see you've got a lot on your mind." His eyes hold a trace of laughter as he looks deeply into hers. She takes a deep breath and closes her eyes. Her mind is, in fact, heavy. *Brother, Brother, what have you done?*

"I think I shall train; would you care to join me?" Magdalena asks.

"I've never hit a princess before."

"I've never hit a barbarian. It shall be a first for us both."

16
Henrick

In the days that followed Cale, Henrick spent much of that time engrossed with drink. Once night fell, he would turn into a mighty Typhan once again. He would stalk his prey through the castle. He would smell her out no matter where she chose to hide. Once he found her, his reward depended upon his mood. Perhaps he would pour wine over her head and laugh at the mess of her. Sometimes, when the animal instinct in him was at its prime, he would give in to the desires. On those nights, he would tell Sabina that if she told a soul about their encounters, two things would happen; one, she would be hanged for treason, and, two, she would break Niklaus's heart. Henrick didn't really understand why he chose to torment the girl. He believed it was to get back at Catrain, at first, for lying with Niklaus when all these years she had been his. It seems that, with the first taste of the crown, she left him.

Yes, he wanted to hurt Catrain, that was for sure. Niklaus and Thea as well, but the more he thought about his nights of hunting, the more he realized that he wasn't doing this for justice or to cause others to feel pain. He was doing this because the castle made him. The stone walls and floors were alive with power; just as they have been for generations. The greatest of men walked these halls, and though they are gone in the flesh, their spirits remain. He has absorbed all those spirits within himself and has become the greatest beast that roams this earth. He is strong and silent, intelligent and brave; he is bold in the face of fear. The souls of his ancestors have made him into something far greater than a man. He is unstoppable.

A knock comes on the open door of Henrick's den that he has turned into his lair. The room is perfect, with many of its walls covered in tapestries that hang from ceiling to near floor, betraying battles won and great families born. The windows are covered in heavy red velvet drapes that he keeps closed at all times. The fireplace is so impressive that a grown man can stand up inside it. This is the only source of light he keeps in the room. The desk and dark velvet chairs are covered in bottles and papers with his scribblings. Henrick sleeps on the floor in front of the fire, surrounded by a mound of animal skins his ancestors killed. The skins of great beasts like himself.

"Come in."

Dagen and Samalt enter the dark den and squint in the dim light, apparently trying to make out the shape of Henrick on the small couch. "May we open the curtains?"

"No, you may not."

Crossing the room carefully, Dagen and Samalt make their way toward Henrick, stepping over the mess of food scraps that litter the floor as they go. They draw up two chairs near Henrick and, brushing crumbs from their surface, take their seats.

"Henrick," Dagen says, clearing his throat, "we have not had the honor of your presence at the council meetings since the falling of Cale. We are five days away from the Typhan attack we promised at the funeral, and there is still no sign of your niece. I understand that Haluk was how you were hoping to form an alliance with the Typhans."

Henrick makes no noise, and the three men sit in silence for a time.

"Okay, here it is, Henrick, brother. I need you to hear me. Can you do that? Can you bloody just listen to me?"

Henrick makes no response to Dagen's pleas.

"After the burning, homes were searched in Cale. The offering records were useful in telling the number of people that lived in each home within the town. We were able to do a count of bodies, and we did not find anyone that we didn't expect. With setting the fires while they were all still asleep, we were sure that only those that actually resided in the home would be present. Therefore, if we found an extra body, it could have been the very person that was fueling the uprising there. It was a long shot, but we tried to no avail. Now, on the edge of town, there was a small farmhouse that we also raided and emptied, but we left the barn intact, as my men were instructed that the animals and food stores within could be brought here to the palace. It was there that we found the evidence of an outside influence in Cale."

Henrick makes a grunting sound but seems unfazed by the development.

Samalt decides he will try. "Your Grace, there were signs of life in that barn. A camp. It was tucked away to where you would have to walk to the far end of the dimly lit loft and duck under beams laced with webs, but once there, the signs of life were everywhere. A bed roll. There were buckets and blankets and food."

"You think it's Maggie?" Henrick speaks at last.

"We don't know for sure." Samalt sighs with a forlorn look in his eye. "I sprawled out on the bed, trying to inhale the covers for something that felt like her. I looked through the dust and webs for the slightest strand of her fair hair. She remains mute for me. She remains just out of my grasp."

"Samalt, why don't you let me handle this?" a frustrated Dagen says. "Henrick, the truth is, we don't know if it was Magdalena. Now, we do have to consider that an entire village rebelled. Because of that, Samalt and I have started to imagine the possibility it was Magdalena. Regardless of how the bed smelled." Dagen shoots a look at Samalt as he says this. "The people of Cale needed something big, a clear sign that we weren't being honest with them. Cale needed someone they could rally around. Magdalena could do that. Her presence could have started the unraveling of the people. Not only is she a very smart girl, but she has also been bred to be a leader."

Henrick sits for a long time, not making a sound, not moving a muscle, just staring at the men. He watches as the men look at one another, shift in their seats, turn away, and glance at the fire. He never takes his eyes off of them. It is great fun, watching them like this. He has to bite the inside of his cheek to keep from smiling as they sit there, wondering if he's truly gone mad. At last, he can't take it any longer and roars with laughter. Henrick laughs until his side hurts and tears come down from his face in streams. Dagen and Samalt just sit there, staring at Henrick and then at each other, then back at Henrick.

Jumping from his spot on the couch, Henrick breaks the spell. "Well, isn't this fun? Not only do you think that my niece is alive, but you also think she is forming a bloody rebellion. People in Masunbria willing to follow a woman? A treacherous woman at that? This is beyond madness. Maggie is dead or long gone. Our plan remains. The Typhans have no idea what Maggie looks like. I say we give them any girl and claim she's a royal. I have one or two in mind, as a matter of fact. Let them be devoured by the beasts of the mountain. Their souls crushed. Their bodies ravaged. Their spirits broken."

"Samalt, can you leave us, please," requests Dagen, not taking his eyes off Henrick.

Once the door closes, Dagen sighs and buries his head in his hands. "I know what you are doing at night, Henrick."

Henrick pauses, the smile falling from his face. He sits back down.

"Most importantly, I know why you are doing it. But, brother, it is time. It is time to come out of the dark. Your kingdom needs you to lead it now. You have stayed too long this time. People have begun to talk. I have told them all that you are in here, planning for great things for Masunbria, that this is part of your process, that you hide away and come out only after you have solved the hardest of riddles. They are buying it for now, but not for long. I know why you hide, Henrick. I know what comes to you in the dark, because it comes to me as well. That is the price we pay for being the soldiers we are. You don't have to face the dark alone, my friend. Since Cale, we have been without a leader. I've been without my brother. It's time to come back."

Dagen leans across the space between them and places a hand on Henrick's shoulder, gripping it gently. Henrick wants to slap Dagen's hand away, laugh at him, call him weak, tell him that his honesty, his confession, has shown his weakness and that Henrick shall now strip him from his post. Instead, he cries. Refusing to meet his friend's face, he lets the tears fall silently to the carpeted floor below. Dagen lets him cry, hand still gripping his shoulder tightly. They sit like that until Henrick thinks he has nothing left.

"Alright, brother," Dagen says, rising and offering a hand to Henrick. "Let's clean you up. We shall go to Kaelonoch. Whoever was living in that barn made it out alive. It only makes sense that their next destination would be the largest village in all of Masunbria."

Henrick, looking momentarily alarmed at the suggestion, exhales deeply before nodding his approval. "Yes, let's go. Dagen, get Niklaus as well. It's time the people see their king."

That afternoon, the sound of two dozen horses echoes through the streets of Kaelonoch. Trumpeters announce their approach, and men with flags parade ahead. The entire procession is dressed in purple and gold livery, to include the horses. A smile spreads across Henrick's face as the sun shines upon his skin. He has been trapped too long inside the castle walls. Gone mad from it watching and judging his every move. But finally, he feels free. He feels as if the weight of his problems lie behind him, and forward is the only way to salvation. As they draw near to the town center, he sees that a crowd has begun to gather. Their faces are painted with both curiosity and a healthy dash of fear.

Niklaus offers a stately wave to those that have come out. A smile is playing on his face that makes him appear younger than he truly is. His expression is shy and vulnerable, and judging by the looks on some of the young women's faces in the audience, it is a practiced look that has suited him well in the past and will continue to in the future. Niklaus, as Henrick is beginning to see, has an innate ability to make you see in him exactly what you are hoping to see and nothing else. *If he were to live, he would actually make a pretty great king.* Not that Henrick is considering allowing that to happen. Dismounting his horse, he looks around slowly, taking it all in, scanning the ever-growing throng of people. In the midst of everything they have been doing, the seizure of the castle, the plotting of their expansion, and the disease of Cale, Henrick realizes now that he has lost sight of what moments like this are like. Moments where people you don't know call out your name or wave to you. Moments where people strain their necks or hoist their children atop their shoulders so they can get just a glimpse of you. He has forgotten how this all feels.

When he was a boy, he would beg his father to take him on his trips to see his people. He would sit tall and proud on his horse, soaking up the attention. His brother, Hadrian, would always wave dramatically and smile like a fool and talk to everyone. Henrick, on the other hand, believing that Hadrian looked like an eager imbecile, would instead straighten his back and remain still. Proud. He would look down upon them, but never at them, just as his father had taught him. Hadrian had always felt sad when they arrived home from their trips with their father. He would talk Henrick to death in their rooms that night about the children he had seen. He would have noticed which ones were not wearing shoes or which ones looked like they hadn't eaten. He would cry over this misfortune, something that disgusted Henrick. He never saw what Henrick saw, which was people that—no matter their life circumstances—still knew and loved the court, still looked at the court to protect them, and still came outside, in all weather, even without shoes, to get a single glimpse of the king and his young princes. That, Henrick knew, even at his young age, was powerful. Niklaus, he can see, understands that too. He understands that the world needs people like them, people they can turn to that will tell them what they can and can't do, people to impose limitations on them and expectations of them. For, Henrick knows, without this, people would live in chaos and nothing more. So he is proud to see that Niklaus doesn't wave like his buffoon of a father and doesn't hug people as he passes or ruffle the hair of small children. He is proud to see that Niklaus knows his place in this life and knows what his people need most from him.

Dagen leads Henrick and Niklaus through the crowd and into the safety of the Kaelonoch tavern, Sordusten Inn, which, having been cleared out moments before, now lies empty aside from the barkeep. Shutting them inside, Henrick can hear Dagen on the other side of the door instructing the people that they will hear from the king soon. That today is a grand day. He bids them to run home and gather the family and wash their faces. Today, he exclaims, they will see and hear their king for the first time since his coronation. It is a little over the top. Henrick will surely remember to mock Dagen for it later. This has started to become a pattern, he thinks. Perhaps Dagen would be best suited for theatre. Henrick looks around the tavern. Bits of light stream through the windows. Small tables and chairs are scattered throughout the room. Each one has been wiped down and the chairs pushed in. It's orderly.

"Your Grace?"

Spinning, Henrick looks questioningly at the barkeep.

"He asked what you wanted to drink, Uncle."

"Wine. Thank you." Henrick sits down atop the stool next to Niklaus, who is reaching for his own cup of wine just as Dagen throws open the door to the tavern.

"Stop! What in the bloody hell are you doing?"

"Uh, having some wine, Dagen. What does it look like I'm doing?" replies Niklaus.

"Well, it looks like you are trying to get yourself killed. That's exactly what it looks like."

"You think this is poison?" mocks Niklaus.

"Could be, or maybe not, but I would rather not test it out on you today."

Niklaus gives a weary rub of his face and looks between the barkeep and Dagen and back again. "Did you poison my wine?"

"No, my lord. I did not."

"See, he didn't," Niklaus says, and grabs his cup and takes a large gulp of his wine before Dagen, running the few feet between them, can reach to stop him.

Niklaus freezes. His hand holding the cup begins to shake, his eyes grow large, and his face turns red. He drops the wood cup to the ground, where it bounces and rolls away, wine spilling across the dusty plank floor. He reaches for the bar to help him rise to his full height. One hand grabbing at his throat, he begins to pull fiercely at the buttons on his collar in an attempt to loosen it.

Henrick jumps to his feet as well and grabs Niklaus's arm.

"Are you okay? What is happening? Can you breathe?" demands Henrick, face full of fear.

Dagen jumps across the bar in one swift leap and draws his dagger on the barkeep. The man raises his arms high above his head, looking at Niklaus with wild eyes.

"What did you do? What's in the wine?" Dagen screams. The man only stares back.

Niklaus continues to tumble and trip, trying to free himself from Henrick. He stumbles his way to the ground, landing on his back, arms outstretched at either side. His head dips one way and then the next, finally resting with his eyes slightly apart, staring at the barkeep through the slits. Henrick stands staring down at his nephew, fear mixed with relief coursing through his body. He hadn't anticipated becoming king this way, this soon, but he will take it. He tries not to smile. He jumps when he hears Dagen roar with anger and raise his arm high above his head to bring the dagger down into the chest of the barkeep.

"Was that what you thought it would be like, Dagen?" says a laughing voice from the floor.

Dagen pauses midstrike. He turns and looks puzzlingly down at the king as he lies, now rolling with laughter, on the wine-soaked dirt of the tavern floor. Dagen releases the collar of the barkeep with such force that the man flies back, and bottles that stand on the shelves behind him topple to the ground. Dagen doesn't say another word. He storms from the tavern, slamming the door behind him.

"You are an idiot; you could have gotten this man killed with your games." Henrick kicks Niklaus hard in the ribs as he lies laughing. "Plus, you have gone and pissed Dagen off. Now I'll have to deal with that. I am the only one who gets to piss him off, got it?"

"Oww, what did you kick me for? I was just having some fun. I wasn't going to let the man get hurt. We have been stuck inside the castle for so long. I just wanted to not be so serious for just a moment."

Niklaus pulls himself back up to the bar, dusting off his clothes as he does so. He extends his hand to the barkeep. "I am sorry if you were startled there. I surely would not have let him harm you. I was just playing with him; you understand, I am sure. I bet men have fun all the time in this establishment. Apparently, I am not allowed to have any. Nope, never. No fun for Niklaus. Ever. If it isn't Dagen telling me what to do, it is this uncle of mine here, or his wife, Thea. Now, to top it all off, I am going to be wed. Then I will have a wife to tell me what to do. Are you married? Uhh, it looks awful. Does it ever end for us men? Say, what is your name?"

"Brom, Brom Anker, Your Majesty," says Brom, shaking the outstretched hand. "And if you don't mind, I think I will pour myself a drink while refiling yours. Seems I could use one."

Niklaus roars with laughter at this, and Henrick rolls his eyes. He decides to take back the nice thoughts he had of Niklaus upon their arrival to town; he really is a buffoon, just in a different sort of way compared to his father.

Once the men have new drinks poured and the mess has been wiped up, Brom takes a stool across from them at Niklaus's insistence. Henrick thinks perhaps he does feel slightly bad about what just happened, after all. They sit in silence for some time, Brom refilling their drinks when they get low. They ask polite questions of Brom about the town and the people, and whether or not his answers are truthful, they are kind and calculated.

"We have asked you many questions. Don't you want to ask us some?" asks Niklaus.

"Oh, well, I don't know. I hadn't thought of that, I suppose." Brom pauses and looks thoughtfully off into the distance. "We have merely five days until the Typhans descend Crask and ravage our kingdom. Have you any luck finding Haluk?"

Niklaus lets out a sharp laugh. "You are bold man, Brom Anker, to be questioning the crown like that."

"Not bold, Your Lordship. I am afraid. Afraid for our people."

Niklaus takes a long drink, eyes never leaving Brom's. After downing what remains of his cup, he sits it down on the bar top and twists it into place until it is perfectly covering an aged, ringed stain appearing on the bar surface.

"Her name is Magdalena," Niklaus says at last. "Maggie. That's what my parents called her. She is an abomination. I assume you get a lot of visitors in this tavern, Brom. Have you seen anyone unusual lately? Perhaps making their rounds from table to table in whispered conversation?"

"No, my lord. People don't have coin for drink. They don't have the energy either. You think Haluk is recruiting an army in Masunbria?"

"Someone is infecting my kingdom, Brom. If it is Maggie, she couldn't be doing it alone. She would need help. If there are those in Kaelonoch hiding her, aiding her—keeping her alive in any way—I will hunt them down and kill every last one of them. Maggie is a disease on our land. She has betrayed her people, and anyone caught with her will be hung as a traitor to the crown. Spread the word, dear Brom, time is running out for Maggie."

17
Magdalena

Brom hastened to Sybbyl and Hagen's home once the livery had marched free from Kaelonoch. He burst through the door with the news of her brother's visit and the threats made against her and anyone who dares stand with her. Magdalena ordered a meeting to be held that very night at Hagen and Sybbyl's home. Willem, Brom, Segan, and Warrick were all present for it. They lit only a few sparse candles and used wool and fabric sacks to cover the windows to darken the home from even the smallest escape of light. This group was her unofficial council. The fact that Segan was a member was strategic on her part. When Magdalena finds herself in his company, she can barely look at him, let alone trust him. He is a sniveling man who cares only for himself. Magdalena knows, however, that it is best to keep snakes in a cage of your own making, rather than letting them slither where they please.

She was irritable the entire meeting. Her brother, having been so close by, sat her on edge, sure, but it was more than that. Everything felt wrong. There was a humming in her veins. It was as if deep down there was a scream waiting to escape. Her irritation did not discriminate. Even those closest to her found their way into the fire. Spying Brom and Liri whispering and linking fingers when they thought no eyes were upon them sent her into a silent rage. *A courtship? How can the two of them possess enough hope left in their hearts for love? Why do they still have a faith in humanity that I no longer possess?* She thinks of the day she stood to walk away from all this. The day she chose to stay rather than have a life, a family, peace. In this moment, she hates Brom and Liri for having a choice in life.

Magdalena poured over her list of recruits. The number, though now well into the hundreds, was still too small. True, with Warrick's revelation, the enemy was no longer a murderous hoard from the mountains, but that did nothing to diminish the seriousness and the deadliness of the approaching conflict with those forces that inhabit and surround the castle. They needed help. They learned from Fani—who had developed a professional relationship with a rather talkative soldier—that Henrick wrote to all the heads of the neighboring kingdoms requesting an increase in offerings. This was an increase, as Warrick pointed out, that was not demanded by the Typhans themselves. It was evident to all that Henrick was growing his own coffers and using the raid to justify his actions. This proclamation might very well enrage a neighboring kingdom enough that they would choose to aide Magdalena in overthrowing Niklaus and Henrick. Of all the kingdoms Henrick would have written to, More would have been asked to send the most, for they had the most to give. It was then decided that they would travel east at first light.

More's support is a longshot, but it is worth taking a chance for it. If their king can be persuaded to help Magdalena, then they might just have a chance. It is an unspoken understanding that making this move, taking this trip, will mean that they can no longer live in hiding. This one act will seal their fate as rebels to the crown, formally. Word will spread that she is alive and is building an alliance, and with that, an army from the castle will be fast on their heels. They have come to a fork in the road. They all know that this act will change the trajectory of their lives. Turning down this road will lead nowhere but battle and, quite possibly, their deaths. The other choice is no better. The people are suffering. The death toll rises each day. To some, what occurred in Cale, though tragic, was a swift end to a life that was proving to be nothing more than a long, slow, painful death.

***

"Aye, you doing alright, my lady?"

Magdalena is startled from her thoughts by the sound of Warrick's voice next to her. She was so deep in her contemplation that she didn't hear his horse approach. They have been riding for More since before the sun peeked over the horizon. The quiet ride in the still-dark morning has given her time to think. Her mind has been a million places, playing out thousands of scenarios. Her mind has been in all places but here on this horse. She has been mindlessly following Willem and Brom as they ride ahead and has nearly forgotten that Warrick is pulling up the rear.

"Yes, Warrick, I am well, thank you. I just have a lot of things on my mind this morning."

"Aye, well, I tend to avoid heavy thinking if at all possible. You should try it. Or perhaps Your Grace believes that this tragedy can be solved between your ears and not with a sword?"

"What are you doing here, Warrick?" she asks wearily.

Warrick looks at Magdalena for a moment without saying a word. She thinks she spots a hint of sadness floating through his gaze, and she instantly regrets not only her words but also her annoyed tone. She didn't mean to hurt him; well, she doesn't think she meant it, anyway. She hasn't been herself lately. It would be difficult for him to understand, given that he has never been responsible to, or answered to, anyone in all of his life. So she assumes. Still, she doesn't want to make enemies of the man. She opens her mouth to begin an apology, but Warrick cuts her off.

"Well, if you are asking what I am doing riding next to you and not behind you, the answer there is that I have been riding all morning staring at your horse's ass, and I thought I would be able to protect ya just as well by your side. We could even keep each other company, if it pleases Your Grace." Sarcasm drips from his lips, but he continues despite the look Magdalena gives him.

"Now, perhaps you are instead asking why I volunteered to accompany you on this trip? If that is your meaning, then I am happy to explain further. It is my belief that out of the whole sodden group, I am the only one who is willing to look you in the eye and tell you if the guy that we're meeting is an imbecile. Of course, you can do what you like with my opinion of the prince, whatever it may be. I just think it is important that you have someone by you who doesn't care at all about pissing you off. I tell ya, Mags, I am really, really good at not caring about pissing people off."

"You seem to not care how much Brom dislikes you."

"He will come around, or he won't. It makes no difference to me."

"You obviously have had plenty of time to form an opinion about our circumstances in Masunbria, yet you have kept mute. Here, though, you tell me that you will give your opinion freely. Why, then, have you chosen to remain silent thus far?"

"Did my silence bother you?" His voice is slightly mischievous near her ear.

"Not at all. I can barely understand what you say when you do speak."

Warrick laughs at this.

"Well, listen carefully, then, my lady, and I will speak slowly. I think you can take your kingdom on your own. In your own way. I don't think you need Mikhail to help you get your castle back or save your people. Not if it means that you have to sell your soul. There is only one person you can trust in this world, Mags, and that's you. Mikhail might promise all sorts of things, but if he falls through on just a one of them, it will be your fault, not his. That's the way your people will see it, anyway. I am certain his help comes with a price. I'd rather not see you pay it. You are strong, Mags. Don't forget that when you meet this prince today."

Magdalena can't help but smile.

"That smile looks good on you, Mags. I do believe it is the first time I've seen it."

"What about you? When will you grace us with a smile?

"I smile plenty," Warrick exclaims in mock shock.

"Ha! Well, I most certainly have never seen it before."

"What is it you speak of? I am smilin' right now."

Magdalena shakes her head as she stares at his handsome, chiseled face, serious as ever. He leans on his horse a fraction closer, bending his opposing frame so his lips are very near to her ear. Magdalena holds her breath. She has never been this close to a man before. She can smell the earth and sweat coming from his body. She feels his hair brush her cheek.

"You were looking at my lips for the smile, but ya need only look into my eyes and you shall see that when I look at you, I always smile."

Magdalena laughs. She can't help herself. She pulls her horse away from Warrick's and looks up to see Brom has spun around and is watching the two of them. His brows are furrowed, and he stares only at Warrick. Magdalena sees all this, but when she looks over at Warrick to see if he, too, has caught the look on Brom's face, she sees he is looking only at her, eyes dancing with mischief.

"Can I ask you something?" she says, gaining composure.

"Anything."

"What's it like, where you are from?"

Warrick looks off for a long moment before turning back to face her. "It is hot and miserable most days. It is loud. The people fill their days with war strategy and building ships for the sea. Their nights are spent toasting to their gods and telling tales of their battles won."

"Do you know the man I was to marry had I gone to the mountains as I was supposed to, the man who would have claimed me for his prize?"

"Ya, I know him." Warrick makes a grunt of a noise.

"What is he like?" She wants to know he is awful. She longs for Warrick to say that he beats women and spits on their faces as they cry, crumpled and dirty on the floor. Warrick seems to consider her question for a long moment before answering.

"He is a broken man. You did well to avoid him."

Magdalena nods in response. She wants to ask him more, but she can tell he isn't going to divulge anything further.

As the sun stretches high in the sky, the group finally enters the heart of More. It is like nothing Magdalena has seen before. There are so many more people here than in Masunbria. The place is so bright she has to squint to focus. In Masunbria the homes are made of cold, gray stone with a soft carpet of moss growing in all the dark cracks and grooves. The ground of her home is softened with lush grass that tickles your toes when you walk barefoot. The forest of Masunbria is so dense everywhere you go that the sun will merely splinter through leaves and trees, casting a scattering of light and dark across the whole of the land. It is quiet; it is magical. More is nothing like that.

It is beautiful, for sure, but it is very different from home. The homes and other buildings near the castle are made with sun-bleached stone that shines white in the hot sun. The sound of the waves crashing into the shore is so loud to her ears that she wonders how anyone can possibly live next to it. It is a constant roar as they come in, faster and faster, one after another, and a giant crash when they break against the rocks, spraying water high into the air. It is deafening in both its sound and its relentlessness. The entire place smells of fish, and there are so many people here that look nothing like herself nor anyone she has seen before.

Their hair, their skin, their language, she can't make sense of any of it. They have large baskets full of beautiful colored spices, and they have large tables with folds of vibrant silk fabrics. She sees a woman—hair straight and black and skin as beautiful as glass—sitting and rocking a small child behind a table loaded heavy with silks and necklaces made of small shells. The child has to be three or four, Magdalena thinks. She looks from the woman to her child and then out to the cold, violent sea and instantly feels a roll of fear over the voyage this woman and her child made. She understands that this woman sits here only after making a journey destined to kill her and her small child. Did she do it out of fear or love? For the choice to do such a thing could only have come from a place of great suffering or a place of great love. Perhaps both. The thought makes her think of her parents and the choice they made to raise her as a boy. She gives a small shiver in the salty breeze.

They reach the gates of the great castle of More. The towers reach high into the cloudless sky. There are no statues depicting grim ways to die. There are flowers, and water fountains, and artfully shaped shrubs, and sun-bleached stone. The castle itself is much more lavish than the one Magdalena has grown up in. She dismounts her horse, biting the inside of her cheek in an attempt to distract herself from the anxiety she feels coursing through her veins. She silently follows Willem and Brom through the gates, Warrick behind her. She stands straight, walks with her head held high, and silently reminds herself to breathe.

Once in the great castle, they are escorted to a room that is lavishly decorated with silk-covered pillows in varying colors.

Some have stitches of intricate gold weaved throughout to mimic a flower or an abstract design. The room is lit by candles, though it is day. She puzzles at the ability to light candles for no reason other than because you like them lit. This royal family has far greater wealth than her own. Magdalena begins to walk through the room, lightly running her fingers over carved wood chairs, touching glass containers holding wine and spirits, feeling the silk of the drapery that hangs from open windows. It is at the window that she pauses to look out at the roaring sea below this high precipice of stone. The sea makes her uncomfortable. It is beautiful, surly, but she can see that it has a mind of its own, intentions of its own. The sea swells and falls as it pleases. Man cannot control the tides, nor the beasts that live below them. The sea, she observes, is the last great thing on this earth that man cannot harness for profit, control for power, or sell to the highest bidder.

"Amazing, isn't it? Beauty and power combined. I imagine the same can be said of you."

Magdalena startles and turns at the voice uncomfortably close to her ear. Before her stands a tall and handsome man with dark hair cut shorter to his head than most men she has ever seen. His skin is dark, and his teeth shine bright white in comparison. His eyes appear as black as night.

"I didn't mean to startle you, Princess Magdalena. I am Mikhail, prince of More and heir to the throne. Actually, with my father's passing, I am set to become king rather quickly. But technicalities, you know." He waves a hand flippantly in the air.

"I was surprised to hear you even existed, but even more shocked that you have come to me."

Magdalena bows and smiles at the man before her. "Thank you, for your hospitality, my lord. I look forward to discussing with you the fate of my kingdom and what, together, we can do about it."

Mikhail lets out a loud, almost forced laugh. "My darling flower, there will be so much time for talk of that sort later. For now, we must get you ready for dinner. I have taken the liberty of choosing a gown for you and have assigned several ladies to wait on you as you bathe and dress. I am certain you would wish to make yourself more presentable to me at once. Luckily for you, my dear, I have at your disposal all things you could require to get you looking less like a war general and more like the princess you really are."

Magdalena stares blankly at Mikhail for a moment, then looks down at her clothes and hands. She bathed just the night prior. Liri presented her with a small, scented soap as a gift, as well as a comb. Bath complete and skin smelling of rose, Liri took Magdalena's hair and added small braids and bits of ribbon to the slowly growing stands. Sybbyl surprised her before she left with a dress she traded for in town, and as she rose that morning, she put the dress on with such care. She knew what it cost Sybbyl, and she loves the dress for that reason. It is the first dress she has ever been given in her life. Though hating the feel of it as compared to trousers, she knows the tender kindness the dress represents. It was a lovely shade of pale pink that complements her complexion well. Brom told her, upon arriving at the small cottage in the early hours, that she looked stunning. She thought she cleaned up rather nicely, all things considered. Now, however, she feels foolish and out of place amongst the finery of the room and the man before her. She feels as if she sticks out as a weed amongst the dozen roses this castle keeps. She couldn't come to him as she has always been—trousers and short hair and boots with mud. Neither could she come to him as a lady in pink and smelling of flowers. She doesn't belong, and seeing the evidence of that truth is crushing. Glancing from Mikhail to Willem, who only offer her a sad smile, she decides to swallow her pride and nods her acquiescence.

"Thank you, my lord. I am grateful for your kindness."

"Kindness has nothing to do with it. I just can't have such a gem remain unpolished. Now, you run along, and I will speak with your men. You just focus on looking your best, and leave the messy negotiations to us." Mikhail smiles that dazzling smile before placing a kiss on the back of her hand.

Magdalena is led away then. Bile climbs her throat, and rage threatens her chest as she follows the attendants to her waiting bath.

18
Henrick

Henrick pulls the reins to slow his horse as it nears the bank of the Miraron River. He dismounts and ties the leather strips to a tree near the river's edge so his horse can drink some of the fresh water. Since returning from his visit to Kaelonoch, he has had a growing desire to wander the grounds. He has found great joy in spending some time in the woods that surround the castle or even just sitting near the river bank. He has refused to allow a guard to accompany him on these trips, against Dagen's furious requests. He wants time alone more than anything else.

He found this particular spot on his journey out yesterday. The water here is slow and lazy as it makes its way around a sharp bend. A spot where, over time, the river has worn a path, determined as it was on the course it felt destined to run. On the edge of the bend sits a large willow tree that is fighting for its established ground. But, little by little, the river will soon wash away the very ground that the roots cling to, and the tree will come crashing down. A tree that has stood for a hundred years will not win against a river with nothing but time and persistence on its side. Henrick hopes he is the river and not the stubborn willow.

A noise behind him causes him to spring to his feet and grab for his sword. He stands at the ready, scanning the tree line for the approaching enemy.

"Henrick, my love. It is just I, Catrain."

"Yeah, well don't expect me to put down my sword, for I fear you will plunge it into my turned back."

Catrain emerges from the trees looking beautiful in a long red dress that was made of a fabric that billows in the breeze. The black bear furs hang loosely from her shoulders, revealing the delicate skin at her collarbone. Gone is the lady in waiting with the eager smile and downcast eyes. Before him stands a woman sure of who she is and her place in this world. Before him stands a future queen.

"What is it that you want, Catrain? I don't like to be disturbed on my rides. It isn't safe out here for you anyway. I assume no one even knows you have left the castle walls?"

"No, no one knows. I wanted to come to see you. I wanted to be the one to tell you, face to face, that the wedding to Niklaus is set. We will wed in one month's time."

"Damnit, Catrain." Henrick snarls between clenched teeth. He begins pacing back and forth in the small opening, kicking the ground subtly as he goes. He is shaking his head back and forth as if he can dislodge the words she has just planted there.

"My darling," says Catrain, approaching him cautiously, "you have done it. Just as I knew you would."

"What are you talking about?" Henrick asks, glaring at her from under his furrowed brow.

"Henrick," Catrain's voice is breathless, and he can't help but be drawn into it. He watches her lips as she says his name once more. He longs to kiss those lips, to feel her breath against his mouth. "My love, you have done it. You promised me that we would be together forever, that nothing in this world would drive us apart. Now, it is true."

Henrick snorts out a laugh as he forces himself to break his gaze from her lips. He turns his back to her for fear he will not have the willpower necessary to keep his distance, to keep from pulling her in and drinking her up.

Coming up behind him, Catrain weaves her arms around his middle and, standing on her toes, presses herself against his back. Her lips tickle the back of his ear as she says, "Don't you see, darling? You, a man of such honor, a man who, above all else, keeps his word, you, my darling, have secured our future in one selfless act. Your love for me, for us, is so shocking that sometimes I don't know how I could have ever been graced with such luck in life. You knew that there was no way we could marry. You knew that I couldn't bear to live my life without you, a fate which was certain. We both knew it. The day was quickly approaching for me to marry some man I didn't love and no longer be a lady in waiting for your wife. I surely would be matched with an old man who would probably treat me rotten, and I would visit the castle on Treaty Day or another celebration day, but that's it. We would never see each other; we would never have each other. But you, in the most selfless act I can fathom, chose to wed me to your nephew. You have given me more than my heart could dream. You have not only secured my spot, forever living under the same roof as you, but you have also given me a kingdom in the process. How, how can a man love so much, and how can I return that love to him? Because of you, we will always be together; we will always have one another."

Henrick remains silent for a moment as he takes in her words. He wants so badly to believe them. The vision he has conjured a thousand times returns, though, and he shoves forcefully away from her grasp on him.

"I know you lie with him already. I know you choose to find his bed at night and not mine. I have seen it with my own eyes. How am I supposed to feel about that? How does that honorable, noble savior feel about that, Catrain?"

Catrain moves to the water's edge to where Henrick stands. Finding a large boulder, she sits atop it and watches the river take chunks of ice with it as it goes.

"He doesn't love me, Henrick. He never will. His love for another is too strong for that. I am blessed, don't you see? I don't have to pretend to love him, and he doesn't have to pretend to love me."

Henrick lets out a snort in reply.

"Sabina. The maid. I caught the two of them together shortly after our betrothal. They were huddled together in the corners of his room. She still had the chamber pot in her hands. He had her pinned, back to the wall, and was whispering in her ear. It must have been something scandalous, as her face turned a deep shade of red and she covered her mouth to stifle a giggle. He bent down then and nuzzled her face and planted kisses across her cheeks and neck. I stood there for a long time watching them. They were so beautifully in love, it reminded me of you and me. I knew then that my life would be just fine. You see, when Thea first encouraged this union, your nephew, well, he was nice to me. He smiled when he saw me, he laughed when appropriate to laugh, and he even held out an arm to me as we walked. This was about the same time you started to pull away from me, no doubt upset with the union. I felt so alone, Henrick. I didn't have you, my one true love, the person who knows me and understands me best, there to help me, and guide me, and console me. I had the pressures from Thea to make this successful, and then I had this strange man that, honestly, I would rather he hate me and treat me poorly than fall in love with me. At least then I could reciprocate the emotion, for I knew from the first moment I saw him that I would never love him."

"You tell me all this, all things that I want to hear, but you don't tell me why you went to his bed. After the wedding, sure, though I would have hated it I would have understood it. But now? I was still here, Catrain."

"I was getting there, Henrick. After I saw Niklaus and Sabina, I knew that I had my freedom. Not only did he not love me, but he was also deeply in love with another. Ours would be a marriage of contract and nothing more. That evening, after dinner, we were taking a walk through the castle. It was then that I brought up what I had seen with Sabina. Niklaus responded with denial and anger, like I assumed, but I remained calm, my face serene until he was finished. I then took his hand and told him that he deserved love and that he deserved happiness. I told him that neither of us had asked for this marriage and that, though I would be a loyal queen to him, I was not going to stand in his way of love and joy. I told him that our marriage was for one purpose, conception of an heir, and nothing more. I told him that once we had an heir and my job was finished, we could be partners in the kingdom and that's it. He was relieved, I think. He told me he was thankful that I understood his love for Sabina. He was the one, then, who set the plan to start immediately on attaining an heir. He told me he respected my feelings and wanted to honor them as well. The quicker I conceived him a son, he said, the quicker we could get on with the lives we had laid before us and not continue walking the path someone else directed us down. I was so happy he understood, Henrick. I lay with him that night, and all I thought of was you and how I was rushing through my obligation as queen so that you and I could be free." Catrain, finishing her tale, sits up straighter and smiles her bright, wide-eyed smile into Henrick's face.

Henrick laughs.

"You are a dumb girl, Catrain. You actually believe that Niklaus proposed lying with you nightly, while unwed, to better your situation and ease your trepidation over marrying a man you didn't love?"

Henrick begins roaring with laughter now, and tears begin streaming down Catrain's face in response. The tears don't faze Henrick in the least. He pushes on. "You have to be the dumbest girl I have ever met. Here I thought all along that you, my beautiful one, was as cunning as my dear Thea. I thought you were smart and patient and not one to make foolish decisions, but here you have proved me sorely wrong."

Catrain begins feverishly wiping the tears from her face as if angry at her own eyes for betraying her. "How dare you, Henrick? You know nothing. You are lying. You are trying to blame me and upset me. I did this for you. I did this for us. I don't believe you," she yells her final exclamation, teeth baring at him as she does so.

Rising from her spot on the rock, Catrain moves away from Henrick and begins pacing the bank. Her hands ball into fists at her sides, and her face and chest appear red as hot coals.

Henrick continues to laugh. He can barely speak from the laughter. "Oh, you stupid girl." he finally chokes out. "It isn't entirely your fault. Niklaus played you for the fool you are. He knew exactly what he was doing. He used your own emotions against you. Thea would never have fallen for it. I give Niklaus a lot of credit though. I didn't know this side of him, but now that I see it, I think that between him and I, our kingdom is going to be in good hands. You need to leave me now, Catrain. You have opened my eyes to who you are. I thank you for that, I really do. I see now that Thea is the perfect woman for me. She is smart and beautiful, and she is my equal in all things. You should go back to Niklaus. You better hope it takes time to conceive that heir, for the anticipation of that will be the only thing guaranteeing your usefulness with him. I am sure the seed has already been planted in his mind that you are not quick enough or cunning enough to be his queen. Once you have given him a son, he will surely send you off to live the life of a recluse somewhere." Henrick spits on the ground near her feet.

Catrain, now sobbing, in what Henrick can only describe as long, disgusting sobs in which bubbles appear and disappear from her nose and her face is red and distorted, storms up to Henrick and, before he has time to draw his attention from the nose bubbles and see what she has planned, raises her hand and smacks him hard across the face. She is gone before the shock of it wears off and he can react. She is running through the woods, a trail of tears and shame following behind her.

Henrick stands there for a moment staring at the path she has just run down. He knows he has gone too far in hurting her. He wanted to punish her, humiliate her, make her hurt like he hurt, but he wasn't able to control the anger and betrayal and took his punishment to the extreme. Though, he is probably right about Niklaus and his motives for lying with Catrain being entirely selfish. After all, he would have done the same thing to a desperate girl like Catrain.

If he is honest with himself, though, which he rarely is, he believes that Niklaus could've been sincere in his words and actions with Catrain. It all could have been just as she perceived it to be. Regardless, he isn't going to feel badly for humiliating her the way he did. She deserved it, even if her interpretation of the events proves to be true. She betrayed him, and she should be punished for it. He will forgive her in time, once he determines that she has suffered enough. And when he does, she will become the most humble and loyal woman to him. She will do his bidding all the days of her life. Catrain will be to him what Thea could never be. Thea is so many wonderful things, but never could he have control over her the way he is about to with Catrain. Catrain will soon need him as much as she needs air to breathe, and after today, she will do anything for him. He is sure of it.

Dinner that evening proves to be just as entertaining as Henrick's trip into the forest was. For the first half of their meal of roasted pheasant and potatoes, he sits and watches, with slightly smug curiosity, he will admit, Catrain avoiding conversation with Niklaus at every opportunity while simultaneously refusing to make eye contact with Henrick. Poor thing is so distraught. *Good.*

"My Lord," Dagen says, clearing his throat as he enters the dining hall, his metal armor clanging as he walks. "I am sorry to interrupt your meal." Dagen waits then, something that Henrick has observed him doing when both Henrick and Niklaus are in the same room. It is as if Dagen addresses the air between them with his precursory "my lord" and then waits patiently to see which one of them acknowledges his presence first. Dagen is Henrick's man, and the fact that Dagen would even want to appear that he is giving Niklaus some sort of respect for his title and position is enough to make Henrick want to disembowel his friend right there in the dining room. Henrick begins to laugh at the thought of the women screaming over Dagen's spilled entrails sliding around the stone floors.

"Henrick, are you alright? You have been acting odd tonight." asks Thea under her breath, placing a hand on Henrick's forearm to whisper closely.

Apparently, his laughter was not quite as internal as he had thought. Perhaps he should tell Thea about the slippery bowels so she can understand his comedic response. This thought makes him roar with laughter. Once he has composed himself, he looks around the room and sees that all eyes have been fixed upon him.

"Terribly sorry, I did not wish to delay the message Dagen is carrying. I had the most interesting conversation today with this simpleton who quite possibly might have been the most naïve woman I have ever met, and I am still in shock over her total lack of understanding of the ways of the world, that I occasionally get overcome with laughter and pity. My dear Thea, if only you could have been there. She truly was a dim star compared to you, my brightest sun."

Smiling at Henrick warmly, Thea places a kiss upon his lips. Henrick returns the kiss with passionate eagerness while keeping one eye on Catrain as he does so. He smiles into Thea's lips as he sees Catrain's attempt to veil her quivering bottom lip with a sloppy drink from her goblet that sends a trail of red down her chin.

"Thank you, Uncle, for that pointless story. I wish I had those minutes back in my life, but alas you have taken them from me." Niklaus rolls his eyes. "Dagen, my man, please continue with your urgent news."

Henrick stares at Niklaus. His hands shake slightly under the table, and he curls them into fists in an attempt to control the force radiating through them. For one, Dagen is his man and no one else's. For two, if Niklaus ever rolls his eyes at him again, he will stab them out with his fork.

Dagen looks at Henrick with a mixture of curiosity and unease. He can see Henrick's beast stirring beneath the surface. He knows him too well to miss the signs that the animal wants to come out to play.

"Yes, well," Dagen responds cautiously, looking away from Henrick and back to Niklaus. "I have come to report that I just received a missive from the kingdom of More." Dagen pulls a folded letter, seal and crest of a three-masted ship still present, though broken. The crest of More. He waves the letter slightly in the air.

"Go on. What is it?" asks Niklaus.

"Turns out that your Magdalena is alive and well and just arrived in More. She is interested in forming an alliance with Mikhail." Dagen consults the note. "Says here that the princess is raising an army of the fiercest warriors to take back her kingdom and stop the lies and oppression occurring under her brother's rule. Joining her is a retired general, a barkeep, and a man who claims to be a Typhan. This man, the Typhan, has asserted that you, Niklaus, have spread fabricated tales in order to breed fear and fill your own pockets. Mikhail threatens Niklaus several times in the missive but also states that he is sending letters to the other kingdoms to inform them of Masunbria's deceit. There is no indication in the letter that he is going to join Magdalena. By the penmanship and state of the paper, it looks as though it was written in haste and anger, before being sent on their fastest horse."

Dagen carefully folds the note back into its original square, eyes cast downward on his task. The room remains silent for a long moment.

Henrick is the one to break the silence. He stands abruptly, wood chair falling to the stone floor with a bang. He screams a cry of frustration as he rakes his forearm over the table, sending plates and goblets crashing to the floor.

Henrick brings a shaking finger to point at Dagen. "What are you still doing here? Load the horses. Gather your men. Bring me Maggie's head, or I shall take yours," he snarls before marching from the room.

19
Magdalena

Magdalena stands outside the dining hall doors a moment, hesitating before entering. She can hear the men inside. Brom is telling a story of some sort, and, as usual, he is quite animated. She can hear Willem's dark sweet chuckle as he listens, and another laugh, perhaps that of Mikhail, comes loud and confident through the wooden doors. She can smell the savory scents of the food inside, and her stomach growls in anticipation. Her skin, which was scrubbed and washed until it shone pink, betrays goose bumps across the flesh of her bare arms.

Mikhail chose for her a blue silk gown so bright and so brilliant that it looks like the pictures she saw as a child of a peacock's feathers. The ladies who waited on her clapped and shrieked with joy at the way the silk of the dress hugged and accentuated her body more than concealed it. Her hair was washed, and scented oils were applied to it, and now it shines brilliantly and is combed back to reveal her long, thin neck. A small, delicate crown of pears was affixed to the top of her head as her only decoration. Mikhail, so she was told, believes a woman is decoration enough and too many jewels just get in the way. Pearls, he believes, are suitable,

215

however, as they betray the majesty of turning something unworthy into something beautiful. She took one look at herself in the large looking glass that hung in the foyer as she descended the stairs, and her breath almost caught in her throat. Not because she looked like the girl she dreamed she could be when she watched her mother dress. No, this wasn't what she wanted. She felt wrong. She felt just as she did when her chest was bound and her hair trimmed short, when she practiced to make her voice an octave lower. She felt like a fraud.

Magdalena, taking a deep breath, straightens her back and walks through the doors of the dining hall. The men stop laughing and talking at the sound of her entrance. The room is aglow with candlelight. A massive gold chandelier, full of what must be nearly fifty candles, hangs from the center of the room over a long, polished table capable of seating more than a dozen. Floor-to-ceiling windows overlooking the ocean have been opened, and the smell of salt and fish hangs heavy in the air. The breeze coming off the water sends a shiver down Magdalena's arms.

Brom appears to have been bringing a drink to his lips just prior to her arrival, and the cup is now frozen midway there as his mouth lies open and slack. Willem smiles at her with such love and tenderness in his eyes like her father would have, if he was here instead. Magdalena smiles graciously at the two men and scans the room. Her eyes trail over vases full of exotic flowers, a yellow bird held within a gilded cage. Her heart is pounding, and she wills her face to remain calm. She wants to find Warrick, she realizes with a slight surprise. She longs to see his steady face and his watchful eyes. She finds him, in his usual stance, resting his back against a wall, able to see the entire room from his position. He is staring at his hands, something he has discovered under the nail of his middle finger. He doesn't look up at all.

"My princess, you are as stunning as the night is long. Please, please come in and sit. A feast has been prepared in your honor. It would delight me to see you enjoy yourself this evening. I have taken great pains to ensure your pleasure." Mikhail emphasizes the last word of his statement, and Magdalena forces the smile to remain on her face in spite of herself.

Mikhail grabs Magdalena by the arm and leads her to the table and an overly cushioned bench. She sits, and he scoots in close next to her. He hands her a glass of wine and raises his own high in the air.

They eat an elaborate meal of smoked herring, seasoned carrots, and wild strawberries and drink the sweetest red wine as entertainers are brought in for their amusement—women who can bend their bodies into odd arrangements, men who juggle fire. Mikhail sits proudly with her at his side. He asks her to tell him how much she is enjoying herself. He fills her wine when it runs low. He traces the back of his hand down her bare arm. He pushes a strand of hair behind her ear. He is attentive, appraising, and kind. He is dressed in dark gray and looks like a storm rolling in with the sea. He is handsome beyond compare. His character appears beyond reproach. And yet, she can't stand him. She fakes it well though. She understands how important this meeting is.

Magdalena grows irritated with all the entertainment. She wants to discuss what her brother has done, not only in Masunbria, but the effects it has had, and will have, on all the kingdoms. She wants to know if Mikhail will help.

"Prince Mikhail, I trust that you have heard from Warrick that the Typhans have not threatened war with our people. They have not descended the mountain, nor have they asked for an increase in offerings. I assume you, too, have been swindled by the newly crowned King Niklaus?" Her choice of words hits a nerve, and she can see a muscle twitch in Mikhail's cheek.

"Your men and I have already discussed this, my sweet. There is no need to talk about this any further." His tone is harsh though he keeps his smile plastered across his face.

"These men do not speak for me, Your Grace. It is I who shall rule Masunbria."

Mikhail's smile falters, and a look of disgust crosses his features for only a moment before he bares his blaringly white teeth. "Don't be brash. It is unbecoming of you. As I have already told your men, if you want my help to save your people, then you will accept my proposal for marriage. Once signed, I will send my army and destroy your brother. More and Masunbria will be one. You will be my queen, and your people will be relieved of the burdens placed upon them by your brother. They might even make it through the winter, if we hurry this along."

A look of shock crosses Magdalena's face as her mind registers his words. *Marriage?* The word is offensive coming from his mouth, and she feels rage seep into her veins. Her head spins from the wine, and she is suddenly very hot. She reaches a shaking hand to her head and pulls the pearls down and lets them fall to the table. Her heart feels as if it is breaking. As Haluk, she would have had respect from Mikhail. He possibly would have even feared her. As Magdalena, she is nothing more than decoration for his arm. She is not taken seriously. She is good for sipping tea and growing heirs and nothing more. She looks down at her borrowed dress and feels that the moment she put it on, a part of her died.

"I think my lady had better retire for the evening. She is looking pale from the festivities," Willem rushes to speak as he stands and takes her arm.

Mikhail gives an exasperated sigh. "It appears she will need some work," he mutters under his breath.

There is a sudden burst of movement out of her peripheral vision before Mikhail is seen tumbling backward off the bench, Warrick on top of him. Warrick's large fists raise and then fall, landing hard on the king's face. Mikhail's guards, who are dining at the far end of the table, jump up and rush to aid their commander. They grab at Warrick, trapping his arms in theirs, but Warrick doesn't cease. He kicks and knees at the prince under him. It takes all four of Mikhail's men to drag Warrick off their leader. The sound of metal rings throughout the room as swords are unsheathed by the guards and, soon to follow, by Willem and Brom, who push Magdalena behind them.

Warrick sends a quick kick to the shin of one of the guards holding him, and his left arm becomes free. He pivots and brings his forehead down on the nose of the guard trapping his right arm. Blood spurts from his nose, and the guard loses his grasp on Warrick's forearm. The remaining two guards aren't fast enough, and Warrick twists and bends as they swing their swords for his head. Drawing his own sword, he joins Willem and Brom, their blades unsheathed and held before them. Mikhail spits a mouthful of blood on the floor as he rolls to rise.

"I make you this vow, Magdalena: you will either be tamed, or you will be sent over the mountains," Mikhail sneers with blood covering his white teeth. There is a buzzing sound that vibrates through the room. An unseen force. It makes the small hairs on Magdalena's arms stand on end.

Magdalena knows they have one chance to run before all of his guards are summoned and they are thrown into his dungeons. Two of Mikhail's guards begin to advance on their group. Warrick swings into action, his sword arcing through the air and slamming into the armored shoulder of one of the guards. The other guard advances on Willem as the third, the one who had been kicked in the shin, takes on Brom. The guard with blood still dripping from his nose has backed Mikhail into a corner. Metal crashes with metal, and Brom is tossed momentarily off balance as he falls back and into Magdalena. Thrown off her feet, her elbow slams into the door. Whirling, she pushes it open and trips into the open hall. Scanning, she sees the way out to her left. Willem is the first through the open door as Magdalena hears a grunt and the sound of a body hitting the floor from behind him.

"Run! Get the horses!" Willem shouts. She obeys. Grabbing the handfuls of the dress in her fists, she takes off through the large wooden doors. Once outside, the bright sun causes her to blink several times as she looks for their horses. She spots them tied up across the small dirt path leading to the gardens. She runs to them and loosens the leather straps from the wood fence. Mounting her horse, she leads the other three back to the entrance of the castle.

From her perch, she tries to peer through the still-open doors. She can't see inside. She can't see if her men are in trouble. She draws a dagger from her leather saddleback and moves to climb down from her horse, to join the fight. A blur from beyond the entrance, and then, at last, Willem bursts through the opening, followed by Brom and, finally, Warrick. Warrick has blood across his tunic, and if it is his or someone else's, she isn't sure. The three men mount their horses, and with a strong snap of the reins, the group begins to weave their way through the bustling streets full of vendors at a breakneck pace.

***

They ride fast and hard, and she remains silent through the journey. For fear of being followed by the now-infuriated Mikhail, they stay off the trails and move slowly over rough terrain. Winding their way through the deep and remote parts of More, they ride until late into the night. They know they must camp and finish the journey at first light. Their horses need water and rest from the exertion their riders demanded of them. She takes a steadying breath and runs her fingers over her brows. She is unsure which is heavier, her body or her mind. Mikhail and all of his finery were an assault on her senses. She is repulsed to think back to that girl who walked into the dining hall with her silks and her eyes lined with coal.

Arriving for the night at a reasonably hidden spot to camp with dense trees and a creek of clean water, Magdalena dismounts her horse and stretches her back in a long arch. Willem and Brom begin offloading their horses, and Warrick takes off to gather wood for the fire without uttering a word to the group. He hasn't spoken the entire journey from More. Willem and Brom talk as they work. They have an easy kinship, even in times of stress. They don't necessarily exclude Magdalena; it is just that she knows she doesn't fit in that way—in any way, really. Magdalena feels this way at Hagen and Sybbyl's as well, a permanent guest. She can't describe it, really, feeling as if you don't belong anywhere. She thinks Warrick perhaps understands this, not just because he is a literal outsider here, but also because his life over the mountains appears to have been so vastly different. It seems he, too, tries to escape, preferring being alone to feeling alone.

"I am going to clean myself up a bit," Magdalena calls. The perfumes and oils that cover her skin have been a trap for the dust of horse hooves, and her skin is coated in grime. She knows one more day won't matter much, and she could easily wait until tomorrow to clean up, when she arrives back at the little cottage, but this is an excuse to leave the two of them and spare them from having to make her feel part of the conversation.

"Alone?" Willem asks.

"Where is Warrick?" says Brom, unable to hide the tone of suspicion that is always present when he speaks of Warrick.

"I'll take a sword. I'll be fine," Magdalena says to Willem, offering him a weak smile as she ignores Brom's question. The men exchange looks as if they are going to disagree, but she quickly turns on her heels and grabs her sword from the sheath and a torch, before making her way through the woods to the cold creek below.

At the creek edge, Magdalena lays down her sword. She tries to gather the flowing dress out of the mud at the water's edge with one hand while reaching the other into the cool water.

"Ahhhhhhh," she yelps as she loses her balance and falls back, landing in the mud. The blue silk dress falls around her. She tries to push herself up, but the mud sucks her hands deeper into its pit. She tries to twist to get on her knees, but the now wet-with-mud and growingly heavier fabric of the dress gets tangled in her legs.

She hears a chuckle behind her. Whipping her head around, she sees Warrick leaning against a tree. Watching.

"Go away, Warrick. I don't need you here to mock me." She hears the childish tone in her voice and its presence only angers her more.

Warrick pushes off of the tree, unfazed, and walks slowly toward her, hands raised in mock surrender. "I am just offering to help."

"Why?"

"Well, because I would love nothing more than for you to be able to successfully wash the last bit of that shit Mikhail off of ya." Warrick studies the mud, looking for a solid spot to anchor his foot. Finding a suitable place, he leans forward and extends his arm to her. She wiggles her fingers free from the mud's grasp and places her hand in his. In one swift pull, she finds herself up and in his embrace. Her legs feel unsteady beneath her as he wraps his arms around her waist and pulls her closer to him. She places her ice-cold, mud-covered hands on his forearms to steady herself. His skin burns beneath her touch. There is only the space of a breath between them. Magdalena looks up to see Warrick looking down at her. His eyes are intense on her face and full of an emotion she can't read. She doesn't move away.

"Warrick," she says wearily. "Warrick, why did you do it? Look at your face." She places her fingers gently near a large gash above his eyebrow that has stopped bleeding but is beginning to swell. "What were you thinking? He is a king, Warrick. His need for vengeance will not care about any political border."

Warrick doesn't reply. Instead, he lifts his hand, her hold on his arm falling away, and he brings his fingers to her face. He brushes her cheek with the back of his swollen and dry-blood-stained knuckles. She doesn't move a muscle. He moves his hand to her hair and runs his fingers through the light blonde locks. Her heart beats hard in her chest, but she doesn't look away from his eyes nor does he from hers. Raising his other hand now, he uses his thumb to trace a line across her jaw and to her chin, where he makes his way up to her lip. Ever so softly, he brushes the pad of his thumb across her bottom lip, and then her top. Magdalena's stomach turns with fear or thrill, she is unsure. Slowly, Warrick bends down and places a soft, gentle kiss upon her lips. He doesn't linger, just stays long enough for her to feel the softness of his lips and the warmth of his breath against her mouth. Lips parting, Warrick moves a step back and looks down at her.

"Ah, Mags," he sighs as he bends his head to whisper in her ear, "if I'd known that all it took for me to be able to hold you in my arms, place my hands on your beautiful face, or even get to kiss your lips was to get my face smashed in, I would have signed up for it long before today."

Magdalena, hesitating slightly, pulls her head back so she can look into his eyes. He had held his position near her ear, so now, with her turned head, their faces are so close they are almost touching. She looks him in the eyes, and there she sees something that makes her both scared and thrilled all at once. She can't turn away, doesn't want to turn away. She can feel his slight breath against her face. She is frozen in this moment, unable to move or speak. Her lips ache to find his once more. She begins to lean slightly forward. Her lips part.

"Hey! Warrick!" a growling yell from the tree line causes Magdalena to jump back. Warrick, she notices, doesn't flinch at all, just closes his eyes in a dramatic and annoyed blink before turning to face the sound.

"Warrick! We are waiting on that wood for the fire. Magdalena, are you alright?" Brom's tone is full of fury as he yells again, making his way awkwardly through the trees toward them.

"I am fine, Brom. I got stuck in the mud on my way into the water. Warrick helped me. He was just heading your way," she calls back. Magdalena suddenly feels foolish and uncomfortable and nervously pushes her hair out of her face. She turns her back on Brom and moves quickly to the creek edge and squats to fill her hands with the cold water. She stays there a moment, pretending to wash her hands and arms, and when she finally dares a look over her shoulder, Warrick is gone.

That night, Magdalena lies under a pile of furs staring into the fire. A man kissed her lips. Growing up, she refused to allow that possibility to ever enter her mind. She asked her parents once what their plan was regarding marriage and heirs, and they brushed her concerns away, told her they would find a solution, figure it out. She knew no matter what action her parents ordered her to take, her lips would never be allowed to meet another man's. She would never feel the line of a whiskered jaw against her outstretched palm. She wouldn't feel the strength of a muscled body held tight against her own. She smiles slightly now as the color rises in her cheeks.

20
Henrick

At Henrick's outburst, Dagen left the castle and went to the only place one went when they wanted answers: the brothel. Surely if a retired army general, a barkeep, and a Typhan were planning an uprising with Magdalena at the helm, young men would be talking, and if they were, it would be with the best Kaelonoch has to offer—Fani.

"My lady, I am sorry to have kept you waiting," Henrick says, entering the den and moving to the chair opposite the woman in red. "I am grateful for this opportunity to sit down with you." Henrick smiles politely, pulling his chair closer to the captive woman.

"My lord, I am the one grateful to have my eyes grace you on this fine day," the woman purrs, bowing her head before Henrick.

Henrick smiles a crooked smile. When she rises, he notices that she eases her shoulders forward, a practiced move that allows Henrick to better glance the skin above the plunging neckline of her dress.

Henrick shakes his head slightly to erase the thoughts creeping up there. "Well then. Fani, it comes to my attention that you know just about everything happening within the boundaries of Masunbria."

"Some men talk more than others," she replies. "What is that you are lookin' to find out about?"

"An uprising. It would seem that Haluk still walks within our borders. Not only that, but we hear on good authority that Haluk is accompanied by at least three men determined to bring war to our kingdom."

"My word!" Fani exclaims with a small shake of her head. "I can't say I know anything about this, unfortunately."

"Can't, or won't?" Henrick growls.

"Your Grace, since your boys came to town, they've been keepin' me awful busy. Plus, ain't no one in town has coin to spend on me. I have boys that talk, but mostly complaints about each other. The people don't have the time or energy for an uprising. Sounds like Haluk is on a fool's errand, if you ask me."

"I am glad my soldiers are keeping you fed with coin," Henrick says, rising from his chair and moving to the only way in or out of the room. He grasps the metal latch and pulls the heavy wood door open. In stumbles a young soldier. His face is pale and coated with a veil of sweat, fear dances in his kind brown eyes, and he walks into the room with shoulders slumped and head bowed.

"Do you recognize who we have here with us?" asks Henrick

The woman attempts a smile, but Henrick can see her chest heave as she struggles to control her racing heart.

"Yes, he is one of your soldiers. I have seen him a time or two." Her voice shakes as she speaks.

"Not just any soldier, Fani. Don't play games with me," Henrick mocks with a wag of his index finger. "I know this one is special to you. I know that this one means something to you. That's why I brought him here. You are a woman that knows more about what's happening in my kingdom than you are letting on. Euric here is going to help loosen that tongue of yours." Henrick steers the scared young man to the desk, his eyes never leaving Fani's. Her confident, almost cocky demeanor has quickly vanished and has been replaced with a rolling trepidation.

"Dagen, if you please?" Henrick smiles at his general. Dagen walks behind the desk and leans forward, grasping the young man's arms and pulling them behind his back. The action pins Euric to the edge of the desk, and his back bends awkwardly, stomach and chest protruding. He can't move; he can't fight. Henrick walks in slow half circles around him. He picks up a knife from the top of the desk, hilt a smooth white stone, and uses the tip of the blade to touch the man's chest and stomach. He runs the gleaming silver blade lightly over Euric's cheek and then across his neck, where his pulse races visibly.

"I know nothing!" Fani screams through clenched teeth as tears form in her eyes.

"The thing is, Fani, I don't believe you." He turns to Euric, and without a moment's hesitation, Henrick plunges the knife into Euric's side. He pulls the blade free, and with it, blood spills out and down the young man's black uniform. Fani lets out a scream as Euric struggles violently against Dagen's grasp.

"Now, Fani, settle down. He won't die from that wound if he gets the help he needs rather quickly. Tell me what I want to know, Fani. Where is Haluk and who is helping her?"

Fani shakes her head as tears stream down her face. She closes her eyes and seems to be weighing the choices before her. After several breaths, she looks resolutely upon Euric's agonized face. "I am so sorry, my love," she whispers into the air. Henrick doesn't hesitate. He plunges his knife into the belly of the soldier, who lets out a blood-curdling scream in response. Fani jumps from her chair and runs to him, placing her hands over the wound. Blood spills out and covers her splayed fingers.

"I have a physician just beyond the door. One word from me and he will save Euric's life. This is your last chance, Fani." Henrick uses the tip of the blade to dig at something under his thumbnail.

"Fine, fine," she screams through tears. "Magdalena resides in Kaelonoch. She is helped by Willem Falk, Brom Anker, and the Typhan—Warrick, something. It is true, she is forming an army against you. They were in More to get an alliance with their king. That's all I know. I swear it. Please get him help. Please help him; he is dying," Fani cries as blood spurts from the lips of her lover. The man sags, and Fani tries to hold him up, tries to help him to his feet. His head lobs to one side, and she eases him down on the ornate rugs of burnt orange and royal blue. She grabs his cheeks with both palms and leans in to kiss his lips. She whispers her love for him as he takes his last breath. Fani rubs his hair from his forehead as she looks into his vacant eyes.

"You will take me to her," Henrick growls.

Fani looks up at Henrick. She looks down at her now-dead lover. She sees the knife that ended his sweet life still in Henrick's hand but resting at his side. She doesn't hesitate, doesn't seem to even think. She grabs the hilt of the knife before Henrick can react and plunges the blade deep into the soft tissue of her stomach.

"Forgive me, Magdalena," Fani sputters as blood soaks her teeth and drips from her chin. She collapses next to Euric and uses what life she has remaining to hug the man close before she, too, breathes her last.

"Great," exclaims Henrick with irritation. "Dagen, get your men to Kaelonoch. Take her with you. Get someone in here to clean up this mess too. Have them bring me a drink as well." Henrick's orders to Dagen come out in rapid succession. His head is beginning to throb from all the screaming.

Dagen is leaning over the desk and staring at the scene on the floor, mouth agape.

"Did you hear me, Dagen?"

"Yes, sorry. I just didn't anticipate any of that." He waves his hand at the scene below. "A pity, she was fun."

The rest of the day, Henrick's headache continues to grow. The pain bursts behind his eyes and wraps its spidery legs around to the base of his skull. By evening, he can barely move without the pain searing through his vision and causing him to become dizzy. He decides to skip his evening meal and hide himself away in the darkened den he has kept as a home during his nights of drunken deviousness. Thea comes in to check on him before dining herself. She sits sweetly next to him, rubbing peppermint oils on his temples and whispering for him to rest well. He is a man who grows more irritable when he isn't well. When his body is not at peak performance, he finds that his mind and thoughts respond in kind. He is annoyed at Thea's attention, but, then again, if she'd paid him no attention, he would have been angry with her for her lack of care and concern. Henrick looks at his body as the ultimate vessel of strength and success. Thea, knowing this about him and knowing that she is in a situation where she can be of no help, leaves him quietly then to lie in the dark as she takes her evening meal. Henrick drifts to sleep.

He is awakened hours later from his deep sleep by guttural screams. They come from down the hall and echo through the castle's stone walls. Jumping up from the couch he is resting on, Henrick reaches for anything he can use as a weapon within the room. *This is it.* Magdalena and her army have chosen this night to lay their attack. Someone must have told her that he is ill, that he is weak and defenseless. There is a traitor in his midst. He must focus himself. His head swims with pain. He grits his teeth. He knows that he must push past the pain, or he will surely die on this night. The screams continue to vibrate in his ears. For a small moment, he considers hiding in this very room. But he dismisses the thought as soon as it comes, not because it would be cowardly, but because if there was a traitor, they surely told Magdalena where he lies this night.

The screaming continues. Wincing in pain, he locates the tool used to stoke the fire and grasps the black, heavy iron in his hand. He steadies his breathing before emerging into the hall. His heart is pounding hard now, along with his head. Perhaps he has been poisoned, he thinks. That would explain the headache. It is too much of a coincidence that he is in such a state just as the castle is being attacked. No, this has been planned too well. Perhaps it is Thea that has betrayed him. She is good with poison. Perhaps the peppermint oil was something else? More poison that would soak in through the skin? That witch. It had to be her. Rage fills his eyes. He will kill the first person he comes across, no matter who it is.

He takes off then, at a dead sprint from the doorway, toward the sound of the screams. He runs down the twisting halls, turning right, then left. He rounds the next corner; the screams are so close now. They are coming from the servants' staircase just ahead. Then they stop, just like that. The halls are silent for a long moment. They have killed the screamer, he thinks. He begins to creep down the rest of the length of the hall, eyes locking on the stairway before him. Suddenly, a kitchen maid appears, staggering up the stairs. Her light gray dress and bare arms glisten in the moonlight from the window as if she was covered in oil. She sees Henrick and stumbles on the last step, catching herself before her knees hit stone.

"Sir," she rasps. "Sir, thank goodness you are here."

Henrick approaches cautiously, iron poker still raised above his shoulder, prepared to swing at any moment. "Who is it? Who goes there?"

"Sir, it is I, Melda from the kitchens. Sir, she is dead. Right there on the stairs. There is so much blood." Melda begins crying harder as she finishes her last statement so that the word *blood* is drawn out and throaty.

"There is an army down those stairs? Who is the *she* that is dead? Who killed her? Is my niece there? Is she waiting for me?"

"I don't reckon I know, sir. I haven't seen anyone in the castle. I just came up to find her because the torches, they weren't lit, sir. I was bringing me a torch and heading up the stairs, lightin' as I go. That's when I saw her, lying there with so much blood."

She is making no sense. Henrick leans his body to peer down the winding staircase, and he can see the faint glow from where the girl has apparently dropped her torch. This could be a trick. This kitchen maid could be in on the attack and trying to lure him down the stairs where he will have little defense. He will not fall for it.

"Show me," he growls. "You go first down the stairs, and you show me what you have seen."

She shakes her head violently and begins to cry harder, but Henrick pulls her up forcefully and spins her around. With one solid push, she stumbles to the opening of the stairs. Her entire body shakes as she slowly begins her descent. Henrick follows, fire poker held at the ready.

Henrick sees the hair first, a blanket of auburn spilled across the stone stairs. Next, he sees the blood. The thick red blood looks black and appears to glisten in the light of their torch. Henrick reaches the torch above his head to light the mounted one that hugs the stone. The scene explodes in light. Sabina lies on the stairs, a gash across her throat.

***

"Oh no, oh no, this can't be true. This can't be happening," Niklaus yells, tears running down his face and saliva spurting from his mouth at each wail. Sabina has been removed from the stairs and taken to the kitchen, where her body now lies on the working table in the center of the room. She has been wrapped in white cloths, and a bandage encircles the wound at her throat, though Henrick can't understand why someone would go through the trouble. The kitchen maid who found her has been sent to bed after downing a glass of strong wine.

Niklaus sits on the old wooden stool in the kitchen, smoothing her hair with one hand while rubbing her still cheek with the other. His emotions over the past hour since she was discovered have gone from terror, to anger, to a guttural sadness and back again, to start the cycle once more. Any doubt that his love for Sabina wasn't a deep, pure, all-encompassing passion was thrown out by now. Catrain herself had thought it proper to excuse herself from the scene and had patted her betrothed lightly on the arm as she moved quickly for her rooms. No one appears shocked at his love and devotion. Sabina and Niklaus have known each other since they were children. They knew the awkward years of their early life. They watched each other grow and change to man and woman. They liked long before they loved. Henrick stays by his nephew's side. Thea too sits with them, shaking her head at the sight and wringing her hands with the fear that someone committed this act within the castle walls. Henrick tries to comfort his wife, holding her hand and kissing her face. He is ashamed now to have thought that she, his most loving wife, was a traitor.

***

Henrick alone remains with Niklaus now, the others having gone to bed. Niklaus has stopped wailing now, and his body is still. Henrick thinks perhaps he has fallen asleep, his head resting next to Sabina's on the worn wood table. Henrick stands from the stool and stretches his back, which has grown uncomfortably cramped.

"Did you do this, Uncle?" murmurs Niklaus, his face still buried in his arm.

"What did you say?"

Niklaus lifts his head and looks Henrick in the eye. "Did you kill Sabina?"

Henrick is confused at the accusation. How could Niklaus possibly think that? He himself cradled and carried the girl down the stairs to lay her gently here. He was the one to warm water for the maids to clean her face. He has sat here all night to witness Niklaus's mourning. He is hurt by the accusation.

"You pain me, Nephew. Your words cut me like a new blade. I think it is time for me to retire for the evening." Henrick moves to leave, anger and pain coursing through his veins.

Niklaus reaches out his hand and catches Henrick by the forearm. Henrick stiffens prepares for a fight. In one swift motion, Niklaus rises and wraps his arms around his uncle, holding him tightly. Shocked by the tight embrace, Henrick freezes for a moment, then softens and wraps his arms around the young man before him. Niklaus begins to sob again.

"I am so sorry, Uncle. I am so sorry. I just have never felt pain like this before. I can barely breathe. I have no idea how to make the pain stop."

Henrick pats Niklaus's back softly. "I know, Son, I know. You must not be afraid of the pain though. You must embrace it. Grow comfortable with the hard, jagged edges of it. This pain is going to change you."

"I don't want it, Uncle. I just want her."

"I know, Niklaus. I know."

"Who did this to her, Uncle?" Niklaus sobs.

"I will soon find out, my son. I promise." Henrick places a soft kiss on his nephew's forehead, a seal to the vow he has just made.

21
Magdalena

Magdalena closes her eyes and breathes in the damp woody scent of her homeland. It is a stark contrast from the smell of the salt and the fish. Gone, too, is the crushing sound of the sea and of a busy marketplace, and, replacing it, is the silence that only can come from the forest. She feels the relief that comes at the end of a long journey, the final push through the deep trees before they emerge onto the farm she has called home. All have been silent today. Even Warrick has been lost in his thoughts. He has taken up his position from the rear, and any glance she casts back is met with the side of his head as his face scans the perimeter.

The woods are full of hidden life, and each twig that breaks or bush that rustles sends alarm through her and her companions. Everything has changed now. Now that they have gone to More. Now that she has taken her first step on the path of treason. They all can feel it. As much as Magdalena longs for her small bed in an upstairs loft, she knows that her life there will come to end sooner rather than later. To protect Hagen, Sybbyl, and Liri, she must go. She hopes she can have just one more night with them. One more night to sit by a fire and read aloud. One more night of warm wine and the smell of herbs seeping on a stove. The scraping sound of Hagen whittling a small horse at the table. One more night of an exuberant Liri telling one more lively tale of her favorite chicken in the flock. Little things to anyone else, but not to Magdalena. A life that seemed so strange when she first arrived to it has now come to feel like hope. Like home. Like family.

It pains her to think about this new family now being ripped from her, just as her real family was. She thinks about running then. She recalls how close she came once before. She thinks of the little farm and the little family—a life that will never be. Even if by some chance she does survive this war, and in doing so, the people do allow her to be queen, her life will never be a simple life, not like the one of her dreams. No child born from her will ever have days of lying under the sun reading a book or catching fireflies by night. No, choosing her kingdom will cost her, and any future life she brings to this world, more peace and simplicity than she can even begin to describe. For her child's sake, she will never tell them what it's like to live simply. In fact, she'd rather not think of bringing a child into this world. The life she is returning to is one of policy and etiquette, betrayal and lies. It is no place for children. That could be the only mercy she could offer. Not to live at all. She will do her duty for her people, but she won't resign anyone she loves to a sentence such as that.

She fights back tears as she steers her horse out of the thick trees and looks beyond at the field leading to Hagen and Sybbyl's home.

"Whoa, whoa," Willem says ahead of her to his horse as he raises a hand to stop the procession.

"What is it?" Magdalena calls, pulling the reins to yield her own horse.

"I don't know," Willem calls back. "Something isn't right. There are people here. Horses tied up. Brom, you flank left. I'll take right. Warrick, you take Magdalena back behind the barn. I will come for you when it is safe."

No further discussion is necessary. Brom, a look of panic in his eyes, snaps the reins and makes for his position. Willem, only hesitating a moment to offer Magdalena a weak smile and Warrick a curt nod, heads in his.

"Come on, Mags," Warrick says with a tone that is more curious than alarmed.

Magdalena steers her horse away from the cottage and hears Warrick's horse following closely behind her as she moves to the instructed location. Her heart beats in time with the hooves on the frozen earth. Once there, she dismounts quickly and begins pacing a line through the snow-covered dirt. Her imagination gets the best of her. She sees Samalt in the house, the snake having returned. She imagines how afraid Liri must be. Liri talked often, after that day, about Samalt. He unnerved her. Liri told Magdalena that when Samalt went up to the loft, she collapsed to the floor in fear. She saw the look of the man, the smell of him. She knew he was a man that did not believe in a swift death, that hers would be long and careful: strategic cuts to cause pain but not deep enough to kill. It was Sybbyl that straightened her up before it was too late. Sybbyl wiped her eyes and sat her down, pressing into Liri's palm a small black cloth of dried herbs and closing Liri's hand over them, concealing them. Then she bent low and whispered for Liri not to be afraid. She was to take them all at once, and it would be over before it began. Poison. Magdalena, recalling the story now, fears they have arrived too late. She imagines them there on the floor, eyes void and mouth full of froth.

"I can't stay here. I have to know what's happening," Magdalena says, quickening her paces in the frozen mud.

"I know. You need to stay calm though. Ya need not wear yourself out just in case . . ." He drifts off, leaving his sentence to hang heavy in the air between them.

She can't sit though. Her body hums with an energy that has been cultivated, practiced. Her pupils seem to focus on the tiniest movement of the wind. Her ears appear to hear birds more than a mile away as they strain for any clue as to what is happening at the house. A scream? A clash of metal? Anything. Her legs feel light and her arms strong. She is just about to give up. To round the corner for the house and not look back at what she is sure will be a rather furious Warrick. But then, Willem appears.

He walks slowly toward them, measuring each step, counting his paces. Magdalena can feel the dread sink into her chest. He reaches her and looks up, meeting her eyes. It is something terrible. She knows it for certain now. Her heart drops to her stomach, and she brings a hand to her mouth. Whether she is afraid she will scream or get sick, she doesn't know. She can feel Warrick at her side. They both look expectantly at Willem.

"It's Fani, my lady. Fani is dead. Your Grace, they know you are here, in Kaelonoch. I don't know how, but they do. They know our names. They know Fani was helping us. They know we were in More and that we are forming an army. They are coming for you. They are coming for us all. We must make haste to the woods. We can hide there until we are ready."

A sob escapes her mouth as she turns her back to Willem. She offers not a word. She just walks, as if only she were to get far enough away from his words, they wouldn't be able to reach her, to gain purchase inside her. She begins to walk in the opposite direction of the two men. Not quickly, not slowly, just as someone would walk who has nowhere to go at no particular time. Tears burn her eyes and she lets them fall free in huge waves down her face. Her lungs cry in protest as her body refuses to draw in enough air, as the weight of the news has crushed her chest in on itself.

"My lady! It isn't safe," Willem calls after her.

"I will watch out for her. She just needs a minute, brother," she hears Warrick reply. She doesn't turn around. She doesn't stop making her way toward the woods. If she can just pass the tree line, she thinks, she will be safe in there. The trees will welcome her, and comfort her, and shield her.

Once inside the canopy of branches, she sinks down to the snow-covered ground. Her knees dig into tangles of roots, but she doesn't care. She sobs. She was preparing herself for the fact that others would die fighting this fight for her. She knew it would happen. Those others, the ones that would die, they were always nameless, shapeless figures in her dreams. They were men of dark hair, or maybe light. They were short and tall and strong or not. They had names but she never heard them. In her dreams, they died quietly on the battlefield, slipping almost to sleep, sun on their peaceful faces. People in her dream were sad and would say a word for the souls of those lost, and she knew they had died for her and all she had promised. In her dreams, she would feel a great deal of obligation to them. To keep pushing on, securing the victory, so that their death may not be in vain but rather a great stone step on the precipice of freedom. She would envision the victory and the moment they stood there, proud and tired, and would say aloud a toast to those who didn't live to see the day they saved their people. In her dreams, though, she could never conjure a face to go with the tribute, not a single one of them.

She couldn't decide if her assumption that no one she loved would die in this battle was an act of naïveté or the whisper of a prayer, a message to the beyond in the form of a fantasy. Either way, Fani was not supposed to have died. The people who died were the people on the battlefield. The people eating out of tin near a fire and sleeping in shifts on the ground. The people with dirt on their hands and etched furrows between their brows. Not a woman in a red dress. Never a woman in a red dress.

She sits there for several long moments. The sound of sticks breaking underfoot alerts her to his approach before anything else. Knowing him, even in the small way she does, the noise was intentional. He wanted her to know he was there. For this man knows how to remain invisible and unheard. Most likely, she thinks, he has been there all along. Watching her. Waiting. Warrick kneels down beside her.

"Willem said that men from the castle brought Fani to Kaelonoch. They made a show of nailing her body up in the center of town. They told everyone around that the same would be done to anyone aiding you in treason. Once night fell, your men divided, one group creating a diversion while the other group cut her down. They have brought her here, Mags. It is time."

She rises on unsteady legs and wipes her cheeks. She looks at Warrick's face, searching it for a glint of blame, a flicker of regret, but he wears his mask well. As they make their way toward the cottage, she can see Brom, Willem, and Jonan, each with a shovel in hand, moving and lifting dirt in a sun-soaked spot of the open field. A group of villagers turned soldiers stands off to one side. A cluster of three women she doesn't know stands with Hagen, Sybbyl, and Liri, watching on. The women, she assumes, are friends of Fani's. Certainly, they will believe it her fault that Fani is dead. The entire village must think it. She hesitates in her approach. She sees the cart and Fani lying in it, hair splayed over the worn wood boards. Her dress is soaked in blood. Her face is still and peaceful, and Magdalena can almost imagine the easy laugh and the brilliant smile. *This wasn't supposed to happen.*

"I have heard that the villages bury someone nearly every day. My people are dying, Warrick. This one, though, this death is on me. This death occurred because she helped me. There are going to be so many more before this is over." Magdalena lets out a heavy sigh. Warrick takes her small hand in his large one. He squeezes a reassurance before leading her to the cart. Once there, he bends inside and removes another shovel.

"It's time to dig, Mags." He offers it to her and releases his hold on her hand before retreating from the group to stand alone, to guard the burial. Hesitating, feeling the weight of the tool in her hand, Magdalena walks with eyes cast down to join the three men in burying the body of her friend, the first casualty of her war.

They stand for a long while after Fani has been placed below their feet. Little is spoken. They begin to make their way into the home. Sybbyl and Liri are eager to feed everyone, as it is what they can offer best for comfort. Brom sends the men away to pack their bags and bring the others. They are no longer safe. It is time to go.

Magdalena doesn't want to go inside the little farmhouse. She doesn't want to face those waiting there in an enclosed space. Out here it feels like there is more room for their judgment. The right wind could cast their glares away. Even if they spoke harsh words to her, perhaps out here a bird would fly by at just that moment and capture those words in its beak and be gone before they even found her ears. If she goes inside, there will be no escaping their pain and what may be born out of it.

She does, however, go inside. There was really no other choice. The table and kitchen are full of people, spooning a hearty soup of beans and pork with bits of parsley and oregano into their bellies. Magdalena decides to sit alone near the hearth. She spins her cup of wine to reveal and conceal the stain atop the small three-legged table. No one has spoken to her. Sometimes she feels them looking at her. She feels their eyes casting blame on her for the death of their own. The second death that has stained her hands. Astrid, now Fani. Both young women. Both beloved and full of life. She hears laughing behind her. More tales of Fani are being told, and the more they drink, the funnier they perceive them to be. She doesn't listen. Back and forth goes her cup over the stain. Up to her lips, only to return again and again.

"Can I join ya?" It is Warrick. Who else would it be? He doesn't know these tales either. He is alone here as well, but for a very different reason.

"Are you sure you want to do that? I am terrible company."

He doesn't answer, just sits down opposite her. He stretches his legs out long, takes up space.

"What happened with Fani has made this all the more real for me," Magdalena admits without meeting his eyes. "I have been trained in war. I have read the books on battle strategy. I have studied maps of terrain while working out mock scenarios of attack. I am physically trained with sword, arrow, and dagger. Warrick, I am not emotionally trained for this."

He is silent for so long that Magdalena can't resist, and she looks up to meet his eyes. The gray-blue eyes that look back at her are full of an understanding, a knowing, that sends a chill through her body.

"Perhaps I should go to the Typhans. I can plead with the man who I am promised to. I can create a new treaty. If I tell them how my brother is ruling, they will have to see that soon there will be nothing left of Masunbria to uphold the offerings. You said you knew him, the one I was to wed. Would he see reason to help me?"

"Aye, Mags, I don't think he would be able to say no to you," Warrick says with a sigh. "But by the time you went into Crask and came back out, there would be no helping your people, and you know that. The time to fight is now. Your brother and his greed will kill your people unless you put a stop to him."

"In doing so, I will also kill my people."

"It's not the same."

"Says who? I have made my choice, but I am not so naïve to think I will be unpunished for whatever blood is spilled on my behalf, whether that punishment comes in this life or the next."

She hears him shift in his chair. He reaches across to the space between them and takes her hand in his. She doesn't want his touch or his comfort, and she makes to pull away, but his grip is tight. Her eyes sting with unshed tears, and she blinks hard to try to keep them from falling. The salty drops rebel as their desire to be free from her lids proves too strong to resist. Tears begin to trace down her cheeks. She closes her eyes and shakes her head slightly back and forth. She feels Warrick's thumb lightly grazing her skin as he catches each tear on the callused pad.

"Why do you fight in my war, Warrick?" Magdalena quietly asks.

She hears Warrick take a deep breath before letting it out slowly. "I am not fighting in your war. I am not battling your uncle or your brother. I am thousands of miles away. I am slaying dragons in lands where battle cries are called in a language you wouldn't understand. I have fought this same dragon time and time again. If you sent me off, I would just find another war. That is all I know how to do."

"We are both broken, aren't we?" she says with a harsh laugh.

"Aye, but maybe that means that together we can be whole."

Magdalena opens her eyes to meet his. The man before her frightens her. The things he says, the way he looks at her, the way he makes her feel. She swallows hard before rising on unsteady legs. His hand refuses to let go of hers until the very last moment as she moves to walk away. She heads up the ladder to pack her things and leave the little farm, to take her army to safety and then prepare them for war.

22
Henrick

Henrick stares outside at the gray of winter. The season of death stills hangs heavy across the land. It is fitting, then, that death is precisely what fills the castle walls. Sabina's death. Her death has been most unpleasant for Henrick. He has had to bear witness to the depression of Niklaus. The torment of the boy. Niklaus has become paranoid and fearful of everyone in the castle. There are moments where you risk your own life should you think to step foot in his presence. No one can have a moment of peace due to his wails of sorrow that can be heard echoing down the stone halls. Henrick has tried to be there for the boy, to console him. But now, Henrick has grown weary and annoyed by his moods and will not entertain his behavior, which, if Henrick is being frank, has become just plain selfish. There are only two days remaining before the Typhans are set to return to wreak havoc on the land. Preparation must be made, and Henrick can't waste any more time with Niklaus and his sorrow.

A knock at the door to the den stirs him from his trance. When he doesn't respond to the question the knock asks, the door begins to inch its way open, iron hinges screeching as it does so. Rolling his eyes, he glances to the door, ready to demand peace from whomever is insisting entry. He pauses, though, as the head that appears through the open door is that of the last person he would expect to see. Catrain. He has been avoiding her since the outburst in the forest, and it seems she has been avoiding him as well. Their paths rarely cross now except for the occasional meal, and even that is an uncomfortably charged reunion.

He was working on convincing himself that she was not as beautiful as he once thought. At meals he would watch her chew and imagine the bits of saliva and chicken grease coating her teeth. He would picture her tongue as it slid like a slug in her mouth to move her bread from side to side. Then, just for good measure, he would picture her subsequent bowel movement. The imagery worked, and it would get him through the meal. It was at night, though, that she came to him, visions of her beauty, her skin, her smile. She would haunt him then. During the day, it was easier. During the day, he had almost convinced himself that he didn't love her. Almost.

She smiles a weak crooked smile at him, closes the door gently behind her, and makes her way to sit on the couch near him.

"Why are you here, Catrain?" Henrick's voice is weary.

"I have had a lot of time to think about the words you spoke at the river's edge. Your outburst pained me at first. In time, though, I realized that you were right. Niklaus manipulated me, as you pointed out. I have borne the pain of not only his actions but of what occurred between you and me because of them. I am tired of being in pain, Henrick. I've missed you. I will fight for the man I love, even if it means my head. And that's what I did, Henrick. I fought for you and me with my actions, and I don't regret them at all."

"What actions? What are you talking about?"

"It was me. I killed Sabina. I wanted to hurt Niklaus for deceiving me. I wanted to hurt myself for being so stupid to fall for it and lose you in the process. I wanted to show you how much I love you and only you. I didn't want to sit back and let life happen to me anymore."

Henrick stares at Catrain for a long moment, mouth agape. Rubbing his face, he swears under his breath as he rises and begins pacing the room. Scrolls and papers that line the shelves flutter with each passing. *How could she have done this?* Not the killing, that was what it was; how could she tell him about the killing? Put on him the weight of it?

"Catrain, this changes everything," he finally stutters out. "How could you act so recklessly? This isn't like you."

Catrain remains mute. She holds her head high.

"I must think what we are to do now. I wish you wouldn't have told me this. How am I to clean up this mess?"

Catrain shrugs and rises from her spot on the couch. "I am certain you will do what's best for the kingdom, my lord." She turns and leaves the room without a glance back, her body proud and triumphant as she leaves.

Henrick falls dramatically back on the couch. How has his beloved Catrain becomes a murderess? Niklaus has been in misery since the death of Sabina. He could tell Niklaus the truth, set him free of the pain, and watch Catrain get sent to the executioner's block. Her pretty head would be swiftly removed from her body.

She would die. No, there has to be another way. There is only one person brave enough, cunning enough, loving enough to help him deal with this problem.

***

Henrick hesitates outside the door to his savior, staring at the grain of the wood, hand on the latch. He knows that whatever decision is reached within the walls beyond, his relationship with Catrain is over for good now. She will either be sent to her death or she will be made queen. Either way, she will no longer belong to him, and that's the way it has to be. He takes a steadying breath and pushes open the door.

Thea sits lazily on the small couch drinking tea, a book propped open on her lap. The cream-colored couch with embroidered flowers she is sitting on had been a favorite of his mother's. Seeing Thea there makes Henrick wish that his mother was here too. He can see her now, laughing and drinking tea with his wife. He stares for a moment at the room, lost in a scene of his own creation. In this scene, he imagines a child, his child, playing with wooded blocks on the pink-and-beige rug between the two women. Thea and his mother are so delighted in the child that, even when talking amongst one another, their eyes never meet because they are glued on the cherub that plays before them. To take their eyes from the child for a moment would break the spell of love that courses through the room. Henrick winces. His future will never contain a mother returned from the dead or a child brought to life. Henrick knows this. He shakes himself from the torturous dream and swiftly approaches his wife.

"Good morning, my love." He bends and places a kiss on her forehead and moves to take the chair opposite her, hesitating for an unnoticed moment before sitting on the chair his mother just occupied in his mind moments ago.

"Henrick! What a pleasant surprise to see you so early. What can I do for you? I thought council wasn't meeting until midday? Or am I still no longer welcome?"

Henrick nervously rises and crosses the few feet of space to where she sits. He crouches to the floor at her feet and takes her hands in his, where he kisses them tenderly before laying his head in her lap. She begins to run her fingers through his dark, oiled hair.

"Thea, my beautiful Thea." Henrick sighs as he tilts his head slightly to look up at her. "I am sorry for what has occurred between us. I beg your forgiveness. I need you by my side. You are the most brilliant woman in all the land. Your presence alone makes me want to be something great. That is why I am here today. I am here to confess to you so that I may become better. I am on my knees in front of you begging for both your help and your mercy. You, my most powerful Thea, are the only one who can change my circumstance. Only you can guide me where I must go."

Thea sits for a long moment, hand still playing in Henrick's hair. Henrick lies still and allows the caressing to continue. He is relaxed in a way that has become foreign to him since they came to seize the castle from his brother. He begins to close his eyes and melt deeper into the folds of her purple dress as he surrounds himself with the warmth of her touch and the smell of her skin.

Much time passes before Thea speaks. "Have you come to discuss Catrain at last?"

Henrick pops his head up from her lap and meets her eyes. He searches them quickly but finds no anger or hatred, only exhaustion. He rises then, kisses her hands once more, and takes his place back in the chair across from her. Though he doesn't detect any malice in Thea at the moment, he knows how quickly a woman's emotions can turn, and he decides it best not to be in a position of quite literally offering his neck to her when he speaks something that sets her into a rage. He settles himself and rubs a palm over his stubbled chin, knowing what he must say.

"Well, yes, Thea. This is actually about Catrain, but more accurately it is about the fate of this kingdom as it relates to her."

Thea says nothing, just stares at him, face void of emotion.

She isn't going to make this easy. *Fair enough.* "Catrain came to me and admitted that she was the one to kill Sabina. Her motives for the killing appear to be revenge for Niklaus having a relationship with Sabina for many years, and it seems he wasn't keen on that ending after he and Catrain became betrothed. She killed her in a moment of jealousy, hatred, and fear for her future heirs and their place in the hierarchy, but alas, she is the culprit. I am here today to ask you if we take her head or give her a crown? Which course of action is the right one for the kingdom to prosper?" He sits back in his chair, steeples his fingers, and awaits her sentencing with, he realizes, his breath slightly held tight in his chest.

Thea smiles a wry and crooked smile that doesn't reach her eyes, and she lets out a short, unconvincing laugh. "Catrain slit the throat of Sabina over jealousy of her relationship with Niklaus, huh? Yes, that's not absolutely accurate, I am sure. The truth, I believe, is far more complex than that. No matter her real reasons or motives, and no matter if you know them or not, we can't risk losing her as queen. Especially now that we have this bit of information on her. I thought her a loyalist to our family before, but now, now that we hold the power to control her fate in our hands, Henrick, we have a puppet for a queen. Quite simply put, she will do as we instruct her to do, all the days of her life, or we will see to it that hers is ended rather swiftly at the hand of an executioner. It appears fate has smiled upon our rule once again."

Henrick, never one to discount the divine intervention of his path toward a kingdom of his own, decides to agree with his wife. Destiny was playing out in their favor. "You are brilliant, my wife, just as I knew you would be. How, though, are we going to get her crowned queen with Niklaus in the state he is in?"

"We tell him who killed Sabina," Thea says with a sly smile playing across her face.

***

The air was crisp and full of the scent of decayed leaves the morning her head was cut from her body. Niklaus stood in the front row, his eyes never leaving the scene playing out before him. Catrain stood to his left, holding his hand, emotionless in the pale morning sun. Henrick watched her face the moment the ax fell. She didn't even bat an eye. The girl whose head lobbed into the basket was a kitchen maid of no real consequence, and now, just a few hours away, Henrick can't even remember her name. Sigmund and Thea did the hard work of creating a plausible story for why the girl killed Sabina and hiding enough evidence in her quarters to make the story stick. After all their efforts, Niklaus had no choice but to believe the story laid out before him. In fact, their story was so good, Henrick himself could have believed that Catrain told a tale, and it was, in fact, this nameless, faceless, now headless maid that did the killing that fateful night. Thea, ever the loving aunt to Niklaus, comforted him after the news was broken. She told him that justice would be served but that Sabina would have wanted him to rule. He was doing Sabina a dishonor by not being the man, the king, he was meant to be. Niklaus relented. He would marry Catrain, and together, they would officially be crowned king and queen of Masunbria.

Henrick, though relieved that Catrain's life was spared, finds himself once again unable to sleep. He sits in front of the fire in the den watching the flames lick the expansive hearth. A sudden shadow at his right catches his attention, and he jumps to his feet. He must be dreaming, he thinks, as he looks and sees her beautiful form draped in silks. The lavender fabric hugs her body in all the mounds and valleys that only the figure of a woman possesses. Her dark hair hangs in loose waves over her shoulders, and the ends hover just above her breasts. He stares as she approaches, confused but intrigued by her mystical form.

"Where did you get that?" Henrick asks, indicating the lavender fabric.

A smile plays across her lips. "It was a gift from your wife, actually. She said she had a contact in the silk shops of More bring it over for me. When she gave it to me, she told me it was for me to wear on the night of my wedding when I finally lie with the man who has my heart."

"You owe your life to Thea. She is the one who sent that maid to her death instead of you. She saved you."

"Why did she save me, Henrick?"

Henrick hesitates, not sure how to answer that question without revealing Thea and his intent on ruling through control of Catrain. "I imagine because she loves you. I imagine because you have been with her for many years and she believed you a victim of a broken heart." *There, that sounds plausible.*

Catrain laughs and moves closer to where Henrick is standing. She is inches from him now, and no matter how hard he tries, he can't take his eyes away from her body wrapped up like a present before him.

"Perhaps you are right, but I doubt it. Thea doesn't understand love the way you and I do. She doesn't create inseparable bonds with anyone. I have served her for years, as you said, and in all that time, how many close friends or confidants has she had? None. Not a single woman to call her ally in this world. Thea has lived a life alone because she doesn't understand love and relationships the way you and I do. That's why she spared my life. Because I am the only one who can love you the way she can't, and I am also the only one who will love her too. She needs me alive. You see, Henrick, she knows of us, and she always has. She just knows herself well enough to understand that if you are going to be the great man she wants you to be, then you are going to need me to do what she can't, to love you the way she can't."

"Catrain, I don't think I can share you with Niklaus. I am not that type of man. I don't know if I can even bear it to see you with child, knowing what it took between the two of you for that child to be there. These are things I think about Catrain. These are the things that prevent sleep from coming. I see you, belly swollen, walking around the castle, and I know, I know that it is his hands that splay to feel his child kick. I know that he is the one who possessed you in the night, and now, for nine long months, that part of him will continue to possess you, a constant reminder that you and he will forever be tied. I just can't bear it."

Catrain moves closer still. She takes Henrick's hands in her own and looks up at him. He can smell the sweet wine on her breath, feel her warm body pressing against his. He is weak for her love, she is right. He has missed her so much it hurts.

"Henrick," she whispers, "I have a secret to tell you. For several months now, I have been careless when it comes to you. I have known what days to go into your bed, and I have chosen them wisely. *You* are the man that fills my body with child."

"What? You are . . . you mean . . . ?" Henrick stammers.

"Yes." Catrain smiles up at him. She takes his hand and places it over her small stomach. "What grows in the dark below is of your blood. I am set to be married so soon. No one will know that the child is yours except us. You and I will have a family, a family that was built out of love and not duty, a family that was built from passion and desire. Once our child is born and the heir established, then we can decide how to best handle my husband and your wife. We will be together, Henrick. We will rule side by side as we watch our child grow, and we will give this child many siblings to play with. Don't you see? This has been written in the stars long before this moment. We were brought together for this purpose, I know it."

Henrick is entranced by her words and the world she is describing. He is overwhelmed with emotion—excitement, thrill, bliss—the future she has given him that is so full of hope and promise. He knows that this future would mean the end of his beloved Thea, whom he truly does love and admire. At this moment, though, all he can hear Catrain say is the word *baby*. It plays over and over in his head. Catrain has given him what he wanted most, what Thea could never give him. Tears well in his eyes. He grabs Catrain and pulls her into a deep and passionate kiss before leading her over to the couch.

Lost in their passion, neither of them hears the iron hinge of a door being closed.

23
Magdalena

As quick as they could, Magdalena's army moved from what little comforts their own homes still provided, to a camp established deep in the woods that separated Kaelonoch from the castle to the east and the Crask mountains to the west. The truth Warrick brought to Kaelonoch spread quickly. The people understood they were pawns in a game and nothing more. Magdalena's men spread through the land like wildfire, whispering and retelling and recruiting as many able bodies as possible. Their efforts have paid off. She scans the throng of men setting up small tents, lighting cook fires, and sharpening swords, and she can see the desperation on their faces, one last hope to save their families and themselves.

Her twenty soldiers that sat and signed that first pledge of fealty to her have grown to over two hundred. They are of all ages; some are even father and son. They have come not only from Kaelonoch but also the small neighboring villages that dot the kingdom of Masunbria. Though watching them from up here, it appears that there are a lot of men, Magdalena knows there aren't nearly enough. The wind whips her hair around her face as she tries, from her distant position, to look at the face of each person as they set up camp. She wants to sear their image into her mind. She wants to not let a single one of them go unnoticed.

"My queen, you should really not be so far away without anyone here to protect you."

"I am not a queen, Willem." Magdalena smiles as Willem comes to stand near her. She sees the lines of worry etched around his eyes. They have been there since before they left for More. It doesn't appear he has slept a full night since before her parents were killed.

"No, you aren't, are you? You are something more than that. Your army is quiet but determined."

"They are starving, Willem. I can see that from up here. I am afraid I will let them down. I am afraid that I won't be able to do enough. Regardless of the outcome of this battle, I can't stop thinking of the day the actual Typhans learn of my existence, the day they learn of the terrible thing my parents did. The men below may be able to fight my brother and his army, but even that is a long shot. Willem, there is no way that we alone can fight off the Typhans. You know that."

"One war at a time, my lady. That's what they are doing. Right now, they don't care about you and the lie and the possibilities that could come from that betrayal. They are here because they are starving, as you said. Their children are starving. Your brother created a fictitious circumstance to justify his greed. Those men down there know that their families will not make it through the winter. I want you to grasp that, really grasp that. Those men have one chance to change the fate of their children. They will bury them on a snow-covered hill, or they will risk their lives to fight this war in hopes that once the castle is seized, you will help them to live. They know that the only hope they have is to stand with you. They are all here to survive, and taking the castle is their best chance." As he finishes, Willem exhales deeply, the lines of worry evident on his brow.

Magdalena doesn't respond right away, but she thinks for a long moment as she looks at the lives in the camp below. *One war at a time.* "I understand," she says at last. "Shall we see what we have to work with?"

"After you, my lady." Willem smiles and pats her on the back as they make their way back to camp.

The rest of the day, her men train—many of them unfamiliar with sword work. They line up, one row facing the other. Brom, Willem, and Warrick walk behind them, hands clasped at their lower back, shouting commands or pausing to correct stances. The men use sticks at first until they are ready to yield metal. A large tent has been erected in the middle of camp, and Magdalena unpacks paper and quills to scatter across the slats of wood forming a makeshift table that occupies the center. She listens to the sound of the men outside as she steadies her breath and surveys her work.

Her eyes travel across the dirt floor to the cot in the corner, made up with the brown, scratchy blanket from her bed at Hagen and Sybbyl's home. Atop it lies a small chest from Sybbyl with a variety of herbs wrapped in cloth, the color of the cloth indicating their use. The herbs in the black cloth frighten her. They are the ones to take when no others will help. Sitting on the table next to the bed is a small wooden statue that Hagen whittled for her. It is of a stubborn cow. She picks up the small creature in her hands and plants a tiny kiss on its head as a single tear falls from her eye and lands on the cow's smooth back. She sets the cow down, and her finger traces lightly over the dark blue cover of the storybook Hagen gave her. She didn't finish reading it aloud. Before leaving the tiny cottage, Hagen presented the book to her along with the cow statue. She swore she would return and they would all finish the story together. A trickle of fear causes her stomach to lurch as she wonders if that is a promise she is going to be able to keep. *You can do this. Haluk could do this. Haluk was born for this.*

Those assigned directly to her file into the tent, and she levels her chin and moves to join them at the table. The scouts, the guards, the spies, these are in her charge. She first directs her scouts to scatter through the land and report back on everything from the height of the Miraron River that separates them from the castle to the number of guards seen and which entrance seems the most penetrable. The scouts are young, barely men; they are quick and they are quiet. They are like the rabbits who silently escape their den in search of food but wary of the prey that grows hungry and bold through the dead months of winter.

She grabs quill and ink and draws a rough diagram of the camp, the pass to the castle, the mountains, and the horse path to Kaelonoch and Cale, and she points to the guards the areas she has seen that would allow for easy passage. These are where they shall lie and watch and wait. Those chosen for this duty aren't the strongest, or the most able-bodied, but they are the most able minded. They are here to contribute, and if their physical bodies won't allow them to swing a sword with might or run like a rabbit through the woods, they will aid the cause with their sharp instincts and self-discipline.

The last group that remains is the three women who came to camp. These women were Fani's friends—the women from the burial. The women's job will be to check on families and deliver notes to wives, tucked into the folds of their skirts or down the tops of their dresses. They will listen for news and gossip and return with what they have gleaned. Once battle begins, they will serve to bandage wounds and care for the men injured. In this way, these women of the night with their tattered dresses and plunging necklines are just as, if not more, important than the soldiers themselves. They are not only spies, but they are also the lifeline the men have to their homes, to their wives and children, or mothers and fathers. They are what the men need to stay committed, as these women serve and deliver constant reminders of why they are here in the first place. And if the worst comes to the men, these women will do all they can to keep them alive. To these women, she hands a letter written to Hagen, Sybbyl, and Liri, along with a list of medical supplies she would like the women to find and bring back with them to camp.

Sending those in her charge into the four winds, she busies herself sketching maps from memory. The castle, the grounds, the rooms within. Scouts return, and she adds their notes to more sheets of paper before sending them out once more. The day falls to night, and fires are lit. Magdalena stretches her back, sore from bending over the table all day. She has finished cleaning up the mess from the day's planning. Tomorrow marks the final day in the fortnight her brother and his imposter Typhans gave as a deadline for Haluk to surrender. Niklaus and Henrick have surely heard by now about their visit to More. Magdalena is certain they would wish to convince Mikhail that Magdalena's Typhan was an imposter and that the threat made at the funeral was valid. When night falls tomorrow and Magdalena doesn't surrender, the castle will have no choice but to cause some form of travesty to keep up the farce and not draw unwanted attention from the neighboring kingdoms. One day, maybe two, is all they have left before war must be waged.

Unsure what else to do, she pushes aside the thick cloth door of her tent. Into the night air, she sees the men scattered about, warming their hands over the fire and talking amiably. She stands to the side, not nearing them, just watching them.

She has remained in the shadows with her army. She hasn't addressed them. She has worked with her small faction and that is all. Her charges are easy to talk to—they are young, or weak-bodied, or women. These men around the fire are hunters, and farmers, and fathers, and their voices are as large as their broad frames. She is worried that her presence and her words will not be welcomed by these men. Even if Willem is right and they are putting aside their feelings about her betrayal in order to have one last chance to save their families, certainly seeing her, or hearing her voice, will bring nothing but heaviness to their hearts. It wasn't just that her parents raised her a boy; for twenty years she played the part. She looked these people in the eyes and lied to them time and time again. They trusted she was who she said she was. The question she has asked herself since all this began is, "What would Haluk do?" but she can't form that question in her mind any longer. Haluk is gone. She can't hide behind him, and she knows she must stop hiding behind Willem, Brom, and Warrick.

Her eyes seek out the three leaders of her army. She finds Willem first. Ever the historian, he is deep in the telling of a tale about the old days and of the bravery of the men who came before them. She listens as he paints pictures with his words of men marching down from the great mountain and wild horses finally tamed for battle. He reminds the men they are descendants of those fierce warriors who fought back the Typhans all those years ago. She spots Brom next. He is sitting off to the side with a group of young men. Brom, always the loving, brotherly type, is talking to the men about their families and the future they are securing for them. As a barkeep, he has been a part of people's lives in a way so different than most. He was there in their best times to clink glass and cheers to good fortune, and he was there in their worst, to fill their glasses and offer a warm embrace over shared tears. She hears him talk about marriages and births and encouraging the men to let their hearts lead them into battle because their hearts will always ring true.

She continues walking in the shadows of the firelight, thick black furs draped over her shoulders. She smiles at the men she passes but remains quiet. She sees Warrick up ahead; he is standing so close to the flames that his face appears masked in both shadow and light. He is in the middle of some tale. She pauses to hear and laughs as he swears and talks about glory and blood and guts and all manner of things that disgust. The men laugh and beg for another story.

She is grateful to have these three men, so very different from one another but so essential to her troops and to herself. They make it look so easy. She would have nothing to say to any of the soldiers situated around the fires. She doesn't have the experience in battle that Willem has—she has only read the books and had the tutoring on the art of the beast. She can't talk of love like Brom does, for the one great act of love her parents offered was steeped in selfishness. She also isn't at all funny like Warrick. She is not even close to funny. She doesn't even find herself funny, which she has noticed that most people, even those who are not at all humorous, at least find themselves to occasionally be funny. *What would Haluk do right now?* No, she must stop that. She is strong enough on her own. She doesn't need Haluk.

She pulls tightly at the furs wrapping around her shoulders. She could go inside her tent, where it is much warmer, but the thought of being confined inside seems unbearable. She finds an abandoned fire and takes a seat on a log that was rolled over to it. She absently pokes the fire with a stick as she adds more wood. The smell of the smoke comforts her as she leans forward, huddling into the warmth and closing her eyes. She thinks of her brother now, memories conjured from the quiet, perhaps. She wonders if he ever thinks of her, if he misses her the way she misses him. She can close her eyes and see his face, his crooked smile that would light up a room, his hair, always a bit too long. She can hear his laugh. She inhales deeply trying to calm the emotions stirring at the memories.

The sound of twigs breaking at her left causes her eyes to fly open. It's the quick pace of one of the young scouts, limber as he jumps over fallen trees and ducks under low-hanging branches. He is coming toward camp, and fast. She jumps up and runs to intercept him, scanning the tree line behind him as she moves.

"Here!" she shouts. "I'm here. What is it? What have you seen?"

The scout comes to a stop and takes only the briefest of moments to catch his breath. "A woman, Your Grace. There is a woman on horseback asking to see you. She is alone. She came from the castle though."

"A woman?" Magdalena's mind plays a cruel game for a fraction of a second where it imagines the woman is her mother, or even Astrid. *Impossible.* "Are you sure she is alone? Is she armed?"

"My lady, I sent Leif as fast as he could run around the perimeter of camp. I told him to meet us here. I left the lady with one of the guards."

"Good work, Aric. When the coast is clear, bring her to me." Magdalena offers a pat to the young scout's shoulder. She can feel the excitement radiate off of him. They knew that the deadline day would be marked in some way. It had to be. What role this visiting woman will play is unknown. Magdalena looks to the night sky where not a cloud is present, only the full moon and a blanket of stars. She sees Leif running fast toward them. He gives a swing of his arm in a circle above his head, the signal that the perimeter is clear, and Aric takes off fast to retrieve the visitor. Magdalena moves toward her tent. Pushing the brown flaps of the door aside, Magdalena enters and begins striking the tinderbox to set the candles aflame. She notices her hands are shaking slightly as she holds the licking flame to the wick.

The sound of a man clearing his throat at the tent opening draws her around. There, standing next to him, is a beautiful woman with chestnut curls and skin the color of cinnamon. *Aunt Thea.*

24
Henrick

Henrick once again finds himself seated by the river's edge, alone with his thoughts. The cold wind is blowing down from the mountains, and the river runs as cold as ice. He bends over and places his hands in the cold water, gathering some and bringing it to his lips. The shock of the cold is exhilarating as he swallows.

When he was a boy, he used to love to look for treasure along the river bed. He was certain that the mountain held enormous caves filled with gold and gems and that the river, which snaked its way through the mountains and caves, would, every once in a while, reach out its watery fingers and grab from the cave floor a piece of treasure. This piece would then make its way down the mountain, twisting and turning with each bend, rushing over rocks and tumbling down waterfalls, and perhaps, at that exact moment, it would come swimming by, and all it would take was one lucky boy to be there to grab it. He imagined what it would be like to hold that treasure in his hand knowing that not another man glimpsed it or touched it before. It had been hiding in that cave for as many years as the earth had been created, and he, Henrick, was the first to lay eyes upon it. He had always thrilled at that prospect.

Now even as a grown man, he can't help but look closely at the rushing water or kick the rocks and dirt along the bank, just in case something lies there waiting for him.

Perhaps he will bring his son here one day. The simple thought thrills him. Catrain will certainly put up a fuss about the boy being so near the water, or the wind giving him fever. But Henrick will hold his ground. All little boys deserve great adventures, with the possibility of treasure and the element of danger. And Henrick will be the type of father that gives him just that. They will be the best of friends, and they will spend their days slaying dragons and rescuing damsels in distress. They will spend their evenings curled together in Catrain's arms as she sings them both to sleep, fingers curling in their hair.

For a moment he stops to consider that Thea isn't present in the daydream he has just conjured. He suddenly notices how much this realization pains him. There must be a way for him to have both this and that. Thea and Catrain. A child and a wife. He bends down to the water and looks deep beneath the surface for gold, or answers, or both. With a heavy sigh, he knows he must make his way back to the castle. Looking into the dark water one last time, he smiles at the future he will have on these shores, before turning his back and mounting his horse.

Henrick storms through the main doors shouting for Dagen, Sigmund, Niklaus, and Thea as he goes. He hears a faint response. They are in the great hall. Henrick pushes through the massive carved doors and enters the stately room with its tall windows and glaring portraits. One quick glance, and he can see that Thea is not present.

"Where is my wife?" Henrick snaps.

"I can't find Thea, Your Grace," Dagen replies.

"What do you mean you can't find her?"

As Henrick finishes his question, the doors swing open, and Thea walks into the room. She offers not a greeting as she makes her way purposefully to the oversized fireplace. Her hands are red from cold, and snow has accumulated in the hood of her furs. She slips the heavy black cloaks off and lets them fall to the stone floor with a wet smack.

"Where were you?" Henrick demands.

"I was merely taking a walk."

"In temperatures such as these?"

"Weren't you not just at the river's edge, dear husband? The cold can be therapeutic."

Henrick is annoyed at her tone. Her lips leak mockery with every word. She wants him to beg her to reveal where she has been and with whom. She wants him to feel small and scared and threatened. He will not give her the pleasure.

"Can you two continue your bickering later?" Niklaus asks with a hint of humor. "Tomorrow is a big day for us. Magdalena has already visited More in an attempt to persuade Mikhail to fight on her behalf against us. She has already planted the seed in his mind that all this has been a ruse. The only thing that will hold Mikhail back from believing her is a grand show from the Typhans."

"You are right," Henrick says, eyes still burning into the back of Thea's turned head. "It needs to be big. It needs to be bloody. I think it's time we eliminate another village. Nothing small like Cale this time. I believe we should crush Kaelonoch."

Thea whips around at this declaration, her curls springing out to the sides of her head before bouncing back into place. "You have got to be kidding? You will murder more innocent lives? You can't really expect me to go along with this."

"I don't care what you think anymore, Thea. It has become apparent to me and everyone else in this room that you are too emotionally unstable to participate in this level of governance. The Typhans will attack the largest village in Masunbria. They will slaughter ruthlessly, and it will send a clear message to all the neighboring kingdoms that war has once again come to our land. Their offerings will flood into Masunbria after a show like Kaelonoch. We will grow rich from their fear."

"You are a monster, Henrick. This isn't how it was supposed to go for us."

"There is no us, Thea. I am the lord, and you are merely a lady."

As if his words slapped her, Thea turns on her heels and retreats from the room.

***

"What is wrong with you?" Henrick barks upon his entrance to his den where Sigmund told him Thea sits waiting. He walks purposefully to where she sits, his index finger extended as if an arrow to her heart. "I've had it with you and your moods, Thea."

Thea rises from her chair near the fire and pulls her shawl tighter around her shoulders to combat the change of temperature her movement creates. She walks around the room slowly, biting the lower right portion of her lip as she goes. She reaches the desk that sits in front of the windows overlooking the gardens below. She turns and faces the center of the room and pulls herself up so she is now sitting on the edge of the desk. Henrick, seeing her sit there, has a flash of memory of Catrain on the edge of that very desk while they were entangled together. He shakes his head to remove the memory. Looking back at Thea, he sees her head is cocked to one side and she is studying him. Did she see the flash of memory? Henrick wonders. Impossible, she isn't a mind reader. Thea smiles at him with an unsettling smile that doesn't reach her eyes.

"Catrain," she says, and Henrick's heart thuds in his chest.

"What do you mean Catrain?" he stammers out, trying to control the panic he can hear playing in his voice.

"The wedding will need to be moved up. She is, after all, carrying the heir to the kingdom. Am I correct to assume the child is yours, Henrick?"

Henrick stares at Thea. His mouth opens and then shuts again. He searches his mind for words, but he finds none. He tries again at opening his mouth in hopes that his mind will understand that he intends for a defense or rebuttal to spring forth, but only silence passes his lips. Thea smirks at him from her perch atop the desk. The smile does not stop the tear that fills her eye and begins to trace its way down her cheek. That single tear is soon joined by another and then another. Her face is controlled into a look of disgust and resignation, but she can't mask the tears as they fall from her jaw and into her lap.

"She did it then. I wasn't sure exactly, but your silence has confirmed it. She did what I couldn't do and will be giving you the child you have dreamed of for years."

Fear courses through Henrick's body as he looks upon the heartbreak evident in his wife's face. He was foolish to not think about how Thea would be hurt if she was to discover that Catrain has conceived his child. He was so lost in the idea, in the dream of it all. Last night she gave him such a gift when she confirmed that the seed was planted and was growing strong in her womb. He had such protectiveness and such pride over a stomach that still remained flat as ever but inside held a treasure more precious to him than any kingdom or gold. He felt such joy that he didn't consider how this would destroy Thea.

He knows now, though, that he can't lose her. Thea has been his love for so many years and is the only person in this world who fully understands him. He has torn Thea apart in his quest for a child, and she will watch Catrain's stomach grow with life, and as it does, Thea will begin to die.

"No, Thea, that is not the outcome. Catrain will be giving you the child you have dreamed about for years. She means nothing. She was only to be the one to carry our child, mine and yours, into this world, and then you, my wife, will be the one to raise that child as your own. You will be his mother, and Catrain will not have survived the birth. Don't you see, Thea? It was always going to be for you. This child will be yours. I did this for you, my love." Henrick snaps his mouth shut, having realized he might have taken that last statement a little too far.

Thea makes not a sound as the silent tears rain into her lap. She slowly brings a hand up and places it on her lower stomach, fingers spread over the area designed to grow with child. Henrick rises from his seat and makes his way to Thea. He grasps her face in his hands and gently lifts it to look into her eyes. She hesitates slightly at the gesture, but eventually she meets his gaze.

"My Thea, you are my only love. You forever have been and forever will be. You, my sweet wife, deserve a child. I have seen it, Thea. You will hold a babe in your arms and rock it to sleep. That child will grow and call you Mother. I know I should have told you of my plans with Catrain, of my intention to have her bear our child, but I wasn't sure it would even work. I didn't want to get your hopes up. Now that it has, though, now that our child has been conceived, we must protect the baby that will soon be ours. We must ensure this child survives, because we will not get another chance."

Thea pushes Henrick away and hops off the edge of the desk. She begins to pace the room and wipes at the tears on her face with violence at their betrayal. Finally, she speaks. "You have always thought you were smarter than me, Henrick. You have doubted not only my intelligence but my fortitude as well. You have made grave errors in judgment, dear husband." An unsettling smile spreads across her face as she turns to face Henrick. "I made you. I pulled you up from the dirt in Rekabia. I washed your face and bandaged your wounds, and I gave you a will to live and to fight. This is how you repay me? Well, dear husband, just as I made you, I can certainly break you." Thea walks from the room, head held high. Henrick notices his hands are shaking as he turns to stare out the open door after her. Henrick stays in the room only a moment before the fear of what Thea is planning courses through his body and surges him to action. He takes off down the corridor after her.

He rounds the corner and hears the scream before he can reach the dining hall. As he enters, he sees Thea standing near Catrain, who holds her cheek in pain, the red print of a palm visible under her pale fingers.

"Aunt Thea! What is the meaning of this?" Niklaus yells as he wraps a protective arm around his betrothed's shaking shoulders.

Henrick comes to an abrupt stop. Dagen looks to Henrick, confusion and worry playing across his scarred face.

"Catrain is with child, Niklaus." Thea's voice is shaking with a mix of rage and sorrow.

"That's what this is about?" Niklaus lets out a short laugh. "Aunt, though it is none of your business what Catrain and I do or, shall I say, have done, prior to our wedding night, I can assure you that the news you have presented has only come as a great joy for me to hear, if you understand what I am discreetly trying to say."

"Is that so, Niklaus? You believe that the child she carries is yours? It is hard to say, I must admit, whose child it is, with both yourself and my husband sleeping with her at the same time. Oh, Niklaus, I can tell by your face you didn't know Henrick and Catrain have been having an affair. Well, I wasn't certain either. That was until I began to live in the shadows. My, my, my, Niklaus, what wonderous things you can see when you live in the dark. My husband and Catrain have been entangled in just about every room of this castle. Even, to my horror, they lay together in the spot where your dear Sabina died."

Catrain's eyes are wild with fear. Henrick's face burns red and hot.

"You little whore," Thea continues. "I took you in. I brought you up in this world. It was my plan to crown you queen. This, this is how you repay me? You sleep with my husband and bear his child that I never could conceive? Was it not enough for you to be queen when it so clearly should be me who wears the crown, but you also had to get pregnant? You held my hand, Catrain, when I cried over the empty womb that every month I discovered I had. Why would you do this to me? I couldn't have a child, but I had a husband, and we were happy. That was all I had. You, a girl born from nothing, now has a crown, a kingdom, and a child that should have been mine." Tears are falling from Thea's eyes, and her words are no longer angry but full of years of sorrow spilling out over the table.

Niklaus rises then, and in one swift motion, he is around the edge of the table and upon Henrick. Henrick is too stunned to react, and Niklaus lands a punch square in the jaw. Henrick falls back, knocking a vacant seat over and crashing to the floor. Niklaus is on top of him in a moment, punching at his face. Dagen is there and pulling hard at Niklaus to get him off of Henrick, but the rage coursing through Niklaus makes Dagen no match for him. Henrick, having been shocked by the initial blows, finally regains control and begins defending his face with one forearm while pushing Niklaus's face with his other. The upward movement of Niklaus's forehead by Henrick's free arm is just what Dagen needs to slip his own arm around his neck and tighten his grip in an attempt to choke Niklaus off of Henrick. Niklaus continues to land blow after blow to his uncle's face, arms, and shoulders until finally, the air having been choked from his lungs, he is forced to back up into Dagen. Dagen keeps hold of Niklaus but loosens his forearm at his throat, and Niklaus takes a long gasp of air. Henrick crawls to his feet, and just as Niklaus takes that first large inhale, Henrick draws back and punches him square in the nose. Blood spurts out and across the stone floor. Catrain screams.

Niklaus forces himself to rise, pushing Dagen off of him. Henrick stumbles to his feet as well, and the two men glare at each other, their breath coming fast and sharp.

"I will kill you, Uncle. I am king, and I will see you hang for what you have done. Catrain, don't you worry, you will be next to Henrick swinging from your own rope." Niklaus spits a mouthful of blood in Henrick's face and, turning, pushes Dagen aside and storms from the room. Dagen follows after Niklaus, afraid perhaps that Niklaus is in search of a weapon to make good on his promise.

Henrick wipes the blood-stained spit from his face with the back of his sleeve and turns to glare at the remaining occupants. Catrain is sobbing long, pitiful sobs, having melted to the floor in a pile of fabric. Thea stands stock still staring down at her hands folded in front of her. It is only Henrick that remains, and with him, the two women he loves and a river of despair between them.

25
Magdalena

Magdalena sits at the head of the table within her tent. She is surrounded by men all talking at once. It has been fourteen days since she watched her parents' bodies become engulfed in flames, fourteen days since her home was threatened by Henrick's men disguised as Typhans. In the past fourteen days her people have known nothing but fear—fear of the pending attack that was promised, fear of the increased taxation and the consequences of unpayment, fear of survival if all they own is given to the castle under the guise of sworn protection. For fourteen days Magdalena has feared what this day will bring. Though her army is proof enough that Warrick's assertion that the Typhans aren't coming is being believed, there are still thousands of Masunbrian citizens pouring all they have into Niklaus's coffers. Those sitting at this table know that he will go to extremes to ensure that the goods and funds don't stop flowing.

Brom and Warrick have been training with the men all morning. Magdalena has sent her scouts scurrying through the forest, looking for any signs that Henrick's men are on the move. They have come back with nothing, time and time again. The guards have been increased and a defensive permitter set around the camp. Aunt Thea promised that Henrick wouldn't let the day end in peace. She came to seek an alliance in exchange for freedom and immunity. She would serve as their eyes and ears inside the castle walls, and when the time came, she would make sure they had a way in. She departed the camp with a promise to return as soon as she had credible information on Henrick's next move.

"My lady, your men are in good spirits on this cold day. They are ready both physically and mentally for whatever the day will bring," Brom says confidently.

Magdalena looks up from her map to respond to her dear friend, when she suddenly is stopped before she can speak. She can see over Brom's shoulder, through the open tent flap, a guard coming fast with Aunt Thea, skirts gathered in her fists, struggling to keep up behind him. Even from this distance Magdalena can see the look of devastation on Thea's face. *Niklaus. Something has happened to him.* Magdalena can feel her pulse drum in her neck as terrible images of her little brother's bloodied face flood her imagination.

"Magdalena, what is it?" Worry etches Willem's voice, and he gently shakes her arm.

Ignoring him, Magdalena rises and begins to jog, then run, for the guard and Thea. Reaching Thea, her aunt collapses breathlessly in Magdalena's arms.

"Kaelonoch," Thea croaks out between gasps. "I tried . . ." she breathes ". . . to . . . stop him. I told him he was a monster. Then I tried to distract him with his own mess of a life. I wasn't successful." Tears begin to course down Thea's face as she sinks to the ground.

Fear spreads through Magdalena's veins. She turns and yells to Willem and Brom, who are running in her direction. "Gather our men; we ride to Kaelonoch." Panic drips from her words.

The two men turn and begin shouting orders to the men. Magdalena runs into her tent to gather her things. Her heart is racing, and so is her mind. She grabs at what she can find and runs back out into the cold. She stops abruptly. There is shouting and running, and the camp vibrates with a collective fear and adrenaline that makes the hair on her neck stand up. She runs behind her tent and loosens the reins on her horse and pulls herself up. Steering the horse toward the clearing, she gives a quick snap of the rein as she and the horse join the men running for the same spot. The woods here are thick, and it makes for slow travel by horseback. Beyond the clearing is a small trail. Her horse can make it to Kaelonoch quickly once she reaches the path.

She clears the trees and sees Willem, Warrick, and Brom on horseback gathering men into their formations. She rides up to the front and steadies her horse. She flexes her hands, taking them from the reins one at a time, trying to bring some blood back to them. In her haste, she left her tent without gloves, and now the damp wind is stiffening and stinging against the ever-reddening skin of her hands. She watches as the men move into position, eyes focused intently toward the town many of them call home. Seeing their faces, their worry, she begins to panic. Perhaps there is nothing amiss in Kaelonoch. Perhaps Thea was sent by her uncle and this is all a ruse. Or, she now feels the panic growing, is this actually a trap? Has her uncle stationed men to ambush her forces as they move to Kaelonoch? How does she know Thea can be trusted? How could she not think of that? Thea was sent here yesterday to gain Magdalena's trust, and today to lead her and her men to their death. *A siren.* Panic climbs its way up her throat. She looks around for Willem, Brom, and Warrick to ensure they are preoccupied, and then she slowly begins to back her horse away so as to not draw attention. Her mouth has gone dry. Her breathing is coming sporadically now as if she can't pull enough air to fill her lungs. She slowly steers her horse toward the opening of the trail that will lead her to Kaelonoch. She has to know. She has to find out before she gets anyone killed. She has to see if her uncle is waiting ahead.

Spurring her horse hard in its side, she takes off down the trail, hair whipping her face at the speed. Every bend in the tree line, every turn of the trail, she holds her breath, waiting to see what will be on the other side. But turn after turn, there is nothing. Only the sound of her horse's heavy breath and the beating of his hooves on the trail below. She can see ahead where the path expands. She is nearing town now. She strains her ears for sounds of screams but hears nothing except the heartbeat in her own ears.

Breaching the opening, she brings her horse to a sudden stop. She raises her hand to her mouth to stifle her scream as she scrambles down and draws her sword. There, before her, is the body of a young woman. Magdalena slowly and quietly approaches her. She is lying face up with a discarded basket near her that has been tipped to reveal a mess of broken eggs. Her brown eyes stare blankly at the sky above, and a pool of blood encircles her like a halo in the dirt. Magdalena reaches a shaking hand out and places it on the girl's cheek. Her skin is cold and soft under her palm. Tears begin to fall from Magdalena's eyes and land upon the face of the girl below her. She forces herself to rise, to walk further into town. Breaking free from the buildings that were sheltering her view, she can now see the bodies littered everywhere. She must cover her mouth as screams of terror threaten to escape. All that was left in the town were the elderly, women, and children. Now, it is their bodies that are spread along the dirt road.

Her mind refuses to process what she sees as she continues to walk. There is so much blood, arms and legs twisted garishly underneath bodies, pieces of their lives scattered around their heads. She comes across a young boy and recognizes him instantly. This is Jonan's youngest son. He wasn't yet four years old. He is grasping a small doll that looks like a dog under his arm. She falls to her knees in front of him and pushes back his dirty hair to place her lips upon his sweet head. Her tears soak his skin, and she thinks of the fear he must have felt. She imagines him calling out for his mother. Did he watch her die before him? Did he even understand what was happening to him? She picks him up and cradles him in her arms, planting kisses on his face. She tells him that his daddy loved him and that he wanted so badly to protect him.

A noise behind her tells her that her men have arrived. She can hear them running and screaming, calling out names, before she even turns to see them. Magdalena stands, cradling the boy, and turns to face them. It is chaos on the streets. Jonan spots her. He freezes in place as his face twists with agony. She walks slowly forward, cradling the boy gently as she goes. Jonan is shaking his head violently side to side, trying to deny what his eyes are seeing. Reaching him, she places the child in his arms and chokes on her own tears as she watches the kind man standing before her die inside.

When men cry, it is with such a sound of loss and despair and anguish that it sounds more like that of an animal than a human. Their screams are guttural. Fists hit dirt. She watches them, her hands covered in blood. She watches them pick up their children and crush their little bodies to their chests. She sees them kiss their small faces. She doesn't look away as they run their hands through their wives' blood-stained hair and kiss their cold lips once more. The sound of her men crying is like a thousand drums beating all at once. It vibrates through her chest and seems to crush her heart with its echoes. She watches as her men stumble in a sea of the blood of those they were fighting to protect. She realizes now that this was her uncle's plan. He knew the men didn't fight for her but that they fought for them, their families. Her uncle had decided it was easier to eliminate the very thing that her men cared enough about to go to war over rather than fight her men head-on in battle. Why risk his own men when he could kill hers just by killing their reason to live and to fight?

Magdalena closes her eyes. The sound of the men screaming and wailing, the smell of the blood and the dirt, it is all too much. She can't think. The only word that comes to her mind and escapes her lips is, "Please." That one word, though, evokes all the emotion she is feeling. It is the begging of relief for her men. It is a plea for understanding as to why this occurred. It is a hopeful wish that all this is a dream. It is desperation. It is sorrow. It is futile. Brom is there now, shaking her shoulders and yelling into her face. She can't understand him. The noise is so loud around her and within her. He is pointing now, trying to get her to move. He grabs her elbow and drags her to his horse, where he shoves her up before he mounts. He looks as if he is about to vomit, and he rides away. She looks back at her men. She looks back at the destruction. She closes her eyes then and buries her head into Brom's back as he rides as fast as his horse will carry them out of town.

They arrive at the little path that leads to the farmhouse. Magdalena doesn't wait for Brom to stop. Once he has slowed enough, she scrambles free from the horse and begins to run. She rounds the line of trees that shield the home from the harsh winter winds and comes to an abrupt stop. There, in the large tree that shades the front, are the bodies of Hagen and Sybbyl. They swing freely from a branch, rope tied around their necks. Sybbyl has lost a shoe, and her stocking foot dangles in the breeze.

Magdalena crumbles to the ground at the base of the tree. Tears stream down her face as she extends a shaking hand to retrieve Sybbyl's shoe. She holds it to her chest as she turns her eyes upward. Could she have prevented all of this? If she had just turned herself in, just done as they asked, she could have stopped this from happening. It hits her then, like a punch to her stomach. *Their blood is on my hands. All of it.* She sees that the ugliness inside her, her selfishness, has killed the people of Masunbria. Had she fought her parents and chosen the hard right over the easy wrong, she would have walked through the gate and into those mountains as a child bride. Even at twelve, she should have known better. Most certainly, though, given a chance to do the right thing at twenty, she should have taken it. When Henrick and Niklaus gave her a second chance to save her people, she should have gone. All of this could have been avoided. She has ruined not just the lives of men, but generations of families are gone as well. Children who had an entire future written in the stars are now gone. Her selfishness has killed them all.

Warrick is there now; he is squatting next to her. She hadn't heard him approach. He keeps repeating Liri's name over and over again, and it takes Magdalena a moment to realize it is a question. He is looking for Liri. She turns her head toward the house and hears Brom screaming Liri's name, his throat choked with fear.

"Mags, da ya know where she'd hide?" Warrick is pleading with her to focus.

"The cellar," she mutters in response. Shaking, he pulls her to her feet, and together they take off running for the house. Liri has to have made it, she pleads. She pushes through the front door. Her nose is assaulted with the smell of herbs and yeast, the smell of Sybbyl. It nearly chokes her as the memories flood her vision. She holds back the rising bile that threatens to escape her throat and runs to the cellar opening. She lifts the heavy door in the floor and strains her ears to hear. Nothing. She calls out for Liri. Nothing. She quickly scampers down the stairs and into the dark. She screams Liri's name as she waves her hands blindly in front of her. Her mind thinks for a moment that Liri isn't here, that she has been captured. Tears stream down her face as she takes another step into the dark cellar, and then another. *Someone has to have survived*, she begs. *They have to.* She begins to feel around, looking for the hiding space that she and Liri huddled in once before. Her foot lands on glass, and she hears the crunch as her boot crushes it to pieces. She takes another step and trips. More glass. More pitchers. Her shin hits hard against a shelved rack that once stood against the wall and has now fallen over, its contents scattered and broken across the dirt floor. She feels between the tangles of wood and glass, and her hand lands on a shoe. She splays her fingers to find an ankle and then a calf. It's Liri. She screams for Warrick, and he stumbles from the opposite side of the cellar, bumping and tripping as he makes his way to her in the dark. Liri is trapped under the heavy rack.

"Help me, Warrick," Magdalena pleads.

The two grasp the wood unit and begin to pull. The wood cuts into her palms, and her arms shake with the weight. *We aren't going to be able to lift it.* If they drop it now, it will surely crush Liri. Suddenly, the unit begins to rise higher. Brom is at their side and is straining with all his might to help push the shelves back to their upright position. With one last grunt, Liri is free. Brom brings her into his arms and makes his way up the stairs, where he lays her on the rug in front of the cold fireplace hearth. In the light of day cast from the windows in the room, Magdalena can see the large gash on Liri's forehead and the blood that has stained her face and neck. Brom raises his shaking hands to Liri's face and places them gently on her cheeks. Magdalena tilts her head down so her ear is next to her sweet friend's nose. She holds her breath and prays for the sound of air. Nothing. She closes her eyes and waits.

She feels it rather than hears it. Her white-blonde hair blows just slightly enough to tickle her cheek as Liri breathes the tiniest breaths of life. Magdalena smiles and places her head on Liri's chest, where she cries long sobs of relief.

***

They bury Hagen and Sybbyl as the sun begins its evening descent over the fields of the farmhouse. The golden glow of dusk casts beams that reflect off the freshly fallen snow. Standing at the graveside, Magdalena looks about and sees that the snow has covered the frozen mud, and with it, it has erased any footprints on the earth that belonged to Hagen or Sybbyl. It is as if the farm has been wiped clean of their presence. Gone is the proof of the years Hagen spent walking the farm, tending to his cattle. Erased are the footprints of Sybbyl as she tended her chickens or planted her herbs. The snow has covered them all, filled in all the cracks of their lives. Magdalena wants to push it away, reveal that their existence is still stamped on this earth in the form of a boot print. Nature is quick to move on. It doesn't mourn.

She watches the men lower their bodies down into a single grave they dug. Side by side, they will lie under the earth. Once it is over, they make their way slowly and silently back to camp, unsure what they will find there.

26

Henrick

Henrick's orders were carried out, and the people of Kaelonoch were extinguished. Henrick decided he would not accompany Dagen to witness the destruction. Instead, he sat once more in his den and penned letters to neighboring kingdoms, urging them to see the seriousness of Masunbria's plight. The letters were sent with his fastest horses and, most likely, reached the border before the first sword was even raised in the village. Upon Dagen's return, he sent one of his soldiers to deliver a single piece of parchment to Henrick. On it, Dagen wrote, "It is done. Hardly any men of fighting age remained in the town. She must have them with her." Henrick crumpled the paper and threw it into the hearth. He stood watching the flames taste the paper at first, lick it with its tongue of orangish red, before its hot blue teeth engulfed the scribbled words greedily.

Walking the halls, Henrick can feel the loneliness that is being excreted by the walls of the damp, dark castle. Thea has once again sequestered herself in her study. Sigmund is his only tie to Thea now, and the old man is seen sneaking into and out of the room, offering nothing to Henrick but a sad shake of his old head.

Catrain has locked herself in her own room, and no matter how many times Henrick scratches at her door or whispers through the crack at the hinge, she will not respond. Servants seem to scatter in his presence, and the only company he has is the sound of his boots echoing across the stone floor. *I need a drink.*

In an attempt to avoid accidentally bumping into Niklaus, Henrick decides to sneak down the servants' stairs in pursuit of the warm, numbing effects of a good red wine. Landing off the last stone step with a thud into the warm heat of the kitchen, he is surprised to see Dagen sitting there alone, on a stool, at the large wood slab the kitchen maids use to prepare their meals and cut their potatoes. He has a large wood bowl of soup in front of him, and his spoon has temporarily been halted midway from mouth to bowl. *Does he always eat in here with the servants?* Henrick wonders. He knows, of course, that Dagen has taken many meals at his side upstairs, but he supposes that was only when a formal request was extended for his presence. When that request didn't come, did Dagen sit down here? *How fascinating.*

"Hello, Dagen. It seems we are men that must fend for ourselves. I have come to find some wine." Henrick notices that, even to his own ears, his voice sounds awkward. His words sound more like an apology than a statement of fact. It is as if by stumbling onto Dagen eating like a servant, he has now seen something that Dagen himself would prefer to remain unseen. It is like Henrick has walked in on Dagen naked rather than eating soup. Possibly Dagen would have preferred to be seen in all his glory rather than be seen like a servant. Dagen continues to stare at Henrick, no expression visible on his tired face. *Awkward indeed*, Henrick thinks.

Henrick moves fully into the warm, dimly lit kitchen and begins opening and closing the wood cupboards both high and low, realizing how much noise he is making with every creak of the wood against hinge. He checks shelves lined with jars of herbs, buckets full of dirty potatoes, canisters with cream, boxes with eggs nestled in straw. He finds no wine but succeeds in making himself look like a fool. After checking everywhere imaginable, Henrick stands in the center of the room and lets out a long breath. He doesn't look at Dagen, just above and around him, unsure where his eyes should land but certain that they should avoid the naked man at all costs. He sighs audibly again.

Dagen rises from his spot and crosses the room to a small wooden door that Henrick didn't notice. He pulls it open and, crouching due to the miniscule size of the opening, disappears inside. He returns rather quickly with a bottle of wine and places it on the table, wordlessly. *It's a magic room*, thinks Henrick in astonishment. Dagen pivots again and moves to an upper shelf to pull down two glasses. He uses the bottom edge of his black tunic to wipe the dust from their insides before placing them both on the table. Uncorking the wine, he pours a generous amount of the ruby liquid into each glass. He sits one in front of his bowl and reaches out a hand to Henrick with the other. Henrick hesitates slightly and then crosses the room and takes the glass from Dagen.

"Thank you, Dagen." Henrick takes a long drink to avoid saying more words.

"Would you like some soup?"

Henrick looks up at him, surprised by the question. It does smell wonderful, though, and he is hungry. He nods his head. Dagen moves to the large pot in the fire and grabs a bowl off a nearby shelf and fills it using a large metal ladle. He returns with the soup and motions for Henrick to sit across from him. Henrick obeys. The soup is good. There is chicken floating in a golden broth with celery, carrots, and chunks of potato. The top layer glints from the fat of the chicken in the candlelight. It is a simple dish, nothing that would be served to him or the household, but he can tell that it is a soup that would provide his staff with ample energy to perform their daily tasks. They eat in silence.

"Do you want to know about Kaelonoch?" Dagen asks without looking up from his soup.

"Not really. Do you want to talk about it?" Henrick asks.

"Not really," Dagen admits.

Henrick thinks that now would be a good time to assure his friend that he is fighting a noble fight, that the deaths were just. Unfortunately, Henrick can't seem to find the words. The sound of metal clanging down the servants' stairs releases the moment from its uncomfortable grip. The reprieve is only momentary, though, as the clanging noise belongs to Samalt, of all people.

"Oh, umm, Your Grace." Samalt smooths his black hair flat against his head before bowing to Henrick. Rising, he continues to pet himself as he smiles at them both.

"What is it, Samalt?" Dagen asks at last.

"Well, um, I have some rather unfortunate news."

"Go on," Dagen urges while looking sideways at Henrick.

"The man we sent to the kingdom of Ezers with the missive has returned."

"That was always the plan." Dagen's tone is full of annoyance.

"Right you are, sir. The plan, though, I don't believe, included the king of Ezers accompanying the man back to Masunbria."

"Wait." Henrick furrows his brow as he stares at Samalt. The soup begins to sour in his stomach. "What are you saying exactly?"

"King Alden is waiting for you upstairs, my lord."

"What?" Henrick snaps. His eyes go large in his head. *The king of Ezers has come to Masunbria?* The thought of Henrick's nemesis sends bile to rise in his throat. It has been years since he has looked upon the man. Handsome and arrogant. A flirt with women and ruthless with men. Alden is well known as a troublemaker of a man who takes much joy in causing mischief.

"Does he have an army with him?" Dagen asks.

"Just a small accompaniment," Samalt replies.

"I doubt that," Henrick growls. Samalt may have only seen a small band of soldiers, but if Henrick knows Alden, the man has filled Masunbria with spies. His people adore him, and they show their favor by fiercely protecting him at all costs. Abandoning his soup, Henrick takes the stairs two at a time with Dagen fast behind him. Rounding the corner and into the great room, he spots Niklaus sitting with the king of games himself, the mischief maker. They both hold goblets of wine in hand. Henrick hasn't seen Niklaus since Thea's revelation in the dining hall last night and Niklaus's subsequent threat on Henrick's life. Both men's eyes wordlessly follow Henrick as he walks to the credenza under the guise of filling a goblet with wine. He stares at the glass bottles before him, hoping that it appears he is trying to make a selection, when in reality he is working to get his heart rate calmed and his mind clear. At last, he chooses a bottle and fills his glass, noticing for a moment how his hands shake as he does so. Turning, he surveys the pair. They are both looking up at him expectantly from their velvet settees.

Alden is dressed entirely in black with the exception of the pin at his breast, which is of a blue fish, body snaked in an arch with scales of gemstone that glitter and reflect the light of the candles and hearth. His crest. His brilliant blue eyes seem to match the belly of the fish. Alden rubs a palm over his whiskered jaw as he studies Henrick. Alden looks effortlessly regal in the way he is dressed, and it is a stark contrast to the simple brown trousers, blue shirt, and dirt-covered brown furs Henrick stands before him donning. Rubbing a hand through his hair to slick it back, Henrick attempts to stand a little taller. He moves to take up a chair amongst the cluster of various settees and highbacked chairs that are arranged for entertaining in this corner of the room. He leans back and spreads his arms a bit wider than comfortable on the armrests. He tries to broaden his chest, take up space.

"Alden, it's been a while," Henrick offers at last in greeting.

"We have met before?" Alden replies, a look of confusion crossing his face.

Henrick feels the blood begin to boil in his veins. Of course they've met before, and Alden knows that. This is just another one of his games, a way to make Henrick feel like a fool. *Well, not today, Alden.*

"No, Alden, you are right. It must be my mistake. I know what it is—" Henrick holds a finger up as if an idea has just come to him "—you have one of those faces; you know, ordinary faces, ones that look like everyone else's. I am sure I saw someone like you on my travels, perhaps a guard I encountered, or a merchant, or a servant wiping up shit."

"Right. That must be it." Alden smiles ruefully. "I was just talking to your nephew here about this mess you've gotten yourselves into with the Typhans. Your letter says you were once again attacked this very morning. Now, according to Mikhail, this entire Typhan problem is a farce. He states that you have stolen from More, Skogen, Rekabia, and Ezers."

"Mikhail is delusional. Haluk, as you have come to realize, is a woman, Magdalena. She went to More to seek an army to overthrow Niklaus, the rightful heir to Masunbria. Before leaving for the coast, she found some tall, muscled, barbaric-looking man and brought him to More to trick Mikhail into thinking he was a Typhan. Magdalena is good at deception. Her surviving twenty years as a man is proof of that."

"Mikhail seems rather convinced."

"Tell me, Alden, who do you believe should be ruling Masunbria? Niklaus here, or the first-born child?"

"Without a doubt, Niklaus."

"My point exactly. Can you imagine losing an entire kingdom in the blink of an eye? She is determined to ruin Niklaus's good name. She is vengeful and would rather bring war to this land with the Typhans than do the honorable thing and go with them. She is also desperate and manipulative. It doesn't surprise me that

Mikhail bought her story. He is an idiot. You, however, are not. The Typhans are real, and they are here in Masunbria. None of us are safe. Why do you think my wife isn't here with us? I have ordered her to be locked in her rooms with a member of my trusted council. Niklaus has ordered the same with his betrothed. You've taken a great risk to come here under these circumstances, and I think it best you return home as quickly as you can."

Alden looks curiously at Henrick, a small smile playing on his lips. He chuckles lightly and lifts his wine in a slight toast to Henrick before swallowing the entire glass in one long gulp. There is something not right about him, Henrick thinks. It is as if this man is playing a game that Henrick doesn't even know the rules to.

"Where is she?" Alden turns to ask Niklaus.

"Maggie? She is in the forest, or so we assume. Our men are searching, but the forests of Masunbria are vast, as you must know."

"What will you do when she is returned to you?" Alden looks at both now as he poses this question.

"She will be given to the Typhans just as she should have been eight years ago." Henrick sighs. "Alden, we are doing what we can to recover from my brother's mistakes. Why are you here exactly?" Henrick does nothing to hide the anger rising within him. "Would you like to go to Kaelonoch and see for yourself what these barbarians are capable of? Masunbria protects Ezers from these beasts, and you dare come to my door with accusations? After we have lost so many today and in the days that have preceded? Go home, Alden." Henrick sneers at the man before him.

"Once my property is returned to me, I will go," Alden remarks.

"Your offerings have been given already to the Typhans to try to buy us time. My uncle tells the truth. This threat is real, and we are doing all we can to protect the treaty," Niklaus says.

"Not the offerings. I am here for my sister. It wasn't your letter, Henrick, that brought me here today. It was the second letter that accompanied it."

Henrick and Niklaus look to one another, confusion playing on both their faces. *Sister?* Before a word of question can be spoken, the thick doors to the great room are opened, and a guard enters first, shield held loosely at his side, but the arched blue fish painted on it still visible. Behind him, Catrain.

"Ah, there she is." Alden smiles and rises to cross the room. Catrain holds out her arms, and the two embrace, Alden lifting her slightly off her feet.

"Oh, thank goodness you have come, Brother. I have missed you so." Catrain plants a kiss on Alden's cheek. Henrick stares at the scene before him. He looks between the two, and he can see it so clearly now. How did he miss it before? The same eyes, the same dark hair, even their face shape is similar.

Niklaus finds his words first and jumps to his feet before shouting, "What is the meaning of this? She is a servant in this house. She is my betrothed."

Alden smiles at Niklaus as if he is a small, innocent child. "Niklaus, do you think your parents were the only ones in the land

298

to try to keep their daughters from going into the mountains? The only difference between you and me is that I was born first and, regretfully, my mother's second child died before taking her first breath. Or so we told everyone. In reality, I have kept my dear baby sister safe all these years."

Henrick can't seem to get air to fill his lungs. His head seems to be spinning as he tries desperately to process the words Alden has just spoken. He stares at Catrain in confusion, and he sees the look of pity cross her pretty features.

Niklaus stutters to begin speaking once more, starting and stopping his words before he is finally able to spit out, "Why were you serving my uncle if you are a princess of Ezers? Why were you in Masunbria at all?"

"A brother does what he can to ensure not just the safety of his sister but also that her life means something. At first it was Henrick and securing a place in his household and then in his bed. Once the seizure came, however, Catrain and I knew that there was a very real possibility she could be crowned queen and not just mistress to the king's brother. So we shifted our approach. Since arriving in Masunbria, Catrain has been busy planting seeds throughout the land, and we waited to see which ones would bear fruit." At this statement, Alden spreads his hands in front of him as if to say, "Simple as that." "After the scene last night, though, Catrain wisely realized her time in Masunbria must come to an end. So she sent for me to come and bring her home. Of course I would come to her rescue."

"You always do, dear brother." Catrain smiles at Alden and links her arm in his.

"My child? Catrain? You can't leave. You are with child. Have you not told Alden that fact? What could he possibly do with an unwed pregnant sister?" Henrick stammers out at last.

Catrain cocks her head to one side and lets her bottom lip stick out further than her top in a soft, sad look. Alden stifles a laugh by bringing his hand to his mouth to clear his throat. Henrick sees it then. The lie. He feels as if he will be sick. There never was a child.

27

Magdalena

Liri is with them. Brom holds her in his lap as he maneuvers his horse through the thick forest toward the camp. Her head rests on his shoulder, bobbing slightly with the motion of the horse. She has done little but sleep. She awakened once for just long enough to ask about Hagen and Sybbyl. That news tore her open, and she fell back into her motionless sleep. Warrick and Willem ride silently alongside Magdalena. The quiet between her small procession feels soaked in loss and disbelief. The sounds are of the twigs snapping below horse hooves and the wind blowing through branches above, causing them to creak as they shake. Their small band nears the clearing in the forest. They are almost to the camp now. *What will I find once there? Emptiness?* She really can't blame the men for abandoning the cause, not after what just happened. They have lost their wives, their children, their parents, their sisters.

As they pierce through the last row of trees, a glob of snow drops onto her fur hood as she ducks under a low-hanging branch. Shaking her head free, she looks before her, and she can see the rows of tents silently standing. The makeshift tables and stools for eating together are now covered in snow. There is no smoke, no sign of fire or of life, just rows of brown fabric flapping in the wind and scattered pieces of a man's life littering the snow-fallen ground. A rustle of one of the tents draws Magdalena's attention. There before her stands a small girl, probably eight years old. She has a curious expression on her face. She can't be real, Magdalena thinks. She isn't dressed warm enough for the winter day, but she isn't shivering either. Magdalena wonders for a moment if the girl is a ghost, a child lost in Kaelonoch whose soul has come to look for the one responsible.

Suddenly a man emerges from the tent and jogs toward the girl. He touches her shoulders gently. Magdalena can't hear him but sees him gently reprimand the child as he brings her back toward the tent. Magdalena stops her horse and dismounts. She walks in a daze toward the man and child. Her mouth is slack, and her eyes are unmoving. She feels as though she is in a trance. She is walking to meet her fate. Either there will be men or ghosts before her. Either way, she won't make it out alive, she thinks.

She arrives at the first tent, the one with the man and child who now stand outside the fabric flap of a door, waiting for her. The small girl curtsies, and the man gives a slight bow. His eyes meet hers. They are full of sorrow and exhaustion. His face is pale, and his skin is so thin it appears translucent.

Magdalena stares.

"My lady," the man says. It comes out as more of a question than a statement. "My lady, this is my daughter, Helena. She is . . . she is what remains of my family now. She has no one else, and I didn't know where to take her." There is a catch in the man's voice as if he is trying to dam back a great flood of emotion and heartache.

Magdalena nods.

"Hello, my lady. I am pleased to meet you," says the girl in a small voice.

Magdalena closes her eyes to fight back the tears that threaten to escape at the girl's unwarranted kindness. When she opens them once again, the man is looking at her expectantly, hopefully.

Magdalena crouches down in the snow so she is eye to eye with little Helena. She reaches out and takes both of the girls' cold hands into her own.

"I am very happy to have you here, Helena. You are a brave warrior. Why don't you come to my tent later when your father says it is okay, and I will get you some furs to keep warm with?"

The little girl nods excitedly. Magdalena can see that she, too, has the same dark circles under her eyes and tears puddled within as her father does. The tears don't fall free; they just envelope her eyes like a glass dome as if they will now forever be part of the girl's appearance.

"Thank you, my lady," the man whispers. Magdalena hates him for it. She motions for Willem, who is at her side before she can even finish her summons. She turns and begins to walk into the camp and hears behind her the sounds of Willem embracing the man and the man letting out a short sob into what sounds like the shoulder of his commander. She walks away from the intimacy.

The noise of their arrival acts as a bell or beating drum. Suddenly, tent flaps begin to flip up. One by one, their fabric doors open. Men emerge from them and make their way silently to the place where the snow-covered tables and log stools stand in neat rows, to the place where Magdalena stands. They aren't alone, these men. Some come from their tents with a child, just like Helena, others with what could be a wife or sister. Some bring with them to the row of tables an elderly man or woman. There are survivors other than Helena, Magdalena realizes as she looks from person to person.

The more motion and noise that is made, the more tent flaps that are moved open, and the more people silently walk toward her. Her men have returned. Their hearts are broken and battered, but they are here. What's more, they have brought with them survivors. She didn't assume anyone survived the attacks in Kaelonoch. In the chaos and bloodshed, her mind wasn't able to grasp that as even a possibility, but here they are. Tears fall from Magdalena's eyes as she watches the families take seats around the constructed dining hall.

The men offer the stools to the survivors of the attacks, while they stand behind them. Some place their hands gently on cold and bony shoulders. Brom walks past where Magdalena stands, carrying Liri, and an elderly man hops up to offer him the stool, which Brom gladly takes, balancing the weight of Liri on his lap. Warrick, too, moves past her and embraces a man standing alone in the back of the row of tables. Warrick slaps his back and pulls him in, and Magdalena can see the quivering of the man's shoulders as he returns Warrick's embrace. Magdalena doesn't wipe away the tears that fall. Willem is last to arrive with Helena and her father. They, too, move to join the crowd. It is only

Magdalena that stands before them. As Haluk, she addressed legions of men, masses of civilians. Haluk had perfect, practiced words—bits of speeches written and given for over a decade flooded her mind. Looking out to the faces before her, she realizes for the first time that these people don't need Haluk; they need Magdalena.

"Here we stand, my brothers," she begins as the tears fall silently to the snow below. "We are broken, shattered into a thousand pieces. The wounds inflicted on our souls will never fully heal. For the rest of our days, however long or short they may be, a part of us will never again be whole. But, in each other, we will find the strength to go on, the strength to stand once more. Look around you. Look to your left and to your right. This is your family now. In the depths of our pain and our sorrow, we will find one another. We will find hope there. We will find tenderness there. We will find solidarity there. My brothers and my sisters, I vow that I will do everything in my power to protect you. Your lives and your happiness, however we can measure that now, are my life and my happiness as well. I can't promise you victory, I have never been able to promise that. But I can promise you that I will fight for you until I die. I will not give up. Every time I fall, I will rise again until breath leaves my body.

"You deserve a life free from tyranny, free from starvation, free from fear. The thread of grief has stitched all of us together for the rest of our days. We might not win, this is true, but we will fight for those we buried in Kaelonoch, those that were senselessly murdered. We will fight for those that remain, that they may never know fear or violence like that again. We will fight together.

Never again will someone sit in a castle and play games with your life. Never again are you and your children at the mercy of their whims. Never, ever, again." Her voice has gone from shaking at the start to now a strong echo that vibrates from the trees as she says these last three words.

"Rest, my friends," she says with gentleness. "Heal your wounds, both the ones seen and unseen. Tomorrow, we march. Before first light, we leave this camp for the castle. When the sun finally sets on the day ahead, we will have avenged our fallen, we will have fought for freedom, we will have refused to bow down to an oppressive monarchy. Are you with me? Are you angry enough to be with me? Are you scared enough to be with me? Are you foolish enough to be with me?" Her eyes search the broken souls scattered before her as tears fill her eyes once more.

"I am mad enough," Brom says solemnly as he glances down at Liri's face buried into his shoulder. "I am beyond mad, Your Grace. Those were innocent lives, and they were taken from us in the most gruesome way." Brom bites out these words as a vein throbs in his neck.

"I am scared enough to be with you," Willem says, taking a step forward and turning to face the crowd. "Any monster that could slaughter his own people—innocent men, women, and children, mercilessly killed like that—what else are they capable of? I don't want to find out."

"Aye, well, I guess that leaves foolish for me," Warrick says, forcing a smile. "I will fight at your side tomorrow, my queen. I am foolish enough to think that we are mad enough, and scared enough, to win this war."

A murmur begins to rise from the crowd. *I will fight, my queen. I will fight.* The sound of their hoarse voices blends and carries on the wind, through the twirling snow and straight to the heart of Magdalena. In their whispered words of solidarity to the woman before them, Magdalena feels the final piece of Haluk fall away.

She nods in response, her jaw set in a tight line but tears still falling from her face. "Rest now," she offers as her departing words before she turns and walks to her own tent. Once she is inside and the flaps of the tent close behind her, Magdalena falls on her knees to the floor. She lowers her forehead down until it touches the frozen ground below. Her tears pool in the dirt, and she wraps her arms around her middle in an embrace. The images of Kaelonoch flood her vision as she rocks slightly back and forth. Her mind heavy, she doesn't hear him approach but rather feels strong arms wrapping around her, enveloping her. She can see the pale hairs on the tanned skin and smell the earthy scent of him.

She rises to her knees and turns to face Warrick. He brings the back of his fingers to her face and begins to wipe away the tears that continue to fall. She can feel the heat radiating from his light touch and can smell the sweetness of his breath against her lips. She realizes with a trembling rush that she wants nothing more than to be known by this man. She wants to be seen as the woman she is. She wants him to look at her and find beauty and strength, and not be afraid of their duality. She wants him to know her hands were taught to kill, not to caress. Her body and mind were built for war, not twirling in dresses and times of tea. She wants so badly to be herself, her whole self. She reaches a trembling hand to his whiskered cheek and brushes her fingertips along his jawline. He doesn't move. He is wanting her, willing her, to make the choice. Without a further thought, she reaches out for him and wraps her arms around his neck and threads her fingers through his shoulder-length hair. She pulls his head down to hers, and their lips touch hesitantly, briefly, before finally melding together. Warrick wraps his arms around her waist and pulls her close to him. She moves onto his lap, her legs on either side of his, and she can feel his strong chest against hers as their lips move together and apart. Magdalena's heart is racing in her chest, and her hands are shaking in his hair and on his cheek. She can feel his body beneath her, can feel his desire for her, and the knowledge of it sends a rush of heat throughout her body.

"Oh, Mags—" Warrick's voice sounds thick in his throat "—how our lives could have been. If we'd only known, maybe all this would have been spared."

Magdalena pulls back suddenly so she can look him in the eyes. Her own still swim with tears. She closes her eyes tightly as a realization floods her mind. "It was you? Wasn't it? You were the best of them all. You were the victor, and I, I was to be yours?"

Warrick lets out a breath that it seems he must have been holding since the day he met Magdalena. "Aye, Mags," he says in a whisper.

"Oh," she exclaims as new tears fall from her eyes. "I would have been yours," she confirms, a sad smile spreading across her face.

"You are mine tonight, and I am yours," Warrick says before lifting the edge of Magdalena's tunic over her head. The two come together once more. Their hands attempting to discover and sear into memory at the same time, their lips thirsty for the taste of the other. There, on the cold dirt floor, their bodies move together until two become one.

***

Magdalena emerges from her tent well before dawn's first light. She stands for a moment and breathes in the crisp air before letting it out in a rush. Warrick has already risen and started a fire where her aunt Thea now sits. She studies the older woman for a moment. Thea is grasping her furs tightly around her shoulders, arms crossed over her chest and knuckles white from the force of her hold. She is slumped forward on the fallen log, face peering into the fire and lips moving in a silent whisper. She looks tired, tired in a way that a thousand nights of sleep wouldn't cure. Magdalena grasps the parchment Thea gave to Warrick when she returned to their camp only moments ago. Inside the folded piece of paper is a detailed account of every guard's position in the house and which rooms Henrick and Dagen are occupying. The paper is a death sentence for her husband, and it is written in his wife's own hand.

"Her horse is ready," Warrick says when he comes to stand next to Magdalena. She nods in response, and the two of them approach Thea as if she is a skittish cat that could either pounce or dart to the shadows at any moment.

"Aunt Thea? It's time."

Rising slowly, Thea turns to stand before Magdalena. The wind whips through her chestnut curls. Her body is tense, but her face is void of emotion.

"Are you sure about this? You could stay," Magdalena says, but Thea shakes her head in reply.

"No. There is nothing left for me here. I would rather take my chances out there."

Warrick removes the leather cord from around his neck where a black talisman is attached and places it into Thea's hand. "Show this to the first Typhan you find. They will guide you to my family. This will secure you a spot in my household, but after that, I can't guarantee anything."

"I know," Thea says quietly before closing her fingers over the necklace. She turns to mount her horse but pauses and spins back to face Magdalena once more. "Promise me one thing, Maggie?"

"Sure."

"When you kill Henrick, will you make it fast? I hate him enough to want him dead but love him enough to want it to be painless." She doesn't wait for Magdalena's response before mounting her horse and riding off toward the mountains of Crask. Warrick wraps his arm around Magdalena and plants a small kiss at her temple. Leaning into one another, they silently watch Thea ride away. This day could end with one or both of them dead, and that thought wraps its heavy arms around their shoulders and causes them to pull together closer as the first rays of sun land on their faces.

28
Henrick

Henrick stands, staring out the window in his study and watching the gray clouds descend from the mountains. Snow is quickly approaching. The glass before him is etched with fragments of frost. Tiny, shattered fingers spread from the edges. He puts his forehead on the cold pane and looks down. The air from his nostrils creates two circles of fog in his field of vision. It is a long way down. Not long enough, though, he thinks. He glances over his shoulder at the sleeping figure of Dagen on the couch. His dear friend has been afraid to leave his side. Whether it is fear of what Henrick might do to himself or what Niklaus might do to Henrick, he is unsure.

The young king hasn't been seen since Alden and Catrain departed for Ezers, since the morning Henrick's world was set on fire. Niklaus, he has come to learn, has locked himself in the tallest turret. From there, he drains the bottles of wine before tossing them out the window, aiming for anyone who happens to be below. One of Dagen's men met the bottle at the bottom and now lies unmoving and unresponsive in the stables below. Niklaus was heard cheering when both bottle and man crashed to the frozen earth below. Dagen wanted to kill Niklaus for that. He would have done so, too, if the boy hadn't barricaded himself before climbing the tower. Now Dagen watches over Henrick. Well, he naps in the presence of Henrick. Dagen claims that when his eyes are closed, his sense of hearing is heightened, and from the settee, he will be able to hear the beam of wood lifted from the tower door the second it scrapes free. In reality, he just doesn't want Henrick to be alone.

Henrick's entire world has crumbled before him. It has taken only weeks for his dreams to shatter. He recalls the early morning hours after the castle was taken, the thrill of success. He can see himself now, pacing the great hall, feet bounding with a newfound weightlessness that comes with freedom and opportunity. He howled, he recalls with a silent laugh. Thea feigned annoyance. That night, he slept soundly for the first time since his mother's death. He slept knowing that he would finally have the future he worked so hard to achieve. He wasn't a failure after all. He had a beautiful wife, a lover and confidant, and soon a crown and kingdom. His legacy was coming together bit by bit, stone by stone. He had never once, even in his darkest days, thought he would fail. Someone who wants something so badly can't fail. Someone who puts their heart and soul and blood and sweat and tears into something must have reward in the end. It is only fair. But then, everything went wrong.

He is now a man without his wife, his best friend, his anchor. Her words and her tears as she unraveled herself in the dining hall still echo through his bones as if they have taken up residency in the marrow. Never will he live separate from the pain he caused her. Through his affair with Catrain, he was arrogant in his belief that Thea would be spared from it. He loved Thea; that was never the question. Things were so much more complicated than that. He began to believe, as Catrain did, that somehow, in some part of her heart, Thea not only knew about the union but blessed it. That she turned a blind eye to it.

The revelation that not only was she painfully aware of the union but also physically watched them together frightened him. She knew when and where they lay together. She watched silently from darkened corners. Why? What did she feel while hiding in the shadows? Anger? Hatred? Sorrow? How easy, he thinks, would it have been for her to scream at them both to stop? To yell and hit and throw whatever lay nearby? But she chose instead to sit and witness alone in the dark. She chose to cast her eyes on the gut-wrenching truth of it all and never say a word. That's how he knows she's broken. There was no fight left in her because he took that from her years ago. Now all that remains of her is a shell. His loving, tender savior is now gone.

He is now a man without his crown, his redemption, his honor. He is that small boy once more, the one with a mother who woke up one morning and decided she loved the idea of escape more than she loved him. He is that boy with the skinned-up knee and the father laughing and mocking his tears. He is once again the little brother who fell in love with a beautiful peasant girl only for her to be taken from him by a boy who would be crowned king. He has deserved so much more than what life has given him. He was a good child. He was kind and tender. He was generous with his smile and attentive in his studies. He made people laugh. His parents, before his mother died, would even allow him to sneak into a party they were throwing and entertain the adults with his antics. He loved hearing their applause and seeing his mother's face crack into a wide smile. He craved being seen. It made him feel alive. He craved moments where he felt real and not just a piece of furniture. His life mattering, that was all he asked. *Was that too much? Apparently so.* His life didn't matter when his mother took hers. His life didn't matter when his father gave Hadrian the bride Henrick chose for himself. *Things weren't supposed to end up like this*, Henrick sighs.

He is now a man without his lover, his confidant, his escape. Catrain was planted in Masunbria by her brother. Her love for Henrick wasn't even real. It was a survival tactic, nothing more. She used him. She saw into his soul and gazed upon the brokenness that resided there, and she turned those shards of desperation into ambition. From the beginning, he knew he was selfish to want both Thea and Catrain. How, though, was a man to choose between roots and wings? Both were so desirable. *The child.* That was what nearly broke him. The knowledge that her belly lay bare felt like a massive stone crushing his chest.

Wearily, Henrick lifts his head from the window and pours a glass of wine though he has no taste for it. It won't help anyway. Not anymore. No amount of wine will drive out these demons. He cannot use drink to hide this time, and he knows that.

"Dagen, how did this happen? How have I fallen so far?"

He hears Dagen sigh from his spot on the settee as he opens one eye and aims it at Henrick. Henrick has already asked him these questions, probably a dozen times since they took up confinement in these rooms. Dagen has never had an answer for him. The question worked to awaken him, though, and he, too, pours a glass of wine that he will leave primarily untouched.

Henrick moves to sit opposite Dagen. Resolve in his heart, he knows he must make right what things he can. He takes a small sip and sets his glass down before meeting Dagen's eyes.

"I have failed, Dagen. There is no possibility for me anymore. That means there is no possibility for you either. I release you, brother. I release you from your obligation to me. I will give you plenty of coin, but you must go now. I don't know what will happen, but I do know that every moment you spend with me, the target on your back grows larger and larger. I can't let you fall with me," Henrick says gravely, realizing that in saying this, he is saying goodbye to his only friend.

Dagen doesn't respond immediately. When he does, though, to Henrick's utter irritation, he laughs. Not a small chuckle of a laugh, but a full-bellied roar of laughter. Henrick, knowing not what else to do, stares at him in disbelief.

"What is this, Dagen? Do you find how far I have fallen so funny?"

"No. No," Dagen sighs, bent over, trying to catch his breath. "Henrick, I find it funny you think I am here out of obligation, that you have some sort of hold on me that you must release me from. You see, I must laugh, or else I would be so offended that I would likely break your nose with my fist." Dagen says this last sentence with no trace of humor as his face falls to a serious scowl. "Who do you think you are anyway?"

"Well, I mean," Henrick stammers. "Hadrian forced you to serve me. That is why you are here."

"No, Henrick. That is how I came to know you, but that is not why I am here. I am here because you need me. I am here because you're an idiot who can't seem to stay out of trouble. I am here because you are my brother and I am yours. I thought you knew that."

"I am an idiot, aren't I?"

"Yes. That you are. Do you really see me as a servant you have the power to release?"

"No. No, Dagen. I just don't know how to tell you thank you. I don't know how to say I am sorry. I don't know how to express to you that you've been a good friend to me."

Dagen offers a nod in response, but that's it. Henrick knows he has hurt his pride. He is ashamed for it. It appears that in addition to the multitude of things he can't get right, friendship is also on that list.

A knock on the door sends both men into slight alarm. No one visits. No one dares to. Henrick is a dead man walking. Dagen moves swiftly to the door, sword drawn, and peers out. A breath of a glance is all it takes before the door swings wide and Sigmund shuffles his old, decrepit body into the study.

"Niklaus will kill you if he hears you were in here. I am sure he has spies everywhere and he won't allow a sympathizer to make it until morning," Henrick warns.

"Who would win?" the old man asks dryly.

Henrick looks at Sigmund, puzzled for a moment and then a flash of memory. Simpler days. Carefree days. Days when the biggest question to be answered was when Sigmund would die.

"I would," says Dagen soberly as he pats the back of the old man in greeting before kissing the top of his thin gray hair. He pours Sigmund a glass of wine as the old man arranges his bones into the chair.

"Ah," smiles Sigmund, "that's good, that's good. I always preferred it to be Dagen."

Henrick feels the skin of his face twist in an attempt to smile. He, too, secretly cheered for Dagen to win. There wasn't much in life that went Dagen's way; surely Sigmund's death should. "Why take the risk, old man? What brings you here?" Henrick asks, back to him as he looks out the window as the first flakes of snow begin to drift to the ground.

"I am here to tell you that Thea has gone."

"What do you mean? Where did she go?"

"I have advised her to make her way to Cecily, if she is still alive, that is."

"You knew she was leaving and you didn't stop her? Not only that, but you've sent Thea to the Typhans?" Henrick shouts, face reddening as a vein throbs at his temple.

"Of course I knew she was leaving. Thea could no longer remain here after your betrayal. She would die a slow and agonizing death in the belly of this stone beast. I have great love for Thea. I wasn't going to let that happen to her. If your sister married the best of the Typhans, she might have a position of power within their clans. Thea is a smart woman; she can survive there and possibly even thrive."

"She is barren, Sigmund. All they care about is producing heirs, and Thea can't do that." Henrick is shouting at the old man now, spit spraying from his teeth as he does so. Spinning, he moves to the window to try to calm his breathing. Looking out, he finds a snowflake to follow with his eyes. Down. Down. Down. He hasn't seen his sister since she was twelve years old and he was ten. She came to Henrick's room the morning she was to go into Crask. She sat on the edge of his bed and held his hand as he cried silent tears. She would wed a great warrior who held power. She reminded him of this. She told him that, once she secured her position with the Typhans, she would send for him. She would protect him from their father. No word ever came. Henrick would rise each morning thinking that surely today would be the day the missive would arrive. Each night he cried himself to sleep. *No, Cecily is surely dead, and Thea will be next.*

"I can't believe you would do this to me, Sigmund." Henrick sighs. "I can't believe you would do this to Thea. You've sentenced her to death, old man. Once they realize she isn't useful, they will kill her. Worse, they will use her body for recreation until she gathers the strength and the means to kill herself."

Sigmund takes a long, slow drink of his wine. He lets the ruby liquid slide around his mouth and travel slowly, lazily, down his throat. He sits a little taller in his chair and adjusts his robes. Taking a steadying breath, he replies, "Henrick, you are amiss to assume that Thea can't be found useful for her mind. You are also assuming that Thea is, in fact, barren. She has been fully examined by the court physician you've kept locked up in the dungeons, and it is his medical opinion that there is nothing wrong with Thea's body. He believes it is perfectly capable of bringing a child into this world."

"That can't be possible." Henrick snarls.

"It can be when one considers that it is actually you, Henrick, who is unable to create a child."

At this statement, Henrick hurls across the room, knocking the chair and Sigmund inside it to the ground in one swift pounce. Henrick brings his fist high above his head and lets it rain down on the old man's face. Rearing back, he slams his fist down again, hearing the crack of old bones under his knuckles. Again and again, his fist raises and falls, blood spurting and pooling around the man's head. His wispy gray hairs begin to drip red as Henrick releases all the anger and fury inside of him to the wrinkled face of Sigmund. Henrick, straddling the old man, peers down on what remains of Sigmund's face. Henrick is simultaneously sobbing and gasping for breath as the old man lies motionless beneath him.

That's where he is when it happens. He is down on his knees, staring at the still form of Sigmund. Dagen is standing next to him, staring at the bloody scene before him. It is there in a room littered with broken dreams that the two men inside hear two distinct sounds almost simultaneously. The first is the sound of a wood beam scraping free from a turret tower door. The second is the resounding sound of a battle cry coming from what sounds like more than one hundred men with nothing more to lose. Both sounds can mean only one thing: death has come looking for Henrick.

29

Magdalena

Magdalena's men scream into the night as they storm the castle grounds. They run through the silent gardens and past the enormous stone monuments with their little braided saviors. They move as a great mass of metal and misery down cobbled paths, through trees and over brush. Hearts racing, their breath is visible in the cold moonlight, like puffs of clouds leading the way. There is single-minded concentration in the men. Their body and mind are preparing for war, a magnificent response. Without prodding, without any semblance of conscious effort, their bodies are calling upon instincts that have been cultivated throughout thousands of years of existence, from generations upon generations of people. Magdalena's body hums with a readiness that she can only liken to a predator lurking in the shadows, tracking the movement of its prey.

The metal sword in her right hand feels almost weightless as her arms, ropy with well-honed muscles, swings the blade free from its sheath. She opens and closes her fist, adjusting her grip, as her legs bring her to an abrupt stop in the center of the courtyard. Against her will, her eyes twitch to the spot where just weeks before the bodies of her parents were set aflame as they lay on their adorned pyres.

As predicted, an onslaught of Henrick's guards begin to pour into the courtyard from deep inside the castle itself. Brom shouts commands that seem to not necessarily be heard in the traditional way, but rather the words seem to soak into the bones and tissues of the men who stand with him. Swords and shields ring together in collision. Her men cry out a battle cry for blood and revenge, and it is a sound heavy of sorrow and torment and desperation. It takes mere seconds before the scene in front her erupts into chaos. She wills her feet to move, and at last, they obey as she raises her sword to strike that of her enemy.

The man she faces is strong but not nearly as fast as she. She ducks right and spins left, catching the man off guard, and his swing cuts through nothing but air. Magdalena has him already; any blow she swings will land. But for a reason she can't fathom, she hesitates. The man, regaining his control, turns to her and swings his sword down, aiming for her neck. She quickly raises her shield overhead just in time, and the feeling of his mighty blow vibrates through the shield and down her arm. The man releases the pressure on the shield, and Magdalena jumps quickly back, knowing his aim was to catch her arm raised while holding the shield and strike her exposed abdomen. His sword jabs and misses by just a breath, and in that time, she brings her shield upon his sword in one swift chopping motion. It startles him, but he doesn't drop the blade. Instead, he takes his own shield and slams it forward into Magdalena's face.

Blood shoots from her nose and fills her mouth. Her eyes water viciously. She spits hot blood from between her teeth to the ground as she blinks free the blur of her eyes. She sees him then, the man before her; he is smiling at her. Smiling at her pain. Smiling at her unabated and unintentional tears. The rage she feels in that moment is all she needs. She attacks the man before her, sword swinging high in the air toward his head. The man ducks, just as she knew he would, and she plows into him with her shield at that moment and sends him falling to his back. She brings the edge of her shield down on the bicep of his right arm, and he lets out a howl and releases his sword. Standing over him now, she looks into his face and knows what she must do. There will be no mercy shown for her or her men, just as there was none shown for the people of Cale or of Kaelonoch.

She raises her sword and plunges it down into the exposed throat of the man who lies beneath her. Blood sprays out in a great arching fountain. She forces herself to look at the blood and his eyes and she watches life leave his body.

Heart pounding, Magdalena knows she must move. If she continues to stand still, she will become more of a target than she already is. She looks around. She sees nothing but war and death. She sees blood and twisted bodies and smells sweat and metal. The sound of their swords and shields is deafening as it echoes off the stone walls. She spots Brom and wills his eyes to meet hers. He pierces his sword through the soft middle of a young guard before twirling in search of her. Spotting her, he makes a small nod before bellowing out another battle cry, their men returning the bloodlust-filled scream with equal zeal. She swallows, and it tastes of blood. Crawling on all fours, she nears the metal grate in the ground to her right. The grate is small, barely large enough for a man to fit through, but the metal is thick, and the hinges are all but immobile from disuse. She laces her fingers between the bars, and bracing her feet into the packed earth, she pulls hard. The hinges let out a sound of protest, and her arms shake from the weight and resistance.

"She's going under!" she hears someone yell from behind her.

Turning her head over her shoulder, she sees a royal guard. Blood still dripping from his sword, he begins pushing through the waring men, making his way toward her. She bites down hard on her teeth as she wiggles her legs and butt under the heavy steel grate. Another quick turn of her head, and he is close enough now that she can see his brown eyes, full of hate and locked on her. Her arms shake as she tries to push the grate further up. She has no time. She bends, letting the grate fall hard on her arched back. A scream tears through her chest as she curls into herself and falls down into the darkness below. She lands with a thud on her stomach, the air forced from her lungs in one large swoosh. She tries to pull fresh air in, but her body refuses.

She can hear the man above her. He is shouting for others to join him. She clambers to her knees, tripping in an attempt to get to her feet. She gasps as her diaphragm finally recovers from its shock and pulls air into her lungs. She knows the way, and her only chance of survival is if the men who are crazy enough to follow her down here do not.

Below the castle lies her great-grandfather's life's work, a product of fear and paranoia: miles upon miles of tunnels, stairs, secret halls, and hidden walls. The twists and turns double back on one another and are designed to confuse and frighten those who get trapped inside. There are two other ways out, a secret passage that leads to a hidden door within the fireplace of the great room, and a tunnel leading straight to the Miraron River and a hidden cave where Warrick, Willem, and an army of men wait for her.

These tunnels were Thea's plan for Magdalena and her army. While Aunt Thea was going through some of Henrick's mother's things in her library, she came across a hidden compartment in the desk. Once the lever popped, she discovered a journal inside. Inside the journal was page after page of Henrick's mother's fears regarding her husband and his violent nature.

About halfway through the book, she revealed that she discovered the tunnels. The next dozen or so pages were full of sketches, as she spent her nights not sleeping but mapping her escape. The last few pages of the journal were full of a terrified, slightly manic scrawl, where she revealed that she believed her husband was aware of her desire to escape and that he would kill her. In the last entry, she stated that she was finally ready. She found her way and memorized her route. She would get Henrick and take him through the tunnels and to the river. She wrote that she couldn't save Hadrian, and her sweet Cecily was gone to the Typhans, but she could save her youngest child from the monster she married. She wrote of her love for her children and the life she would make for Henrick, one of days spent in the sun gathering berries, a life of winter nights curled in thick blankets telling stories of giants and brave young boys. Of course, she never made it out. She was dead before dawn, and Henrick never knew anything about the tunnels or her plan to take him with her.

Thea let out slow tears as she lay the book open for Magdalena. She didn't tell Henrick of her discovery, unsure if it was because she hated him or loved him that she kept secret his mother's deep love for her youngest son. Together, Magdalena and Thea retraced the path over and over until it was seared in Magdalena's mind. Now, Magdalena runs, counting steps and turns, running her hand over damp stone to feel her way. She can see the worn pages of the journal in her mind. She can see the frantic scrawl of paces and points. Behind her, she hears the sounds of men who have come down here with her. They shout and run and stumble into one another. They light torches, but the darkness here swallows up the light. Rounding the last corner, she can smell the difference in the air before she spots her first trace of moonlight.

"Mags," Warrick breathes in relief as he pulls her into his arms once she emerges from the grate at the river's edge. She falls into him, head resting for a moment on his chest, as she breathes in the scent of him. Warrick leans back, looks at her face, and then grabs her chin and lifts it, examining the marks that portray her as victor. Her face is covered in a mixture of blood and dirt. Her lip has already begun to swell and so has a spot under her right eye.

"I am fine, Warrick. We must go. They are in the tunnels."

Willem, grabbing Magdalena's shoulder and giving it a squeeze, bends down and kisses her forehead softly, the way a father would welcome home a long-absent daughter. He turns back to the men crouched along the water's edge and makes a chopping motion with his hand. Magdalena turns to the grate and jumps back down, Warrick following close behind. The rest of the men plop one by one into the darkness below. She can hear their quickening breaths as Magdalena silently leads her men through the damp and darkness, back through the maze, and to their destination—the great hall.

Peering through the trap door behind the fireplace, Magdalena sees the great hall is empty. She pushes through, and her men follow. They stand for a moment, taking in the massive room with its floor-to-ceiling windows and portraits of important-looking faces. They can hear the sounds of men running in the space beyond the room. They take only a moment to gather their wits, and then, Warrick leading the way, they run through the doors and into the open hall.

Stunned guards whirl in surprise, and that moment of shock is all Magdalena and her men need. Warrick runs at full speed, his shoulder-length blonde locks flying behind him. His sword is raised and his teeth bared, and he looks every bit the barbarian her people believe him to be as he leaps in the air before bringing his sword down and through the face of the shocked guard before him. He spins and swings and takes out another. He is fast on his feet, as well as strong, and there is something else there, too, something coursing through his veins, unseen but not unnoticed.

Magdalena draws her eyes from him and moves to the doors leading to the courtyard, where she swings them open wide. She is relieved to see a tired, bloody, but still very much alive Brom smiling up at her. She pulls him in for a quick embrace before stepping aside and allowing Brom to lead what men remain with him into the fight. Magdalena stands for a moment at the threshold and looks out at the blood-soaked earth of the courtyard. The bodies of men are littered throughout. She tries to see without seeing, but her brain refuses to participate in the delusion as it recognizes the still form of Jonan, watery brown eyes looking to nowhere as blood drips from his parted lips. Magdalena feels a wave of sadness wash over her. *Reunited with his family at last,* she hopes.

She forces herself to turn away. She knows where Henrick hides, and that's where she is headed. The sight of her fallen men in the courtyard, the look of Jonan's vacant eyes, sends a searing anger through her body. She takes the servants' stairs to her right and ascends them two at a time. Her heart is pounding in her chest, not out of fear but out of determination as she pushes her legs to take her faster up the winding stone stairs. Thea said Henrick and his right hand, Dagen, were hiding away in her father's library.

Running down the stone hall, she pauses outside the closed door. She grips her sword and her shield and takes one steadying breath. She anticipates the door to be barricaded from the inside, but one push and it gives freely, too freely for the force she used to open it, and she stumbles slightly into the room. She nearly trips over an old man who lies in a pool of blood on the ornate rugs, his face smashed in. She steps over him and then spots outstretched legs on the ground, sticking out from behind the settee. Brown boots, black britches. Cautiously she takes small steps toward the furniture shielding the still form and peers over.

"No," she says aloud as she brings a shaking hand to her mouth. She moves quickly around the furniture and drops to her knees, suddenly unable to stand. *Niklaus.* His throat has been slashed open, and the carpets below him are soaked with his blood. She can feel the knees of her pants soak up the now cold proof that life once coursed through his body. She holds shaky fingers near his wound, touching slightly for a pulse though she knows one won't exist. The gaping wound is sticky on her skin, and the feel of it on her fingers makes her want to throw up. She takes his face in her hands and cradles his cheeks as she looks down upon him. His eyes are open and staring blankly up at the ceiling overhead. She brushes his dark hair off his forehead before bending over and planting a kiss on his brow. The tears drip onto his face and roll down his stubbled cheek. She remains bent over as she covers his features in her tears.

"I am sorry, dear brother," she whispers into his forehead, lips brushing his skin as she speaks. "I am sorry for the lies. I am sorry for what those lies made you feel you had to do. I know now how badly I hurt you."

"Mags!" she can hear Warrick yelling from outside in the hall. She takes one last look at her little brother. *I love you.* Turning, she picks up her sword and shield and heads to the door. She turns and looks back once more. She thinks of their adventures. Their silly games. Their shared laughter. *It was all real, even if it was all soaked in such heavy lies.*

"Maaaaaags!"

"Here, Warrick, I am here." Tearing her eyes away from Niklaus, she runs out into the corridor.

"He's gone. Your uncle escaped. The castle is yours."

***

She has moved in a daze since rising from her dead brother's side. She led her army to tend the wounded and gather the dead. It is these images that haunt her now, three days later: the sight of the lifeless men, the screams of those that still clung to a sliver of life. Two-thirds of her men were found dead. A dozen others didn't make it a day longer before succumbing to their wounds. Their bodies were taken to towns, villages, and farms across Masunbria to be buried with those they loved, on land they cherished. Anyone well enough to dig a grave went.

The castle, full of life and love in her childhood, has now turned to a place of tears and blood for Magdalena. She longs to return to the little cottage. She wants to feel the thick covers, smell the lingering scent of herbs and bread, hear the scraping of Hagen's knife against wood. It is in those fantasies she remembers that what made the cottage a safe, happy place is no longer there—Hagen and Sybbyl. Her uncle took them from her just as he took her parents and her brother.

Those men still alive have temporarily left the castle to return to their homes, seeking what loved ones remain and assessing their losses, both physical and emotional. The castle is quiet, and she sits alone in the great hall. The candles are lit, though the gray of daylight seeps through the floor-to-ceiling windows. Their flame is a comfort, a kiss, a tender embrace as shadows dance across the faces of her family that look upon her. Her own portrait hangs near the fireplace, and she studies herself now. No, not herself; she studies Haluk. Wearing a high-necked white tunic under a navy jacket adorned with the gold crest of Masunbria, her icy blue eyes look to the open room with an intensity to them that is alarming.

Her fair skin is painted taut with lines visible on her forehead and between her brow as if she is furrowing in concentration. Her lips are unsmiling, and her strong jaw is set in a hard line. Her fair hair, cut short and slicked back from her forehead, is topped with a crown adorned with spinel gems in the color of blood. She sighs into the empty room and reaches for a bottle of wine and a cup. She pours herself a full glass and takes a long, slow sip.

Her brother is to be burned on the altar today, a grace she has offered him in death as an atonement for her betrayal. While navigating the grounds in search of those fallen, a fresh grave had been discovered. It was marked *Sabina Anker*, Brom's sister. Her dear friend was torn open at the revelation, so much so that Magdalena ordered one of her fastest scouts to ride to camp and bring Liri to comfort him. She watched from the window as the two of them held one another, knees buried in the dirt of the earth Sabina lay below. So much death. So much sadness. Somehow though, in the middle of all the loss, there was also something found. Brom and Liri are evidence of that. Their love for one another has only been made stronger in the loss of Hagen, Sybbyl, and Sabina. They hold one another, and in that embrace, they find the strength to rise.

They aren't alone in that feeling either. Magdalena longs for Warrick now. She needs his steady presence, his strong hands to hold her shaking ones. She hasn't allowed herself to think about what's next, to think about how she will be crowned queen of Masunbria, the first of her kind, that she will rule not as Haluk but as Magdalena. She has tried to keep her mind from wandering to the dangers the crown on her head will bring to her kingdom. The only imagining she has allowed is a life with Warrick.

A creak at the door. The sound of silent feet on stone. She knows it's him and doesn't bother to look up. He seems to be able to sense her distress. It is as if his mind is wired to receive a signal from hers once her thoughts become too heavy. He crosses the room to the chair across from her and pours a glass of wine. She looks up at his tired, dirt- and sweat-stained face as he takes a swallow before grimacing in disgust. She smiles, finding comfort in his desire to be close to her even if the drink available is appalling to his palate.

"You know you could bring ale next time, Warrick," she offers.

"So you've said, Mags. But then what would I have to complain about?"

"Oh, I am sure you would find something. You don't seem to like being inside these walls."

"Aye, I don't. I don't know how you people can tolerate these living conditions." He shifts uncomfortably in the cushioned velvet chair that seems too small for his large frame.

Magdalena lets out a small laugh before taking another sip of her wine. She stares once again at the portrait of Haluk. Warrick, following her eyes, turns his body to look upon the painting. He lets out a sigh, sets his glass down, and rises to stand before her. He takes her glass in his hand and sets it aside before pulling her to her feet. Magdalena looks up at him, studying his face. Her own eyes swim with unshed tears—tears over the loss, tears over the weight of all the lies, tears over the fear for what tomorrow will bring. Warrick wraps his strong arms around her and pulls her into him. She rests her head against his chest and can hear his strong heart beating below, can feel the warmth on her cheek, and can smell the scent of earth and fire on his tunic. She wraps her arms around his middle and splays her fingers across his back. They stand like that for a long time, just holding one another, her tears dampening his chest.

"What now, Warrick?" she mutters against him. He gently pulls her away and looks down at her. He smiles, as true of a smile as she has seen come across his lips.

"We keep fighting, Mags. We fight for your people and their happiness. We fight for freedom from my people and the pain and hardship they inflict." At her look of despair at all that lies before them, Warrick brings his hand to her cheek and gently cups it while looking deep into her eyes. "Mags, we also fight for this." He leans down and kisses her on her lips, long and slow, drinking one another. He pulls back and runs the pad of his thumb under her eye to catch a tear. "We fight to make whole all the places we are broken, to heal the wounds that our families caused so we don't inflict the same ones on those we love. We fight to be seen as the people we truly are and not the lie or legend that precedes us. I love you, Magdalena. I want to spend my whole life loving you, if that is what you want too? I want to love you as the warrior you are. I want to serve you as you sit on your throne and breathe life back into this kingdom."

She can feel her hands shake against his broad back. She can be both this and that. She can be brave and afraid, she can be strong and tender, she can be seen as a woman and someone deserving of the crown. She will fight until her last breath. She will fight for her friends and her kingdom. She will fight for this man and his love. Above all, she will fight to become herself.

LB Swanson lives with her husband and three kids in the Heart of Illinois. When she's not writing, you can find her going on hikes, working in the garden, sipping wine while doing a puzzle, or cheering her kids on from the bleachers. She is a foodie who loves antiques, old buildings, sports, and fairytales.